gossip

ALSO BY BETH GUTCHEON

Good-bye and Amen
Leeway Cottage
More Than You Know
Five Fortunes
Saying Grace
Domestic Pleasures
Still Missing
The New Girls

gossip

Beth Gutcheon

WILLIAM MORROW
An Imprint of HarperCollins*Publishers*

GOSSIP. Copyright © 2012 by Beth Gutcheon. All rights reserved. Printed in the United States of America. No part of this book may be used or reproduced in any manner whatsoever without written permission except in the case of brief quotations embodied in critical articles and reviews. For information address HarperCollins Publishers, 10 East 53rd Street, New York, NY 10022.

HarperCollins books may be purchased for educational, business, or sales promotional use. For information please write: Special Markets Department, HarperCollins Publishers, 10 East 53rd Street, New York, NY 10022.

FIRST EDITION

Designed by Jamie Lynn Kerner

Library of Congress Cataloging-in-Publication Data has been applied for.

ISBN 978-0-06-193142-0

12 13 14 15 16   OV/RRD   10 9 8 7 6 5 4 3 2 1

For Eden Ross Lipson

gossip

YOU WERE ASKING ABOUT DINAH WAINWRIGHT," I SAID TO Judy Mellincroft, once we got her bodice basted. Mrs. Oba was on the floor with her mouth full of pins, taking up the hem of a sleek wine-colored evening sheath. Judy is so tiny that we have to reconstruct everything she buys, but it's worth it. She loves the designers I carry, and she's out in my clothes every day for lunch and most nights during the season, a walking advertisement for the shop, and I don't even have to give her a discount.

Having a storefront on Madison Avenue is usually a boon, but that day I could have wished for an appointment-only operation upstairs somewhere off the avenues. We'd had more walk-in traffic in two days than in the prior two years, and everyone who rang the bell tracked muddy slush in along with their curiosity. The sky was heavy and there were huge puddles at the street corners where the grates were still clotted with snow. And inside we felt like animals in the zoo.

I had a beautiful taffeta opera coat in the window, my winter staple. I don't carry fur anymore, even as trimming—so much has changed since I first opened—but this is one evening coat that is as warm as fur and doesn't make you look like a stuffed cabbage. However, the gawkers pretending to study it were not thinking of upgrading their wardrobes.

Could we talk about fur for just a minute? When whoever it was wrote of "nature, red in tooth and claw," he could have been talking about the kind of mayhem an ermine can cause in a henhouse. They kill for pleasure. My father tried keeping chickens for a while. Believe me, the sight of those slack, defenseless feathered bodies lying on the floor of the coop with their throats ripped open while the rest of the flock screams in terror is enough to make a fur wearer out of anybody. Ermine, on clothes, the emblem of kings. You know what it is really, an ermine? A stoat in winter. Their coats change color except for a flick of black at the ends of their tails. They have no intention of eating the chickens; they're in it for the screaming.

Sorry. The point is, it was a hard day. I had Dinah Wainwright in the back fitting room, trying to give her some privacy, but Judy must have heard her voice. If Dinah's voice were a color it would be magenta, a warm color as vital as blood, mixed with that dark blue of late evening sky and with something rich and brown, like chocolate. It's not so much that the voice carries as that it draws you. You want to hear what she's talking about. In our school days, when you heard a peal of that voice laughing, you wanted to be there, where the fun was.

Nowadays when she laughs there's a rattle in the undertones, like someone shaking a jar of buttons. Dinah didn't stop smoking nearly soon enough. A great way to get Dinah to do something was to tell her she shouldn't do it.

I couldn't blame Judy for asking. I'd been described in the tabloids as "a friend of the family," apparently because I'd answered the phones. But if I *had* minded her asking, I couldn't have shown it. You don't keep your customers by being touchy. I probably should have taken Dinah straight upstairs to the workroom, but it happened to be stacked with samples for spring we hadn't had a chance to sort and price yet.

I don't think you can really understand this story without

knowing how long we all have been in each other's lives. Dinah and I met in 1960 when we were fifteen, the day we both arrived at boarding school. I was a scholarship student at Miss Pratt's, which nobody knew. So was Dinah, which everybody knew, because she told them.

My first day at school was indelible, mostly not in a good way. For our classmates, arriving at school was a family affair. They came in station wagons with their parents. On the sidewalk they shrieked greetings to friends. They sang out "man on floor" when someone's father or brother entered the dorm lugging a trunk, as if they were characters in a cozy British movie like *The Belles of St. Trinian's*. I had come alone and was watching the street from the window of the room I'd been assigned, wondering how many days it was until I could go home for Christmas vacation, when behind me that oboe voice said, "You would be Loviah French."

She even pronounced it right, LOV-i-uh. Dinah was already dressed like the quintessential Miss Pratt's girl, in a knee-length skirt, charcoal kneesocks, and a shell-pink sweater over her matching blouse. She lounged against the doorjamb, a marvelous creature with huge blue eyes and mad dark hair.

"Lovie," I said.

Dinah walked in, taking inventory of my suitcase open on the chest at the foot of the bed, at the little framed pictures I'd put out of my parents, my sisters and brother, and my dog.

"Well, I knew you weren't Sherry Wanamaker," Dinah said. That, according to the name cards on the outside of our door, was the name of my roommate.

"Do you know her?"

"I don't *know* her, but they're in the papers all the time."

"They are?"

"I don't think they are the department store people, but I know they're all blond. While you are more . . ."

"Mouse-colored," I said, quoting my mother. My first experience of hearing something I had no intention of saying out loud offering itself to Dinah.

She looked at me with a flicker of special interest.

"I'm Dinah Kittredge," she said. "I'm from Canaan Hamlet, the village huddled against the famous gates of Canaan Woods. I'm here on scholarship. Where are you from?"

I had no idea what Canaan Woods was. "Maine."

"The Main Line?"

"The state."

"I've been to Maine. What part?"

"Ellsworth."

She looked blank. I said, "West of Mount Desert, and east of everything else."

"And you're *here* because it's where all the best people go?"

"My grandmother went here. I'm named for her. I think my parents expected a different kind of daughter entirely." I'd done it again, completely lost control of my mouth. And when I saw that it pleased her, I suppose it was inevitable that I'd go on doing it.

"Come see my room," she said. I left my unpacked clothes and went. She had pictures of her parents and her two sisters in pretty frames on her dresser, and she had brought her own bedspread and had a Kennedy/Johnson campaign poster on her wall. She was, as far as I could tell that fall, the only Democrat in the student body, which bothered her not one whit. We sat together listening to Ella Fitzgerald sing Cole Porter on her record player as the dorm filled up around us.

By the time I went back to my own room, Sherry Wanamaker, blond as advertised, was all settled in, laughing with three upperclassmen she knew from New York. We were never soul mates when we were in school, but Sherry's been wonderful to me since I opened the shop. She has me dress her daughters, and I did all the clothes for her last wedding.

I HAD A HARD TIME ADJUSTING TO LIFE AT MISS PRATT'S. DINAH USED to say I was a middle child trapped in the body of a firstborn. I had to do everything first in my family, first to go to kindergarten at The Big School, first to go to sleepaway camp, first to go away to school, and all of it scared me, usually for good reason. At Miss Pratt's I could see the minute I looked into the closet I shared with Sherry that my clothes weren't right—my mother had made most of them. My shoes were generic Oxfords, not the kind with a flap over the laces from Abercrombie & Fitch. My cable-knit sweater was made by machine, not hand-knit in Hong Kong. The color didn't have that jewel-like intensity of the real ones, and the buttons were flat. I noticed Sherry noticing.

So did Dinah. Dinah saw everything. Her own clothes were real. She may not have had as many as other girls, but her blouses had Peter Pan collars and came from the McMullen shop. She had a cable-knit cardigan in emerald green with matching yarn-covered ball buttons. On Saturday nights when we dressed up, her crisp blue-and-white dress was a Lanz, not a copy. Dinah watched everyone, and somehow she knew exactly what to do, and also saw who got it wrong, and how they handled it. She gathered information. She was at ease with the girls with famous names and all the right connections, and they accepted her—in fact flocked to her—as it began to be known that she could do a flawless imitation of the science teacher's speech impediment or of the rolling walk of the Latin teacher whose right leg was shorter than her left. But really her secret was that she was at ease, not a small trick when you're fifteen, and she never pretended to be anything she wasn't. She was ruthless about those who did.

One autumn morning after breakfast, I was in the dorm bathroom, in one of the stalls, when I heard Sherry Wanamaker talking to someone else about her roommate, Harriet High School. (It was true that I'd gone to public school before coming to Miss Pratt's.) Mortified, I stayed where I was until the warning bell rang for class and the dorm emptied out, so no one would know that I had overheard. But as I was rushing up the hill to French class, Dinah joined me. She said, "You can't mind Sherry. She doesn't know she's mean."

It wasn't at all what I was expecting, and it made me laugh. That was the moment I began to really trust her. Of course Dinah was right; Sherry wasn't thinking about me, she was just making a friend. A wink, a knowing remark to someone she wanted to be close to, and she established a bond. Even my own dotty mother, with her homemade clothes and disastrous cooking, would occasionally describe someone as "N.O.C.D." Not our class, dear.

I did wonder how Dinah knew I'd heard. Saw my shoes under the stall door, I suppose. My not-quite-right shoes. Dinah's protection changed everything about Miss Pratt's for me.

People like . . . well, like my poor mother with her superiority complex, based on nothing so American as accomplishment, needed walls between them and the people outside the gates. If you weren't up on the ramparts with your cauldron of boiling oil, full of Harriet High School and Not Our Class, Dear, someone might notice that *your* shoes weren't quite right either. But Dinah wasn't like that. She knew who she was; she lived outside the walls and preferred it. She could go in and out of the gates at will. She could even afford to bring people like me right up to her campfire. What she knew was that soon the most confident and amusing inmates would be outside with us, singing rude songs and telling ghost stories. I never would have made friends myself with all those girls with the famous names, girls with influential parents. Confident girls who made us laugh and would one day invite us to their coming-out parties. I was almost always the quiet one at the outer edge of the circle, but I was welcome to join their reindeer games if I wanted to, and knowing I was under Dinah's wing meant that girls who might otherwise have looked through me, and even the teachers with famous mean streaks who had seen me as fair game, began to assume I must have some hidden depths. And of course I did. We all do.

As I came to understand much later, Avis Binney's social credentials were impeccable. Her father was a partner at the whitest of white shoe law firms and her mother came from one of the Dutch families of old New York; there is a tiny triangular park in lower Manhattan named for one of her direct ancestors and a street in the financial district named for another. At one time there had been in the family a famous estate north of the city, a favorite haunt of the painters of the Hudson River School, but the closest Avis had ever been to it was to visit its vistas in frames hanging at the New-York Historical Society. Perhaps it was that experience, of looking into pictures as if looking out a window from a life that wasn't hers but might have been, that made art so important to her.

You would have thought that, with her brains and breeding, she'd have been made for Miss Pratt's and it for her, but you would have been wrong. Miss Pratt's at mid-century wanted girls to be bubbly, cheerful, and easy to manage. Avis was hard to read, and shy even when she was a senior. To us new girls, her shyness registered as unearned hauteur, perhaps because she was tall and bony and frightened of making social errors; when she wasn't sure how to react, she often simply remained quiet. This made others suspect snobbery.

Avis was the only child of older parents. Her father, George Binney, had been nearly fifty when she was born; her mother was ten years younger but was still what was known in those days as an elderly primipara. Siblings for Avis were not contemplated. An older friend of mine described Alma Binney as a stern and humor-less woman, fond of bridge and club life, who agreed with most of her social set that Franklin Roosevelt was a traitor to his class and family. Avis's parents were much involved with each other and with their various boards and pastimes. Avis was mostly raised by a thin-lipped Scottish nanny who stayed up all night pacing in panic when the moon was full because it reminded her of bomb-ing raids on bright nights during the Blitz.

Throughout her childhood and youth Avis was far more at ease around adults than children; she understood better what they wanted, and how to please them, than she ever did with her class-mates. She knew that among her mother's friends it was assumed that George Binney would predecease Alma, as husbands tended to do, and that Alma would enjoy a long and decorous widow-hood for which she was calmly preparing. Instead, Alma suffered a massive stroke in her sleep when she was forty-nine, and as she herself would have put it, woke up dead. Avis was eight.

Alma had been dead not quite a full year before George mar-ried Belinda Ray, a magazine editor and self-described party girl who had come to New York from rural Ohio to attend Barnard College, fallen in love with city life, and stayed. She was as differ-ent from Alma as chalk from cheese, fun loving, irreverent, and beautiful. Having never been a mother, she functioned less as a parent to Avis than as an unusual but trustworthy pal. It made a great change in Avis's life, and after a period of confusion and standoffishness on Avis's part, which Belinda ignored, they be-came friends. Even in later years when Belinda had grown rather grand, she was known everywhere as a thoroughly nice woman.

In her own age group at Miss Pratt's, Avis was respected by

most and loved by two or three. The younger girls, however, were less likely to see the point of her. New girls tended to prefer the seniors who were warm and affectionate, or mad, bad, and dangerous to know. Avis understood this and had long since made her peace with it, since her passions were not social. On a grand tour of Europe Avis had discovered Velázquez at the Prado in Madrid, and stood transfixed before first one and then another portrait of Philip IV with his long jaw, swollen lower lip, and sad droopy eyes. The pictures made him so present and human that it made Avis hungry for more; seeing them was like reading the beginning of a story you then couldn't discover the ending to. She wanted to know how it felt to wear those doublet things, to be never alone, to marry your own niece, to lose that beautiful prince, Carlos Baltazar. She hated it when children died. She had questions for Queen Mariana too, and for the lady-in-waiting, who looked so much like her roommate Cynthia, who was offering the tiny princess a plate of fruit in *Las Meninas*. Did they all really love the dwarves, or were they afraid of them? Avis was afraid of them. The rest of the group was ready to leave the museum and find some lunch when the tour leader did a head count and had to backtrack through half the galleries to find Avis and haul her off to where she was supposed to be.

When Avis returned to school, the History of Art teacher, one of the best and meanest teachers at Miss Pratt's, watched her commitment to this new passion first with skepticism, then with an amused pleasure in trying to find its false bottom or trick latches, and finally with admiration. Her classes had inspired scores of girls to major in art history in college and then to while away a year or two in internships at the Met in New York or the MFA in

Boston before marriage, but a girl with an actual vocation came along far more rarely. By her senior year, when we first knew her and Avis had taken all the art history courses the school offered, the teacher did something she would normally have considered far above her pay grade; she designed an individual tutorial for Avis on Spanish painters from Pacheco to Sorolla. So Avis got out of taking Domestic Arts or something else she didn't care about to fill out her schedule.

Nothing, however, could provide her a bolt-hole from the school's famous social traditions, which had once, in its days as a finishing school, been its most important aspect. Equipping young ladies to converse graciously with companions they had no interest in was still seen as a key aspect of a Miss Pratt's education. Accordingly, each new girl was assigned a senior girl as her "date" for Saturday nights, a different senior for fall, winter, and spring terms, and yet others for special occasions. These arrangements occasionally led to real friendships, but most often they were regarded with anxious horror by the new girls. The older girls minded the whole business less, as the "dates" mirrored the roles of girls in the outside world, with the seniors playing the boys. The seniors sat with their own friends or roommates while the dates sat glumly by, attempting to fit in. But some seniors, and Avis was one, never got over the discomfort of these forced intimacies. I imagine she may have reacted with inner dismay to the news that her assigned companion for the annual winter Ice Cream Concert was popular, self-assured iconoclastic Dinah Kittredge. Avis's only contact with Dinah up to then had been her duty as library proctor to ask Dinah and her friends to stop erupting in laughter during study hall.

The Ice Cream Concert was always a classical performance of some kind, followed by ice cream, so the girls would look forward to the event even if they were sporty or lowbrow philistines who knew nothing of classical music, and many of us were. All that the new girls knew for sure was that we must wear velvet skirts and Capezio flats to this concert, as the clothing list that came with our acceptance letters had specified. By the time Dinah and I arrived at Avis's door I knew my velvet skirt was wrong. It looked homemade, with a broad embroidered tape of vaguely Slavic design for a waistband. No one else had a homemade skirt or a contrasting waistband, and all too clearly my mother had had trouble setting the zipper, as the velvet was sewn into a pucker at the base of it. Avis of course noticed this at once, but I sensed that she felt not satirical but sorry about me and my skirt, and I wished she could keep me and protect me, but my date was a girl on the next floor up; instructed on how to find the right room, I left Avis alone with Dinah.

Dinah hated it. She was an alpha girl and she especially didn't like being paired with those who, though senior to her, were not class leaders, or beloved, or notorious. Avis also had an unfortunate haircut that winter, a severe bob that made her neck even longer and her nose more prominent. They had fallen silent by the time my date and I caught up with them on the porch and we all sallied forth into the dark evening.

My date was a jock named Lonnie whose long lank blond hair made her look like an Afghan hound. The four of us crunched grimly along in the new snow, the crisp winter night air sharp with woodsmoke in our nostrils. The grand houses that lined the village street loomed dark on all sides of us with yellow lamplight glowing from their window eyes as we joined the chattering flood of girls heading from all parts of the campus toward the cloakroom door at the side of the dining hall.

Avis's roommate had been saving places for Avis and Dinah at the table in the corner where she was sitting with her tiny date, a very young freshman with tight curls and thick glasses magnifying mournful eyes. Through the soup course and then the mystery meat, the four of them made laborious conversation about chemistry, which the roommate loved and Avis didn't and neither of the new girls had taken yet. At my table we were trying to talk about Baroque music.

No dessert was served at dinner, since there would be ice cream later. There were rumors about how wonderful the ice cream would be. Monotony and deprivation make a fine petri dish for rumors about almost anything. These rumors were wrong; the ice cream, served in slabs, was that grim supermarket stuff that came in stripes, one chocolate, one vanilla, and one strawberry. I remember that forty years on, and I don't even care about sweets. But the music! They didn't stint there. They had the Juilliard String Quartet and the program started with a Brahms that was transporting.

In retrospect some believed it was a piece of snobbish malevolence that the headmistress, who had certainly told us not to rattle our programs or unwrap cough drops once the music began, did not also point out that you don't clap between movements of a classical piece. Of course there would be girls who did not know that in advance. Of course there would be girls who started clapping when the bows were rested. Would be and were, and one of them was Dinah.

It was a tiny moment. She wasn't the only one. But Dinah was proud, as most are when young and ignorant, and thin-skinned about offenses to her dignity. She stilled her hands the instant she realized Avis hadn't moved, but not before a hot shock of humiliation had flashed through her system. She had wanted to show that she was alive to this new beauty, or simply to demonstrate the sophistication of her taste. We all did. Avis didn't correct her or in any way contribute to her embarrassment. But Dinah never forgave her for seeing.

I'M MAKING IT SOUND AS IF DINAH WAS MY BEST FRIEND. SHE wasn't at all. My best friend was a girl named Meg Colbert who came from the Northeast Kingdom in Vermont. Meg and I bonded over the fetal pig we dissected together in sophomore biology class. She was very shy and homesick (though remarkably cold-blooded about the pig), and later told me she had cried every single day she was at school our first year. There was a soul mate for me. It was Dinah who told me that the town Meg came from was Colbert, Vermont. It was the kind of thing Dinah knew.

Meg and I roomed together junior and senior years and were thoroughly happy together. I went home with her for spring vacation both years. She lived on a farm, threadbare but so beautiful you could practically eat the views. Her father kept dairy cattle, and her mother taught piano and played the organ at church. Meg kept chickens. And there were horses. We went cantering in those gorgeous spring-green pastures, through those endless woods, every day it wasn't raining. Heaven.

Meg is dead now. She married a boy she'd grown up with, stayed in the Northeast Kingdom, and died in childbirth. She was home alone when her labor started, and a snowstorm had knocked down the power lines and blocked the roads. The town's one ambulance was already out and stuck somewhere. Then a falling branch ripped Meg's phone line off the side of her house, and by the time someone got there to check on her, it was too late. They found her on the floor of the kitchen in a sea of blood, cradling the dead telephone. Her daughter lived, but she's an odd one, and never comes to the city.

SUCH AN INTERESTING QUESTION, WHETHER MEAN PEOPLE KNOW THEY are mean. Thinking of Dinah always makes me wonder about that.

Did you know that the origin of the word *gossip* in English is "god-sibling"? It's the talk between people who are godparents to the same child, people who have a legitimate loving interest in the person they talk about. It's talk that weaves a net of support and connection beneath the people you want to protect. I am godmother to Dinah's son Nicholas. My gossip, Nick's godfather, is Stewie Brumder, a great pal of Dinah's then husband Richard Wainwright. I haven't seen Stewie since Dinah's divorce. Really, I'm not sure I've seen him since the christening. Interesting how things change: the people you thought would be friends forever disappear, and others become more and more important to you over time.

Mrs. Oba and I tend to close the shop at lunchtime, and eat our lunch together in the upstairs workroom, surrounded by the ladykins of our best customers. I don't worry about losing business by closing; most of ours is by appointment. The workroom has a huge cutting table, though we make almost nothing from scratch anymore. Where there used to be floor-to-ceiling fabric bolts, now we have our racks of ready-to-wear in sizes from two to twenty. We don't keep much on the floor downstairs, just enough to let passersby know it's a dress shop. My ladies will come in and say, "I need something for the PEN Gala," and we get to work.

We know everything about them. We know which ones are allergic to wool, so all their winter skirts and trousers have to be lined. Avis has scars on her chest from skin cancers, so we never show her décolletage. Mrs. Crittenden is unusually proud of her arms, which to my taste speak too eloquently of the gym, so we try to put her into romantic shirts with flowing sleeves, but she's not having it.

We know what balls they go to, who's getting married and with what color scheme, who's had a mastectomy or a tummy tuck. They know much less about us. Most of them think Mrs. Oba speaks only Japanese. That's fine with her; she's there to tailor, not to sell. Selling is my job.

I met Dinah's parents and sisters several times when they came to school and took us out to lunch. Unlike me, Dinah adored her parents. Her father taught English at the private day school inside the Canaan Woods compound. Dinah and her sisters attended the school for free as faculty children, and some other outsiders were bused in from surrounding towns, but most of the students came from inside the gates. I learned from Dinah not to call the houses "mansions." If you're a tourist or a servant, it's a mansion. If you or your friends live there, it's a big house. Mrs. Kittredge sold real estate, mostly big houses inside Canaan Woods. Dinah was proud that her father was everyone's favorite teacher at the school, and even prouder that her mother worked and made more money than Mr. Kittredge.

Context is everything. I began to really understand Dinah when I went to stay with her. The June we graduated, about nine of us were invited to a deb party at the Canaan Woods Casino. I was the only one invited to stay at Dinah's house.

Mother had offered to make me a dress for the dance, but Grandmother Loviah could be heard rolling her eyes even on the phone. She sent me to Mrs. Bachman, her saleswoman at Saks. (Her saleswoman! Who knew you could have your own? The beginning of my real education.) We chose a very pretty floor-length A-line gown with cap sleeves in lemon-yellow taffeta, and I wore it to everything that season. Jackie Kennedy was in the White House, and the dress was pure homage. It was brilliantly made; I still keep it in a cloth bag in the workroom. When we made more clothes from scratch than we do now, I used it to show my workers how the seams are finished, and how beautifully the sleeves are set. I know now that yellow is not my color, but I didn't then; when I wore that dress I felt beautiful. My first experience with clothes as emotional armor instead of the badge of the misfit.

Grandmother Loviah clearly viewed that dress as an investment. She thought if I had a good dress and a string of real pearls, I'd catch a husband. A husband of our class, dear. In her day, very few girls went to college. They were "finished," they "came out," they got married. Clergymen blessed the debutantes every June, just as they blessed the foxhounds in the fall.

Well, the dress *was* a good investment; it was the beginning of my métier. But I can hear Granny spinning like a dervish in her grave up in Trinity Church Cemetery, that a grandchild of hers would keep a shop.

Dinah's house existed on a different planet from where I grew up. Dinah's father was lanky and handsome, a very tweed-jacket-and-corduroy-pants kind of man. Her mother was a wonderful cook—in fact the whole family cooks well. They cooked together. My first night there, Dinah's little sister Treena asked me how much stock she needed for two cups of risotto—as if I knew what risotto was. She thought all grown-ups knew. Mrs. Kittredge, whose hair had been white since her twenties, had deep blue eyes and a wide smile. She dressed in stockings and pumps and a series of suits that looked much better than they were because she cut the cheap buttons off and sewed on very good ones she bought at a special shop in the city. The buttons were always black, so she could wear everything with one or two pairs of really good black shoes. You can't fake quality in shoes, but I used the button trick for years.

When Dinah took me up to see the grammar school she had gone to, I began to understand precisely how her childhood had shaped Dinah's stance in the world. The school was on top of the ridge behind the lake, a sprawling campus with a half-timbered main building that had been added to many times to make room for the best of everything. There was a new gym, a new preschool, and a new science lab. There were two vast playing fields, and a spectacular view of the wooded compound below. Canaan Woods was shaped like a bowl, with the lake at the bottom like a sil-ver mirror, and slate roofs gleaming among the trees. The houses were mostly hidden by leafy woods except for those beautiful blue-gray slants of slate. Many had six or eight bedrooms, many had tennis courts or swimming pools, little glimmering splinters of aqua or green glimpsed through the leaves far below us. All got you access to the Canaan Woods Hunt Club (foxhunting), the Rod and Game Club (the other kind of hunting), the Yacht Club (this was a joke, it was mostly a boathouse down by the lake where members kept their little sailing dinghies and canoes), and the Casino, where you could eat lunch or dinner, play cards, dance on Friday nights, lounge around the swimming pool in summer, or stump in on frozen feet for hot chocolate beside the fire after an afternoon of skating in winter.

Dinah was full of stories of childhood friends and happy times at school. And yet when we stood together looking down at the roofs and the lake, the Casino sprawling beside the water and far beyond, the stone bell tower of the Episcopal church and the thick stone piers of the big iron gates, she said, "It's a little like living in a zoo." Clearly what she liked was being welcome here, passing for a native, but really belonging outside, with the layer of irony that gave all her observations about who the people in the big houses were, and how they were shaped by what they took for granted, and who she was, and which was better.

Going to the deb party with Dinah gave me courage. Her dress was midnight blue satin and had a Paris label; they'd bought it at a consignment shop on Upper Madison. "It had been worn once, if that," Mrs. Kittredge said, shaking her head. "In Europe, you know, you buy the very best you can afford and then you wear it over and over again. I went all the way through college with one very good wool skirt and three cashmere sweaters."

DESPITE MY GRANDMOTHER'S BEST EFFORTS, AND DESPITE A GREAT DEAL of fun I had that season, I did not find a husband. As things have worked out, I think we can conclude that I wasn't looking. Apparently the vision of domestic bliss provided by my parents carried more weight with me than all the romantic stories we'd read and cultural promptings we lived with.

My father's latest flash in the pan had flared and gone out that spring. I don't remember what it was—a new kind of car wash, I think. All my classmates were going to college in the fall. I had gotten into the college I wanted to attend but hadn't been offered enough scholarship money. Grandmother Loviah was unmoved. She had other grandchildren to worry about. She would pay for me to go to the Katharine Gibbs Secretarial School, if I wanted to be a secretary. I did not. Mrs. Wanamaker made a call on my behalf to her couturiere, the famous Philomena, and on July first, I started work in her atelier on Seventh Avenue. The famous Philomena was not an easy person to work for, but to me, it was like throwing Br'er Rabbit into the briar patch.

WE'VE BEEN UNUSUALLY BUSY IN THE SHOP THIS WEEK, FOR OBVIOUS reasons. Mrs. S, a client we haven't seen in four years, bought an $8,000 ball gown yesterday. While we were fitting her, she said, as if it had just occurred to her, "Oh Loviah, aren't you a friend of Dinah Wainwright's?" (She pronounced it Lov-I-ah.)

I hummed something. Pins in the mouth are so useful.

Eventually Mrs. S said, "I don't know her very *well*. I've read her for years, of course."

I took out my pins and said, "I think Bradley is going to love you in this dress. It's elegant, and it shows off your beautiful little waist."

"Bradley likes elegant," she said doubtfully. This is a woman whose idea of glamour is her breasts falling out of her blouse. She tried again.

"I think Dinah might be interested in our apartment. It's finished, finally. Alexa Hampton did it. I'd be glad to have her come and have a look."

"She doesn't really do that kind of writing much anymore."

"I know, but she does sometimes."

"But perhaps this wouldn't be the time."

"No. Of course. I just meant. Later on, you could mention it to her. Or I could give her a ring in a month or two, if you had her number."

"Yes. Do you want to come in for a final fitting on Thursday, or shall we just send this along to your apartment when Mrs. Oba is finished? Why don't we send it, won't that be most convenient for you?"

When she had gone, Mrs. Oba asked, "Would the English word be *strumpet*?" She does amuse me.

At least we got her out of the shop before Avis arrived.

WHEN WE WERE YOUNG, I SAW AVIS BINNEY AS ONE OF THOSE IMPOSsible sophisticates, girls raised in New York who all knew each other from Chapin or Brearley or Spence, who'd been to Barclay's Dancing Classes together, who went to Gstaad or Hobe Sound for Christmas. Of course, I know her far better now.

Her stepmother, Belinda, was a beauty into very old age, and a lot of fun. We made her a dinner suit for her ninetieth birthday party, in emerald taffeta with an Elizabethan collar that framed her face. Even when she was dying, Belinda had her hair and nails done every week; she said the worse you felt, the more important it was to look your best. The week before she died her saleswoman at Bergdorf's sent up a pair of sensationally expensive black snakeskin stiletto heels on approval, and she bought them. Such a hopeful thing to do, and the shoes *did* show off her beautiful legs. Avis buried her in them.

In looks, regrettably, Avis took after her father, whom I never met. When we were in school she resembled nothing so much as a young emu, which made her name unfortunate to those who'd had any Latin. Now in late middle age, she has such poise that she's achieved a distinction, if not a beauty.

A cadre from the press corps that had trailed her there was camped outside my shop when Avis and I came downstairs after her fitting. (I'd learned my lesson by then and taken her up to the workroom.) We could see them through the showroom windows. She turned to me with a look of panic. In the past I have had my own reasons for wanting to be able to enter or leave my workrooms without being seen, so many years ago my friend bought me a small flat in the apartment block that abuts the building the shop is in. We broke through the walls to allow me to reach my apartment through a door at the back of the workroom. I led Avis back upstairs, into my flat, and down to the lobby, where she could exit onto a side street once the doorman hailed her a taxi.

WHEN DINAH WENT OFF TO VASSAR, AND I WENT TO WORK FOR Philomena, that summer of 1963, I expected our lives would diverge, but the opposite happened. I was renting a walk-up near Second Avenue, east of Bloomingdale's, with a convertible couch in the living room, and Dinah was dating an acting student at Juilliard. She came into town to see him all the time, often catching the train from Poughkeepsie after her last class on Wednesday and staying through the weekend, usually with me. How she got through her course work I'll never know, except that she had never had to work very hard at school, which was either a blessing or a curse.

Neither Tommy nor Dinah had two beans to rub together, but they managed to see every play worth talking about. She and I lived in two different time zones. I was up at six and in bed by ten; Dinah slept half the day and had lunch before she dressed to go out in the evening. I loved having her there. I loved hearing about college life and the nightlife and I loved having company my own age. At work, the only people under forty were the models, who, unless we were showing a new collection, sat around all day in their underwear, waiting for Madame P to call them in to have fabric draped on them. (Philomena famously designed without drawings, cutting directly into the cloth.) The models didn't talk much to the likes of me, except to say, "Tuna salad, no mayo, and Fresca, please."

When there was a show I really wanted to see, Tommy and Dinah took me with them. They had lots of tricks, but one time I remember, it worked like this: we dressed in our glad rags. Dinah had a stretchy silver lamé sheath dress that accentuated her curves, and I had a knockoff Rudi Gernreich I had made myself. Our skirts were so short we couldn't cross our legs when we sat down. Dinah wore eyelashes that looked like tarantulas, and her lipstick was almost white. When I couldn't bring myself to adopt the *ma-quillage à la mode*, she said, "All right, you can pretend to be my nurse."

At the theater, Dinah strolled to the door as if she were Katharine Hepburn and said, "Miss Kittredge, party of two. We're on the list."

The usher looked puzzled. "I need to see your tickets, miss."

"No, no, we're on Mr. Patten's list," said Dinah. "Brad is expecting us." Mr. Patten was a producer she'd never met. Brad Taliaferro was the star of the play. Just then, Tommy appeared holding a clipboard.

"Can I help?" he asked the usher.

"Dinah Kittredge," said Herself, looking relieved. "We're on Mr. Patten's list, friends of Brad Taliaferro." She even knew to pronounce it Tolliver.

Tommy ran his finger down his clipboard, looked troubled, then said to the usher, "I'll take care of it." The usher was thoroughly relieved, and we were led off to the house seats, side aisle, third row. In gratitude a seat was found for Tommy in the back, he told us at intermission. After the curtain call, Tommy tapped another usher with his clipboard and murmured, "Brad is expecting Miss Kittredge in his dressing room. Could you?" We were all three led backstage, down a rackety flight of stairs, through a boiler room where the dressers ironed and mended costumes, then up two more flights of stairs. The usher knocked on a door, announced, "Mr. Taliaferro, your friends are here," and left us. The famous voice called *"Entrez,"* and we did.

Here was the toast of Broadway in a grimy terry cloth robe with a jar of cold cream in one hand and a weird net on his scalp where moments before had been his glorious thatch of ash blond hair, which was now perched on a wig stand on the counter. He looked at us with happy expectation as we trooped in. After his smile faded only one degree, he said "And you are . . . ?"

"Absolutely nobody," said Dinah, and Brad (we soon called him Brad) laughed.

"Marvelous! What would you like to drink?"

The friends he was really expecting arrived while he was in the shower. They were much entertained by the story of how we got there and insisted on taking us with them to dinner. I didn't get to bed until three, and Tommy and Dinah went on with them afterward to some place like the Peppermint Lounge where, it was claimed, society girls in miniskirts and go-go boots did the Twist on top of the tables.

I'd almost forgotten how much fun those days were. Dinah would disappear for long stretches when she had exams or papers due. Then she'd reappear, full of appetite and news. She and Tommy broke up, but it hardly put a hitch in their friendship. We still see Brad, although his salad days are behind him and he is not always such good company now. Tommy finally grew into his slightly crumpled face around the time he turned forty and began getting lead roles. He's been nominated twice for an Oscar, and Dinah thinks that this year will be his year.

Next she took up with a rising young editor at the *Herald Tribune.* When the *Trib* folded, he moved to the *Times,* and when she finished college Dinah went to work there too. She used to love to say that she slept her way to the middle and made it the rest of the way on talent.

DINAH COULD REALLY WRITE. I ALWAYS THOUGHT WE'D SEE HER NAME in lights, one way or another, that she'd go to Hollywood and make movies, or write famous plays, or at least win a Pulitzer for journalism. Gloria Emerson was reporting from Vietnam for the *Times,* Gloria Steinem had founded *Ms.* magazine. Things were changing for women and we who had Known Her When thought we'd see Dinah on the barricades. Instead, at the *Times* she dutifully wrote about family, food, furniture, or fashion for the ghetto of the women's pages, left the office at five, and was out virtually every night building her Rolodex. She went to art openings, book parties, discotheque openings, luxury product launches, and even celebrity funerals. Sometimes she was on assignment, but much more often she just found a way to be where the heat was being generated, for its own sake. Andy Warhol noticed her. So did Charlotte Curtis, who was writing about society for the *Times* in a way it had never been done before. By the time the serious women of the *Times* started making common cause to sue the paper for sex discrimination, Dinah had moved on. She'd been offered a job by Simon Snyder, who was writing a must-read society/celebrity gossip column called "New York Eye" for a new downtown tabloid which Dinah liked to call "The Fishwrap."

She told me, "I kept running into Simon. He finally said 'Honey, you're out here every night at all the same places I am, you might as well be paid to be there.'" He said if she worked for him he could go home and get some sleep, but in fact his hiring Dinah was more like his being in two places at once. At the showroom, you could *see* their column selling papers. When our ladies came in to see a collection, they'd sit in their spindly gilt chairs waiting for the show to start, open their salmon-colored tabloids to page eight, read "New York Eye," then throw the paper away.

During my first years with Mme. P, I was mainly a gofer. I'd carry fabric swatches to our button lady and our belt lady with Madame's instructions. When the fabric salesmen came with their bolts of gorgeous cloths for Madame to choose among, I'd help haul them over to her and back again, carry them to the window to show the color in natural light, or unfold several yards of this weave and that so she could see how they draped. When important clients came in to order the numbers they'd liked at the collection, I'd help to dress the models who showed them the clothes. Once in a while the vendeuse would have me take a client's measurements while they discussed variations to the dress we would make for her. Our vendeuse was a marvelous creature named Mme. Olitsky, rumored to be a White Russian princess, though in her off-hours she was known to lapse into one hell of a Wisconsin accent. Perhaps there had been a Prince Olitsky. She was tiny with huge red-framed glasses, always impeccably dressed, usually in Philomena, but now and again in skillful Paris knockoffs from Orbach's. (Society ladies like Mrs. Wanamaker, who wore our clothes everywhere, got discounts, but the staff didn't.) Mme. O spoke beautiful French, good Italian, and passable German, and took me under her wing after my fichu disaster.

A week in which we showed a collection was very high pressure. A runway was brought in and set up in the showroom.

All week we were juggling the seating, so that the second Mrs. Rockefeller wasn't at the same showing as the first, and that the buyer from Neiman Marcus wouldn't run into the buyer from Dayton's in the hall. We had our own models plus two or three others backstage. I'd be assigned a particular model and had to keep the lists of what dresses to put on her in what order, along with everything that went with each costume: shoes, hose, jewelry, scarves, and hats. It was hot and crowded behind the stage, and not all the models bathed as often as one would wish.

At the winter show the second year I worked there, Mme. Olitsky was out front greeting the invitees and showing them to their seats while Mme. P checked all the lists and accessories one last time. As often happened, especially at moments of tension, she found something not exactly to her liking. This time, her eyes fell on me. *"Vous, mademoiselle! Arrêtez ça!* Take this back to the twelfth floor, *maintenant, vite vite!"* It sounded as if its imperfection was my fault in the first place. I was to race with this spangley velvet scarf to the rhinestone crimper, have him fix it, and bring it right back. Perhaps she was giving me a chance to shine, as normally only Marjorie, the brilliant Trinidadian who managed all the physical properties, would have been entrusted to leave the atelier at such a moment. But maybe I was just the first person she saw.

I ran like the wind to the crimper. I presented the fichu and relayed Madame's instructions, in French. I sped back to my post, kneeling among the forest of naked model legs as skirts came off and evening gowns were wriggled on. Size nine feet were put into size ten pumps with lumps of tissue crammed into the toes, missing bracelets were found and fastened, queries, complaints, and swear words made a sotto voce hum drowned out in front by the music now emanating from the record player. It was the "Anvil Chorus," I think.

Out on the stage, Mme. P gave her own commentary on each design as the models marched out, turned, posed, and marched back, passing each other as they went. It was unusual for a designer to perform this role, but Mme. P was famous for it. For the finale, all six of the models would be onstage in evening gowns, each with a fichu of a different style and color. Except that when the moment came, there were six girls and only five fichus. Red satin, green peau de soie, ivory chiffon, blue watered silk with seed pearls, burgundy cashmere, but no black velvet with rhinestones. I had forgotten to wait to bring it back. Madame's eyes alone, when she came backstage after taking her bows, could have singed hair. Marjorie tried to hide me the rest of the afternoon, and for days afterward I crept around the studio, pretending not to cast a shadow, not sure if I even had a job anymore, though the very unpleasant things Madame had yelled at me had not included the word "*terminée.*"

DINAH ROARED WITH LAUGHTER WHEN I TOLD HER THE FICHU STORY, which wasn't quite the reaction I had hoped for. She, after all, was comfortably ensconced in an ivy-covered dormitory with three meals a day paid for, even if she did have to maintain a B average to keep her scholarships. But later, when she went to work for "New York Eye," she was a huge help to me with Mme. Philomena. She'd come to our collections and plant items in the column about them. "What chanteuse in a hit Broadway musical was seen ordering Philomena's new Grecian Column cocktail dress in three different colors of silk charmeuse? Maybe the rumors about her very well-heeled new inamorato are true." The actress and Mme. P both loved it, as long as the inamorato's wife in Rome, also a sometime client of Mme. P, didn't catch on. Mme. P began asking why I didn't bring that charming Mlle. Dinah around more often, especially after Dinah persuaded the very young, very photogenic wife of a major New York philanthropist to model the bridal gown in our spring collection that year. (Which was 1971. I just looked it up.) It was an innovation at the time to send a non-professional out on the runway, but it turned into a PR coup—it proved that our clothes could be worn by a younger customer and caused demand for seats at our shows to skyrocket. And got Dinah a very nice scoop for her column. "Would *you* take to the fashion runway in Mme. Philomena's bridal offering, as pretty Bettina Cosgrove did last week, if you could wear a size six? Can't say for sure, kids, but Dinah Might." The column ran with a photograph of Bettina in our dress.

Bettina, who later became a particular friend of mine, had married a man whose terrifying former wife vowed that Bettina and her husband would eat dinner at home alone every night of their married life. But Bettina had nerve and a surprising cunning on her side, plus a press agent. We lost the former Mrs. Cosgrove as a customer, along with a few of her friends, but more than replaced them with a new, younger group who wanted their pictures in the paper too, and not just when they chaired a junior benefit. Bettina was well pleased because it induced several fashionable hosts to invite the Cosgroves to dinner, even over their wives' objections. And Dinah was given her own column to run in place of "New York Eye" every Friday, entitled "Dinah Might."

MEG COLBERT WAS MARRIED ON A SUMMER WEEKEND THAT YEAR IN her father's cow pasture. She wore a white Mexican peasant dress trimmed with white eyelet. Her sister, the matron of honor, wore cornflower blue, and her bridesmaids, including me, wore soft, vaguely Empire dresses like nightgowns in different pastel shades, wreathes of daisies on our heads, and bare feet. I learned I was the only one among these girls who varnished her nails or owned a girdle. I learned that it was very wrong to refer to us as "girls," and that in some circles, shaving your armpits was a political act. Once again, I'd been reading all the wrong magazines.

The minister wore sandals and little round wire-rimmed glasses, and the wedding march, played by a local jug band, was the Beatles song "When I'm Sixty-Four." Toasts were drunk in fizzy cider that packed quite a wallop, brewed by the bearded philosopher from the next farm over. We square-danced in the dairy barn, and when the full moon was high, the bride and groom, still in their wedding clothes, departed on horseback. It was incredibly romantic, and the first wedding I'd ever been to where the newlyweds turned up in jeans the next morning to join all their friends for breakfast.

A lot of fates were sealed that night. Certainly Meg's. One of the groomsmen introduced a game in which you whirl around and around holding a broomstick while everyone claps and then at a signal, drop the stick and try to jump over it. The second fellow who tried it missed the jump by a mile, fell over, and cracked his head on a stall door and nearly put his eye out, but later he married the bridesmaid who drove him to the hospital. And I met a man who changed my life. He was Meg's godfather. We were the only two people there from New York, and he gave me a ride back into the city Sunday evening.

PROBABLY THE MAN WHO MOST CHANGED AVIS'S LIFE WAS VIC-
tor Greenwood. We went together to his funeral three
years ago and afterward she told me the story of what
turned out to be her job interview.

She'd been one of the bright young things from the *Social Register* working at Sotheby Parke Bernet when Victor noticed something special in her and asked her to come see him. This was in
1970. When she went to her boss to ask for an hour off one afternoon, he said, "Victor Greenwood asked you to come to his house?"

"Yes."

"Why you? He doesn't collect Old Masters."

"I have no idea," said Avis. "He was mooching around some
Dutch still lifes while we were preparing the catalogue, and he
started asking me questions."

"What kind of questions?"

"Which one was better. More important. If I could buy one
painting in the gallery, money no object, which one would I buy."

Her boss had laughed. "That's Victor. Well, go, of course. Give
me a call when you're done, I'd love to know what he wants."

Although she was twenty-eight and probably as toothsome as
she would ever be in her life, Avis didn't imagine Mr. Greenwood
wanted her body. His taste in women was well known, and she
wasn't it. Naturally I asked what she wore. She said she had chosen her usual uniform of very simply cut grays and blacks that
caused her roommate to call her the Art Nun. Apparently this
had been the right call.

She'd arrived on time at his house, a five-story limestone edifice in a French château style on a quiet side street in the east seventies, and been shown into a vast room on the second floor hung with nineteenth-century paintings. The butler offered her coffee, tea, or a cocktail but she had declined, not thinking she would wait as long as she eventually did. When her host failed to appear, she got up and began to examine the paintings. One small Caillebotte she recognized at once as having been sold by Sotheby's two seasons before for a record sum for the artist. To a dealer named Gordon Hall, she thought. And he'd sold it to Greenwood for even more? Or he'd been bidding for Greenwood all along? Greenwood was squirrelly, everyone in the auction business knew. Sometimes he came to the auctions himself and bid, sometimes he came but sat like a stone Buddha while someone in the annex room was bidding for him, sometimes he bid by phone, and sometimes he was bidding by secret agreement with the auctioneer when he pulled his ear or took off his glasses. He enjoyed the sport of it.

Avis was lost in a painting of a young girl sitting in a wood with a boy lying on the grass beside her when she realized Greenwood was in the room watching her.

"What do you think?" He was looking pleased with himself.

"This is Edward Arthur Walton, isn't it?"

His eyebrows went up. "Very good."

"But isn't this *The Daydream*? I thought it was a lost work."

"Someone found it."

Someone who obviously knew well what Greenwood was looking for. She turned back to the painting.

"Do you like it?" He was observing her like a cat studying a cricket.

"I do like the Naturalists. But I'm surprised *you* do."

"Why?"

"Most people like either the Impressionists or the realists, but not both."

"Is that so." He seemed amused. "And which do you like?"

"I like both."

"What don't you like?"

"In paintings?"

"Yes."

She considered. "I don't think I like surrealism very much."

She was beginning to wonder if he would apologize for keeping her waiting so long. But instead he crossed the room and stood before an Eakins, one of his absurdly beautiful shirtless young men, rowing on a river.

"What's the best picture in this room?"

"I can't answer that."

"Why not?"

"You know why not," she said, and then realized she'd been rude. He didn't seem to mind.

"Then what's the most important?"

"For me? The Caillebotte."

"Why?"

"Because he painted so little and it's a very good one."

"But very small."

"Size isn't everything." Oh god. Was that suggestive? She wished the butler would come back. What the hell was she doing here?

"What's your favorite Eakins?"

"The portrait of Louis Kenton."

"Why?"

"Because I love portraits. Because he floats there in space, looking unhinged and sad."

"Kenton was Eakins's brother-in-law, wasn't he?"

She smiled. "You do your homework."

"Only a fool would spend this kind of money without doing his homework. You didn't think I was a fool, did you?"

"I did not."

"Why do you like portraits?"

"I like it that you can stare at them and wonder about them the way you can't with actual people. You have time."

"I like that picture too, but I don't see Kenton as sad, I see him as weak. An interesting subject, weak men. Did you know that he hit his wife in the face and she had to run away from him in the middle of the night?"

"I did. But he isn't doing it in the painting. In the painting he's alone and sad."

"Why do women tolerate men like that? I'd kick him down the stairs."

Greenwood was tall, and she realized, powerfully built, although he didn't move or dress like an athlete.

She said, "This is really not my field."

"No. I'd buy the Kenton, though. Would you?"

She turned and looked at him. Okay, it's a test, she thought. I'm good at tests.

"Yes. I don't think the Met is selling, but there's an oil study of it at the Farnsworth we might take a shot at."

He grinned. "Now how do you know that?"

"I told you. It's my favorite Eakins."

"There's a Renoir coming up at your spring sales."

"*Le Pecheur?*"

"How much do you think it will go for?"

She quoted him the estimate.

They moved to a picture of a river in spring, with a rowboat. "Is this Seurat worth that much?"

A thoroughly loaded question. She said, "I can't tell you."

"Should I sell the Seurat and buy the Renoir?"

"No."

"Why not?"

"Because you already have two Renoirs in this room alone and that's enough."

"Really."

"Yes."

"Two paintings by one artist are enough?"

"No, two Renoirs in one room are enough. You can see too many Renoirs, and once you have, they all start to look like cake frosting."

He laughed aloud. "Did Henry offer you anything? What would you like? Tea? A drink?"

"Coffee, please."

He went to the door and pressed a buzzer hidden behind a damask hanging.

Henry arrived with a silver tray bearing a Georgian silver coffee service, a plate of cookies, a can of Tab, and a glass of ice. He settled the tray and poured the Tab, as if he were serving Perrier-Jouët, as a grizzled dachshund trotted in at the open door, stopped in the middle of the room, glared at Avis, and started to bark.

"Mabel! Stop it," said Greenwood, in a tone that said he had long given up hope that Mabel would obey him in anything. "Do you mind dogs?"

"Love them."

They sat down together on a sofa and Mabel jumped up between them, still growling softly at Avis.

"Hello, little girl," Avis said to the dog. She offered her hand. Mabel sniffed it and fell silent, appearing mollified. Avis leaned forward to pour herself a cup of coffee, and Mabel lunged, teeth bared, at her nose. Fortunately, in her surprise, Avis laughed.

"No, that's enough!" said Greenwood angrily, seizing Mabel. He carried the dog to the door, threw her into the hall, then pulled the door closed. Then he apologized, a thing she guessed he had little practice at.

"Don't worry," said Avis, truly unruffled. "I was brought up by women like that." Mabel reminded her strongly of her nanny, Miss Burns. This appeared to delight her host.

He said, "I'd like you to work for me."

There was silence. As often when she didn't know what to do, Avis did nothing.

"You don't have to leave Sotheby's," he said. "I'd just like to be able to ask you questions from time to time. Give me your opinions. Maybe bid for me now and then."

"But you don't collect Old Masters," she said.

"I don't?"

Another silence.

"Wouldn't it be a conflict of interest?" she asked.

"No. Why would it?"

She couldn't think of a reason.

"Ask your boss. I'm not asking you to do anything shady. I'm still learning, you know. Always learning. I don't have time to get a fancy degree, so I like to be able to call on people who know more than I do. But I don't like to take advantage of people, and no one takes advantage of me. I'll make sure you earn your money."

"There are a lot of people who know more than *I* do."

"I know. Some of them work for me too." He drained his glass, making a sibilant gurgling sound around the ice. Then he stood and said, "Come with me."

She followed him out of the room and up the stairs with growing misgiving. On the third floor he led her down a long hallway to a small round room in something like a turret. It was lined floor to ceiling with dark carved glass-front cases that had surely come from some Old World library that predated this house by several centuries. "This is the treasure room. Your boss has been in the room downstairs, but he's never seen this."

She wanted to ask why not, but Greenwood added, "It's always good to hold something back. Come here."

He led her to a vitrine that held what looked to be Egyptian glass statuettes and ornaments, medieval icons, and some coins.

"Did you know that glass is actually a liquid?" he asked. "It's supercooled, so it seems stable at temperatures where ice would melt. But in fact glass is melting all the time, just very slowly. With pieces as old as this, many millennia, you can measure the slump." He was smiling at his pieces as he spoke, as if they were pets.

He tapped on the pane at a gold ring with a coat of arms worked in glass and enamels.

"Do you know what that is?"

"May I see it?"

He took his key ring from his pocket, unlocked the case, and opened the front. Then he waited to see what she would do.

Very carefully, she removed the ring and turned it around to examine the underside of the bezel. He gave a laughing bark.

"That's what I thought," he said.

Behind the crest, worn next to the skin, was an enameled green grasshopper.

"How did you know? Have you seen one before?"

"A Gresham grasshopper ring? Never. I didn't know there were any in this country."

"Aha. And my point is, *this* isn't your field either."

A GRADUATE OF OUR BOARDING SCHOOL WAS AT THAT TIME THE social secretary to the First Lady of the United States. My grandmother made dismissive remarks about "ladies marketing their social graces," but I could see that rather than being a drawback in that extremely populist mood of the early 1970s, my otherwise fairly useless boarding school education was an advantage in the industry in which I found myself. I had also by chance chosen one of the few fields in which it was not a hindrance to be a woman.

Mme. Philomena thought a good next step for me would be one of the fashion magazines, where I could be an ambassador for her collections. She offered to put in a word with Mrs. Vreeland at *Vogue,* or with China Machado at *Harper's Bazaar,* and I was tempted; magazine jobs were glamorous. But when glamour is a perk of the job, the salary is generally reduced by whatever the employer discovers the glamour is worth, and I had my living to make.

Mme. Olitsky thought that I might make a buyer for one of the department stores. But the buyers I had met at the atelier could be beastly; they had power, and it seemed to make them rude. Power always presents a challenge to the average mortal soul. Still, there is usually a point in any process where there's a chance of grace. In film, the casting director owns the happiest moment, when the project has a green light, talented people are being told Yes, and everyone is full of hope. In fashion, you might think it's the moment the designer emerges to applause after presenting a collection, but you'd be forgetting how many collections fail, not to mention the pressures of paying suppliers and banks, guessing what people will want in six months when the clothes are actually in stores, or the chances that your best ideas will be knocked off and lining someone else's pocket before you can get them to market. No, I'd say the best moment in fashion is the point of sale. The moment an actual human wants to buy the dress and wear it out of the store.

I realize this is a minority opinion.

Selling is a service profession. It's not waiting on tables, but it's in the category. It doesn't suit everybody, but it suits me; there are worse things in life than serving.

I wanted to be Mme. Olitsky. Mme. Philomena already had her vendeuse; it was time for me to find someone who needed what I was good at. Mrs. Bachman at Saks, my grandmother's saleswoman, had maintained an interest in me. She came to Mme. P's shows, though of course she didn't buy from us, since she got a hefty employee discount at her own store. She came to see what our customer was wearing and what she liked from our line. Once in a while she took me to lunch, clanking with heavy gold bracelets and piling up Kent cigarette butts stained with scarlet lipstick in her ashtray. When at last I sent her my résumé, she called me and said in her marvelous ruined voice, "Your grandmother will never forgive me."

When I told Mme. Philomena I was leaving, you'd have thought she'd caught me selling her toiles to the competition. "I have nurtured you! I've spent years training you!" she howled in French. When she was not exercising her Gallic charm, she often looked like a man in a bouffant wig. That day she wore heavy green eye shadow and had a run in her stocking. Apparently I was a hurt bird she'd been plying with worms, and now I'd had the ingratitude to take flight. It was good, I thought, that she hadn't taken up nursing.

Mme. Olitsky assured me that Mme. P would get over it. "She doesn't like it any better when her protégées stay too long— she likes them to move on and shine, so she can claim she made them." Mme. Olitsky took me to lunch on my last day and gave me a little book called *Your Future in the Fashion World,* wishing me luck and signed with affection. The book covered every job except selling.

THAT SAME YEAR, 1972, DINAH'S OLDEST SON WAS BORN. SHE CALLED me at six in the morning. "Eight pounds six ounces," she crowed. "I was a star! All natural, not even aspirin!" I went to the hospital after work with a plush panda and a helium balloon. Dinah was glowing, and the room was filled with flowers and tributes. Her sisters were with her when I came in.

"Have you seen the baby?" they cried. "Doesn't he look just like Daddy?"

I had seen him through the nursery glass, and he did.

"Richard is furious," said Dinah, beaming. "He claims I must have conceived by parthenogenesis." Just then Richard walked in, looking goofy with joy, kissed her and handed her a milk shake, which she fell upon with happy greed.

Simon Snyder, the impresario of "New York Eye," appeared and declared, "My god, it looks like a funeral home," as a nurse came in with another arrangement of flowers.

"The biggest ones are all from press agents," Dinah said.

"These must be from an actual friend. Oh isn't that nice, Constantia Lord! That's really so sweet of her! Do you know Constantia?" she asked me. "You'd love her. I'll introduce you."

"I do know her, but I'd love to see her again."

Dinah paused for an infinitesimal beat. "You do know her? How?"

"We happened to be staying at the same house in Southampton one weekend," I said. Another beat.

"Whose house?" Simon demanded. He had seated himself on Dinah's bed and was passing around the chocolate truffles he'd brought her.

I reluctantly named a much-photographed hostess of the day. "Really," said Dinah again. "That sounds amusing," making it sound as if she'd rather be trussed and grilled over open flame.

"She's a very good customer."

"Is she." I knew she was waiting for more information.

"There was someone she wanted me to meet," I said.

"I'll bet. Monty, the chinless wonder?"

As a matter of fact, it *had* been the hostess's son Monty, who was a very sweet man though unlikely in my view to provide her with grandchildren.

"He's a marvelous bridge player," I said.

"Bridge!" Dinah laughed her famous laugh. "Bridge! You spent a weekend in Southampton playing bridge with Monty Mayhew? Lovie, you do surprise me."

There was quite a stretch after that when every time she called me, Dinah would say, "Am I taking you away from your bridge game?"

DINAH'S MARRIAGE TO RICHARD WAINWRIGHT HAD SURPRISED MANY, including me. I thought she was in love with a photo-realist painter named Barney she'd been half living with in SoHo, or what became SoHo, I'm not sure it had a name yet in those days. Richard, by contrast, was the most conventional man I'd ever seen her with. Dinah had met him at a boarding school glee club dance, then run across him years later on one of her nightlife prowls. He was quite wonderful in his way, handsome, solid, and with a cheerful wit. But he came from a town outside Chicago so like Canaan Woods that it might as well have been the same place. The Wainwrights were country club people, Junior League people, people who'd never met a Negro who wasn't a servant. Richard was far more than that, but he wasn't in New York because he was fleeing where he came from, as Dinah and I were. He was in New York because he'd been offered a job with J. P. Morgan when he got out of Dartmouth and thought it would be neat to live here. The fact that Dinah could hear her companion utter a sentence like that and remain serene proved to me that she loved him, but there was also the fact that Richard Jr. was on the way.

They found a huge rent-controlled apartment on East Eighty-sixth Street across from Carl Schurz Park, and Dinah began a sort of salon, supper every Sunday night for a rotating cast of hundreds from all the worlds she and Simon Snyder inhabited, the theater, fashion, music, books, the art world, society friends, and of course a selection of Richard's more eligible colleagues. Invitations were prized, and Richard happily bankrolled it all and stood around on the edges, smiling. This was the New York he had hoped for. No one was terribly interested in talking to him, but he met most of the people one read about in the gossip columns, and he generally thought it was very entertaining. He was an easy man to please.

I was invited to perhaps one in three of Dinah's Sundays. I couldn't always go, as at that time I often went to the country on weekends with my friend, the man I had met at Meg's wedding. He had inherited a house in northwestern Connecticut that we both adored. But when we were in town he enjoyed going, and the crowd was always eclectic enough that his presence wasn't surprising. Few even realized we were together, and those who did wouldn't have talked about it. What happened at Dinah's was never reported outside, unless by Dinah herself, and she protected her friends. She protected me, by making sure my friend and his famously difficult wife were elaborately mentioned as a couple whenever Althea deigned to come up from Palm Beach or back from Paris or Rio to attend some grand function with him.

RICHARD JR., CALLED RJ, WAS ALL BOY, EARLY TO WALK AND LATE TO talk. I remember him wheeling around the kitchen on his little plastic motorcycle with frightening skill while Dinah was cooking. He could steer in reverse better than I could. I brought him the record of *Free to Be . . . You and Me,* which was supposed to teach him that boys could express their true feelings, and I suppose it worked because from the get-go he freely showed that what he loved best in the world were trucks and guns. Show him all the flowers and birdies you wanted, he'd look politely and blink with those huge brown eyes, but let him catch sight of a big rig and he'd go "brmmm, brmmm" and jig with excitement.

Dinah was working as hard as ever the first few years of RJ's life, reporting with Simon on "Eye" and writing "Dinah Might" for Fridays. She collected so much material for the columns at her weekend gatherings—people told her everything, they couldn't seem to help it—that she didn't have to go out as much in the evenings, but she was still very much the girl about town, turning out for friends' openings and concerts and whatever sounded amusing. Sometimes they kept the nanny overnight and Richard went with her, but mostly he stayed home with RJ in the evenings.

Dinah was pregnant again, with Nicholas, when a society lady named Serena Tate showed up in my department at Saks one day. This must have been late 1974. I was rushing around the selling floor with an armload of debutante gowns and found her browsing among the Halstons. She was Colombian, and had been a dancer—with the Joffrey, I think—and still had a dancer's body, with a dancer's turned-out feet and a neat dark head on a swan neck. I had helped Mme. Olitsky with her chez Philomena.

She said in her elegant Latin accent, "Lovie, how nice to see you. You're looking radiant." I was surprised she remembered me.

"I'm so sorry, I have an appointment in minutes, Mrs. Tate, but I'd love to help you. Are you looking for something special?"

"I do need a dress for an evening wedding, but there's no great hurry."

I got my book, and we made an appointment for a late morning the next week.

"And if you're not too pressed, perhaps I could take you to lunch afterward," she added. This was, believe me, unusual. Mrs. Tate was decades older than I, at least I thought so at the time, and we shared few if any common points of biography. I began to demur.

She put a finger on my wrist briefly, looked at me very directly, and said, "Please."

"Well then . . . of course, that would be lovely." I watched her walk toward the elevators without another glance at the Halstons. She had not come in to shop. I was still watching, noting how still she stood and how self-contained she was, as if she never entirely lost the sense that even holding a pose in the corps de ballet while the premiers danced, she was part of the performance. She didn't shift her weight or check her sleeve for lint the way most people do when alone.

Then my debutante arrived, with her very determined mother.

SERENA TOOK ME TO LA GRENOUILLE, WHICH WORRIED ME FOR TWO reasons. French food is rich, and I usually eat only fruit during the day. And, I only got an hour off for lunch.

"Don't worry," she said, seeing me glance at my wristwatch. "Marjorie is a great friend; you have permission." Marjorie Bachman, my boss.

So now I was worried for a third reason. La Grenouille cost a fortune. What did she want from me?

She ordered for us, and I can remember to this day what we ate; I'd never tasted food like that in my life. I also remember how easily she made the time pass, how she made me feel witty and likeable and as if there needn't be a hidden agenda beyond the pleasure of my company.

But there was, of course. It arrived with our coffee soufflés. (With a pitcher of crème anglaise, if you're wondering, and a plate of tiny petits fours.)

"I don't know if you've met Simon Snyder?" she said, a question. In fact, Simon was one of the things in Dinah's life I envied. He and Dinah shared a completely congruent sense of humor. I always think of one of the Sunday salons, when Dinah and Simon collapsed in a corner, undone by the giggles. The collector Victor Greenwood was there that day with a Swedish actress, and I think there was a Hindu swami as well. Allen Ginsberg came with a poet Dinah knew from Vassar, and after a while he took off all his clothes and recited, quite beautifully I thought. Everyone wanted to know what Dinah and Simon found so funny, and neither of them could explain it without setting each other off again. Later I learned that a self-important impresaria someone had brought and no one had liked was found to have pissed in her chair. Ruined the upholstery, of course, but Richard would have it redone.

"A really beautiful man," said Serena of Simon. "Such a profile. And, of course, so amusing."

I agreed. Serena made a tiny hole in her soufflé and poured in a slim stream of the crème. Showing me, in the politest way possible, what to do with it. She took a microscopic bite.

"I have learned lately that there's another side to Mr. Snyder," she said. "Not a nice one."

Uh-oh. I'd suspected I wasn't going to like this, and I didn't.

"One way or another, he . . . well, he met an old friend whom I knew very well before I came to New York, who apparently was indiscreet. Mr. Snyder asked me rather pointedly how my husband would take the news that my previous love, before I met him, was a woman."

I sat silent. Serena mistook my silence, and went on. "And that she wasn't the first . . . or the last. I made the mistake of making it clear that my husband would not take it well."

I still didn't know what to say.

"I'm not a public person," she said with sudden passion. "We live quietly. Why should anyone care about our lives?"

Which was perhaps disingenuous. They may have lived quietly for zillionaire philanthropists, but there were always going to be a few hundred thousand people who wanted to know why a man with net worth in the high eight figures had married Serena and not somebody else, and at least half of them for no reason at all would hope to learn it wasn't going well. But surely her frustration was understandable.

Serena said, "He wants me to pay him not to print it."

"What?"

Why do people say that when they're surprised? I had *heard* her . . .

"Yes. And . . . Loviah, I have children. They love their father. They love me. My husband loves me. But he *would* divorce me if . . ."

"You can't be sure."

She raised a hand. "Be sure, I can. To know would be bad enough for Leo. To see it in the paper, to know his friends all knew . . . Unforgivable."

We sat looking at each other. I was shocked and distressed, because I had finally guessed why she was telling me.

"I know I'm to blame. It's never all right to do wrong because you think no one will find out. I betrayed my husband, and I may deserve to be punished. But not this way, not by him. And I doubt I'm the only one Mr. Snyder has done this to."

I didn't know what to say, so I said nothing.

"I can pay Mr. Snyder. I already have, more than once. What I find I can't bear is never knowing when he is going to pop up again, and how much he'll want the next time." Another spell of silence, and then she said what I knew she would: "What I'd like you to do, if you will, kind Loviah, is arrange a meeting for me with your friend Dinah Wainwright."

I DIDN'T TELL DINAH WHAT IT WAS ABOUT. SHE SAID YES BECAUSE SHE likes knowing famous people, but she was going to like this even less than I did.

We had one of two choices. We could meet someplace discreet, which would raise questions if anyone happened to see us, or we could meet at the center of Serena's universe, where everyone she knew would see and no one would think it odd. We chose the latter, the Upper East Side canteen for people who wore the kinds of clothes Mrs. Bachman and I sold. It was also the hub of social gossip for the people Dinah wrote about.

There was a very noisy table in the middle of the room that suited us nicely, giving cover. We settled in, Serena exchanged air kisses with several friends. A society walker and publicist came over to greet Dinah, and Mrs. William F. Buckley stopped to speak to Serena and me, which was nice of her, though it made Dinah look at me sharply. She wanted to know how we'd met, but

I didn't explain, so Dinah excused herself and crossed the room to chat up an aging movie diva at the bar, just to show she could.

When Serena finally came to her point, late in the meal as she had with me, Dinah listened intently but otherwise held her poker face. She asked questions like the journalist she was. How were the approaches made? she asked. How much money had Serena paid Simon? How exactly were the demands couched? How was Serena accounting for the money at home?

Serena handled it all with perfect cool. She didn't try to protect herself, she never faltered or fudged her account. And if I realized that in her attempt to escape one professional trader in information, she was delivering herself to another, hung by her hooves and ready for slaughter, Serena certainly did too. For a time during the meal I grew afraid that Dinah might react by protecting Simon and selling out Serena. Dinah loves knowing things about others that no one else knows, and of course the knowing wasn't what interested her. It was letting others know that she knew.

Work changes you. Mine has changed me. Work changes everyone, builds certain skills and habits while others atrophy. And as I've said, Dinah loved her job.

This is what she said when she finally spoke. "Can you explain this? Why are some gay men so bitchy about lesbians?" The word jarred Serena, and she looked down at her plate.

The waiter came and I ordered coffee; the other two seemed paralyzed. After he'd come and gone, Dinah said to Serena, "Is there a number where I can reach you?"

Knowing that Mr. Tate, mostly retired, worked from home and a call from Dinah would be very hard to explain to him, I said, "Call me. I can call Serena." Serena shot me a look of pure gratitude, glanced at her watch, and said "I have to run. Thank you for coming, please stay. Order whatever you want."

Dinah watched Serena sign a chit and hand it to the bartender. "House account," she said. "Let's order champagne." I thought she was kidding, but she wasn't. She ordered a bottle of Veuve Clicquot and profiteroles. When the bottle came, she leaned back in her chair, raised her glass to me, and said, "I'm pretending we're rich."

The aging movie star came over and joined us. She'd clearly taken a drop or two. She had recently married well, a Wall Street tycoon whose name you would recognize, and was trying to learn a new role. When she'd settled herself on the banquette and tossed her vermilion hair, she said to Dinah, "Who do you have to fuck in this town to get on the board at the Met?" Dinah roared with laughter. And, of course, knew the answer, not that the mechanism was quite the one the movie star had suggested.

A WEEK OR SO LATER I HAD A PHONE MESSAGE FROM SERENA, AND RANG the house. When her husband answered, I said, "This is Loviah French from Saks, for Mrs. Tate," and Mr. Tate said cheerfully, "Uh-oh, this phone call is going to cost me money." In fact it did. Serena came in the next day and bought a Norell suit from me. She was thin and tense and didn't look well. She asked if I'd heard from Dinah. I hadn't and didn't know what to say.

Then one evening as I was about to leave for the day, Dinah appeared in the door of my little cubicle and said, "Do you have a minute?" I did. "Good," she said. "Buy me a drink."

Nowadays a pregnant woman wouldn't drink or smoke unless she wanted her friends to call the police, but *autres temps, autres moeurs.* We walked up Fifth Avenue, dodging the tourist throngs of summer, to the King Cole Bar at the St. Regis. When we had settled into the cool semidarkness and had our vodka gimlets before us, Dinah had lit a cigarette, and I said, "So?"

"I just resigned," she said.

I was stunned. "From your job?"

"Well, duh." She raised her glass to me and took a deep swallow. Then: "Of course, I hoped your Mrs. Tate was a fantasist. There was nothing odd in Simon's office files. But I couldn't figure out what her game was, if that story wasn't true. Two days ago, Simon happened to leave his briefcase under his desk when he went to lunch. I happened to look into it."

She lit another cigarette from the butt of her first. "He had a number of files with no names on them, but one of them was Serena's. There were what looked like verbatim quotes from a woman named Luisa who had clearly known Serena very very well. Names, dates, everything. Simon's memory for dialogue is scary accurate, I've learned the hard way. Him and Truman Capote. Let's hope *he's* not planning a nonfiction novel."

"What kind of dialogue was it? A woman scorned?"

"I doubt it. I think she was just enjoying the reaction she was getting and didn't realize who she was talking to. Simon is *very* charming, you know."

"And Serena wasn't the only one?"

Dinah shook her head.

"Bald-faced blackmail?"

"Well, he wasn't putting it like that. He was inviting them to 'invest' in a new magazine he was starting."

"I take it you confronted him."

"This morning." She put her face in her hands, pressing her eyelids with her fingertips. "It was horrible." Her nail polish was chipped. "He called me vicious names. He said everyone in our business does it. I said they don't, and pointed out he could go to jail. He said I just wanted his job. I said I didn't. He said 'Prove it.'"

My Dinah. I could see the scene.

"He said that if anyone ever, *ever* heard about this, Serena's name would be all over Liz Smith in a New York minute. I said I didn't want to ruin him, I just want him to stop."

"Did he believe you?"

She shook her head. "People who do things like that believe that everyone else is just like them. The only way to prove there was a principle at stake was to quit. So I did."

"Even though you *do* want his job."

She nodded.

"Didn't the suits want to know why you were going?"

"Not really. They will tomorrow. Today they just wished me well and assumed I want to stay home with my children."

"And what *are* you going to do?"

"Stay home with my children. Another Women's Libber bites the dust."

The next morning, in Simon Snyder's last column for "The Fishwrap," he announced he was moving west to a new field of endeavor, then sang an aria to old friends, good times, and how much he had loved New York. Simon at his best.

There are five people other than Simon and Dinah and me who knew for sure what had happened. Dinah went to them one by one and gave them their files back. One man actually wept.

And to this day, Dinah misses that job, and that friendship. You never really get over someone you've laughed with like that.

STILL, AT THE TIME, ONE FELT THAT WHEN ONE DOOR CLOSES, MANY more open. Dinah's quitting looked like a temporary hitch in an inevitable upward trajectory. Dinah was a star. She could write, she could talk, she could cook, she knew everyone. She was happily married to a good man. Why shouldn't it all just get better and better? We rarely recognize these turning pylons in life when we round them, though they're easy enough to spot in retrospect.

Nicholas was born on a morning in late September 1975. New York was golden, with the fresh snap of new beginnings in the air, of back to school, of clean slates. The trees were beginning to turn, but flowers still bloomed in the sidewalk beds along the side streets. I used my lunch hour to run up to Lenox Hill to greet the new arrival, and took Dinah a blue satin bed jacket. She asked me to be Nicky's godmother, and I cried.

He was a beautiful baby. He had a mad shock of dark hair, like Dinah's, and his skin had none of the scaly stuff or red blotches newborns often have. Of course I was prejudiced from the first; I felt a rush of something I'd never felt before when I held him. Mother Nature working her little tricks. His tiny fingers with their miniature nails grasped my thumb and held fast, and it made me giddy, it was so sweet.

The christening was at the Church of the Heavenly Rest on the Upper East Side, which many of its members like to call the

Church of the Overly Dressed. Richard was a regular communicant. He'd been a cradle Episcopalian, lapsed like so many of us in his teens, when we had all the answers and knew we would live forever, but RJ's birth had changed that. It wasn't Saul on the road to Damascus, he didn't talk about Jesus or faith or anything, but it was important to him. Anyway, it was lovely. Richard's parents and brother came from Chicago, and Dinah's family came down from Canaan Hamlet. When our part of the service arrived, Stewie Brumder and I went up to the font with Dinah and Richard. I carried the baby, who wore the same long, lace Wainwright family christening dress RJ had worn, still smelling of mothballs. When the priest took the baby in the crook of his arm and began to work his voodoo with the holy water, Nicholas opened his eyes and looked startled, but too interested to cry. My grandmother always said babies should cry at christenings, it's the sound of the devil leaving them. But she also said that a broken mirror meant seven years of bad luck, and referred to an unforeseen difficulty as "the nigger in the woodpile." Nicholas was angelic, sunny, and easy, except when he wasn't.

Dinah was besotted with him. She had nursed RJ for a month or two, but then she'd gone back to work and left him with a Haitian nanny. She nursed Nicky for almost a year. There was a great deal of talk in those years about feeding on a schedule or "nursing on demand." I don't remember how RJ was raised, but Nicky was definitely on demand. Dinah didn't see any point in thwarting him in anything.

RJ was having a hardish time adjusting to the new arrival. On one evening visit I rode up in the elevator with the plumber; RJ had flushed an orange down the toilet. His first words to his brother, when he came home from the hospital, were "Here, baby—eat soap." He was a sturdy three-year-old by then.

After Nicky was born, Dinah's Sunday salons changed. She started including families, and the event evolved into a cheerful madhouse of little boys rampaging through the living room while more and more of the grown-ups debated whether television, even *Sesame Street,* was a blessing or a curse, and how young a child could be sent to day care, and fewer and fewer wanted to talk about the new production of *Uncle Vanya* or whether Ford was right to have pardoned Nixon. Nicky started walking, then talking; RJ started preschool.

And then there was the spring morning I was walking to work and came upon Richard Wainwright leaving the Cabot Hotel with a young woman who was definitely not his wife.

It could have been a power breakfast, but why at a tiny hotel on a side street? And the girl wasn't dressed for business; she was wearing a long skirt and flat sandals and a newsboy cap which, I must say, became her. And there was the way they kissed goodbye as Richard put her into a cab.

What a bite of poisoned apple. As the cab pulled away, Richard straightened, smiling, and looked at the spring sky and the flowering trees on the street, scattering white petals on the sidewalk like a shower of warm snow. For a moment he was a man on top of the world. Then he saw me standing across the street, thunderstruck.

What would *you* do?

There was no right answer. No one is thanked for bearing news like that. What did I know about what went on in that marriage? And of course there was my own situation. I was in no position to tell tales.

But. I was Dinah's friend. How could it be right for me to know something so important about her life that she didn't know? What did the office of friendship require in this case?

I went to visit Dinah and the boys that weekend. Nicky was now two and a half. His hair had stayed dark and his eyes had stayed blue, and he had the world's longest eyelashes. We took the children to Carl Schurz Park and talked while Dinah pushed Nicky on a swing and five-year-old RJ raced around whooping. She was talking, I remember, about wanting to get back to work. She had some book ideas; we always thought someday she'd be on the best-seller list. Making the rounds of talk shows. Maybe having a talk show of her own. I asked if Richard had been out of town that week. Just for a night, she said. He was working on a deal in Toronto.

I asked if he supported her going back to work. She seemed surprised by the question. Whatever she did was fine with Richard. Richard was Richard.

And when Richard came home that afternoon and found us sitting together in the kitchen, drinking tea while the boys played with Legos at our feet, he looked at me as if I were a poltergeist, rattling the silver spoons in the drawer and causing the lights to flick on and off in his marriage. Dinah noticed nothing unusual. Richard made an excuse and left the apartment again, as if he didn't expect the place to be still standing when he got back.

I never told her. That left me the dislikable quandary of whether to come around as often as usual or stay away. I didn't want to stay away; there might be a time coming when Dinah would really need me. But what if she found out how long I had known, and had sat smiling and chatting while a bomb was ticking away under her chair? If it blew it was going to cover us all with scalding slime, not just Dinah.

Damned no matter what you do. Why do people think knowing secrets is fun? It was a miserable summer for me, as I guess it was for Richard too. The spark didn't get to the end of the fuse until one evening in October, when he hired a sitter and took Dinah out to dinner so they could "talk." People say that the betrayed spouse already knows on some level, but Dinah didn't. She thought he was going to say he wanted another child.

She was shattered. And if Richard thought she would take it quietly because they were in public, he was dead wrong about that. There are still people thirty years later whom Dinah won't speak to because they were in the restaurant that night. On some molecular level, she blew apart, and when the pieces settled, which took years, she was never again the person she'd been before.

You could say that if she'd paid more attention to Richard she would have known, or it wouldn't have happened, but that doesn't make it true. I believe Richard was stunned to learn he could hurt her that much. He doesn't have an unkind bone in his body, Richard, but you can still do plenty of damage by failing to imagine other people's realities.

At least he was serious about the girl, who has the old-fashioned name of Charlotte. She had worked for the decorator who was redoing his office. He married her as soon as the divorce was final, and they moved to Ardsley, where she tends her garden and raised their three daughters. Richard seems to be very content with Charlotte, and looking back it's hard to imagine that he and Dinah ever thought they could build a life together. It's hard to suppose that a man as involved in playing squash and watching golf on television as he is could ever have been just as happy at Dinah's Sundays.

Dinah kept the rent-controlled apartment and has never left it. She pays less than a thousand dollars a month for space that would go now, at market rates, for, oh, twenty times that. For decades her friends have said that if she was ever hit by a bus or a falling piano, the police would instantly arrest her landlord.

Richard felt so guilty about the divorce that he didn't make a very good advocate for himself. Dinah got full custody of the boys, child support for as long as they lived at home, full tuition for wherever they wanted to go to school, and alimony until she remarried, with cost of living adjustments built in. And it can't have occurred to Richard, fundamentally fair as he is, that she would stay so angry for so long that he'd be supporting her for life.

THAT WAS A DIFFICULT WINTER. MY FRIEND'S VERY IMPOSING wife, Althea, had a health event and came home to be treated at Memorial Sloan-Kettering. Surgery and chemo didn't seem to slow her down. She turned up in *Women's Wear Daily* every five minutes, wearing a series of turbans on her bald head that were so becoming to her it started a craze. For a while half the fashionable women of New York looked like escapees from the Kasbah.

Naturally, I kept a low profile, avoided Althea's haunts, and was on my own a great deal. I took piano lessons and conversational French. Suddenly without plans for the weekends, I took a ballet class with Dinah for exercise. Thanksgiving was a can of turkey hash in my apartment. I thought if I stayed home all day my friend might shake free for an hour or two, but he didn't. I began to hate my silent answering machine.

I did go to Dinah's for Christmas and took too many presents for Nicky. Christmas night she and I went out to see *The Buddy Holly Story* so that Richard could spend time at the apartment with RJ and Nicky. When we got back both boys were in tears, and by the time he left, we all were, Richard included. Christmas is a cruel time for sad people.

Nicky was a terror that winter. At a birthday party for an older child in the building, he came unglued because none of the shiny presents was for him. When the birthday girl wouldn't give him a wooden puzzle he'd fastened onto, although she wasn't playing with it herself, he ran at her and bit her hard on the arm. The child's mother got to Nicky in a flash, pulled him off her daughter, and bit him back, yelling, "How do you like it?" as Nicky howled in disbelief. Then Dinah snatched Nicky, shouting, "Don't you touch my child!" as the hostess yelled that it was the only way children would learn what it felt like. For years afterward the two families wouldn't ride in the same elevator. And I'm sorry to report that Dinah began to dine out on the story, so Nicky quickly learned that the whole thing had been somehow funny.

Mrs. Bachman retired in the spring, and though she'd recommended me, the store thought I was too young to head the department; they brought in a woman from Neiman Marcus named Marylin Coombs. We had a rocky start together and never entirely recovered. Different manners, different styles. She had a big sense of humor, and many of our out-of-town clients adored her.

It was also that winter when I ran across Avis Binney again, after so many years, at the opera. January 1979, *Luisa Miller*; I recently found the *Playbill*. I still remember the way the colors of the women's costumes drew your eye to Luisa, who alone was wearing blue. A client had given me tickets at the last minute, two in the middle of the fifth row. The price of each one was about what I paid to rent my apartment for a month. Having failed to find an escort at such short notice, I'd put my coat on my empty seat and sat reading the program, waiting for the lights to dim. "I'm just alone because this was so last-minute, you see . . ." I explained in my head to no one. "My friend would have loved to come, but he . . ." and a couple arrived at the seats on the other side of my coat chair. I kept my eyes down but could see that the lady was turning a very expensive fur inside out and preparing to stuff it under her chair. "Please," I said, "share my personal closet," and I patted the spare seat.

"Are you sure?" said the grateful couple, who were already piling their coats on top of mine. They were silver people, with gleaming gray hair and expensive teeth. "How nice of you."

Then came a tap on my shoulder from the row behind me. I turned, and Avis said, "Lovie French? I *thought* that was your profile . . ."

As the house lights went down and the chandelier rose I was suddenly part of the fabric of the great city, not an odd pea alone in a pod, but the sort of woman who runs into pals from boarding school at the opera. The sort of woman who is remembered by the glamorous older girls. Though I knew, of course, that her remembering reflected well on Avis, not on me. She is a woman who notices the quiet soul in the corner.

Avis was wearing a cushion-cut diamond on her wedding ring finger, but her companion that night was Teddy Tomalin, a dapper young bachelor who later became a great friend of mine. She insisted I join them in the Belmont Room at intermission. No standing in line at the lobby bar with the hoi polloi for us.

"So you're in New York now," said Avis while Teddy went to get us champagne. "Tell me everything, what are you doing?"

I gave her my card, dreading her reaction. Surely she supposed, given my fancy orchestra seats, that I was some rich man's wife, spending my days lunching at Le Cirque. But she read the card and cried, "How wonderful! Does that mean you get to run barefoot through the collections and buy everything on discount? I will come straight to you for my clothes from now on." And she did.

She dresses very well, Avis. She is a realist in the fitting room. Her figure is slim, with no bottom to speak of. Even now, she never wears trousers in town. She wears skirts just below the knee, and beautiful shoes that show off her narrow calves and feet. She knew to avoid the big-shoulder styles of the 1980s, when so many women looked as if their jackets still had the hangers in them. Armani is too masculine for her, but Chanel is very good, and now she mostly wears a German designer I've found, who does feminine clothes with clean lines but beautiful details.

She made a professional appointment with me soon after the opera night, and we spent several hours trying clothes for day and for evening. She'd say, "Oh, isn't that pretty, I've always wanted to wear that color," and try on whatever I'd brought her. Everything that season was a gray-green color called Wintermint and it was a disaster on her; it made her skin sallow and her eyes dull, as she had known it would. Gradually I learned. She is marvelous in strong warm colors or black. Black more and more, now that her hair is white. Now, black probably forever.

Next, she invited me to a Sunday luncheon party. Her apartment was on Fifth Avenue. The dining room windows are just above treetop level with a charming view of the Children's Zoo in Central Park. The living room was done in glowing brocades with real Empire French furniture and everywhere vitrines full of objets d'art. I met two new clients that day who have stayed very faithful over the years. Marylin gets the high rollers from South America, but I've built up a steady base of the ladies who live between Carnegie Hill and East Fifty-seventh Street, and Avis helped a lot.

The lunch was not just for ladies. It was much more like a dinner party, with ten at table, a cocktail beforehand, four courses, and three kinds of wine. As I remember, Teddy Tomalin the opera buff was there, as well as Avis's business partner, the art dealer Gordon Hall, the zillionaire collector Victor Greenwood with a vavavoom lady friend, and an aging literary lion who had once shot one of his wives and had just published a memoir. I was seated on the right hand of Avis's husband, Harrison Metcalf. He was twenty years older than Avis, in a bespoke tweed jacket and Lobb shoes, with a beautiful head of reddish blond hair. We talked about his pre-Columbian art collection, which was all around us, and about which he was fascinating, at least early in the meal. His other great passion was polo, about which I also knew a little. After that lunch I was often included when Avis entertained important clients, because I was "good with Harrison." He and I truly liked each other, I think, though by the time I got home that first Sunday I was wishing desperately for a nap, and wondering who these people were that they could eat and drink like that for hours in the middle of the day.

Avis had season tickets to the Met, very good ones as I've said, and Harrison didn't indulge, so Avis was often looking for a companion. She was good enough to put me on her list, and she enjoyed educating my taste. Later we sat through the entire Ring together, but I was a less successful student of Wagner than of the Italians. She forgave me. It was during my first *Otello* when she told me shyly at intermission that she was pregnant.

"Harrison wants a boy," she said. He had twin daughters by a former marriage, girls now in their early twenties. "We're calling the bump Cyril."

"What do the older sisters say?"

She laughed. "They call him The Little Trustbuster."

The daughters were good-natured blonds, very much the image of their father. They also called Avis "Wicked Stepmummy" and appeared to be very fond of her. We met at the Metcalfs' Christmas party and bonded at the eggnog bowl. Hilary was at Bank Street taking a teaching degree, and Catherine was working at *Glamour* magazine. Avis's own stepmother, Belinda Binney, was at that party as well.

Belinda had snow-white hair, like Avis's now, beautifully coiffed. She was wearing a long evening dress in bottle-green velvet, evidently going on to a formal dinner. She looked me up and down that evening in a way I've seen people look over horses they might buy. I almost showed her my teeth. "I'm pleased that we meet at last," she said.

"Yes, I'm so glad Avis and I have reconnected."

"That's not what I meant. I'm on the board at the Public Library with Gil Flood."

My friend. For a moment my heart seemed to stop in my chest. I thought, *This is it, this is what I've been dreading.* She's going to call me a harlot and have me removed and thrown into a snowbank. She went on, "I must come and see you. Avis is looking so well since you've taken her in hand."

Naturally I said that would please me. "Madame Philomena says wonderful things about you too," she added, as if I'd applied for work at the CIA and she was in charge of my background check. Then: "I don't suppose you've *met* Althea?"

I didn't dare react.

"I can't bear her," said Mrs. Binney. "Never trust a woman who is disliked by her servants."

More useful information from another planet. But Belinda and I were friends from that evening until her death, and I miss her still.

CYRIL WAS A GIRL. SHE WAS BORN IN MARCH 1980 AND NAMED GRA-
ciela for her paternal grandmother, and called Grace by everyone.
She was entered for Miss Pratt's the week she was born and had
more hand-smocked dresses than any child I've ever known. One
evening, fresh from her bath, she escaped from her nanny and
ran up the hall, pink and naked, clutching her yellow bath duck.
She succeeded in getting all the way to the den where her parents
were having cocktails, and proudly presented her trophy to her
mother, saying, "Duck! Duck!" Avis was so enchanted she had
little yellow ducks embroidered on Grace's bathrobe, her sheets,
her towels, and the hems of her dresses.

IT HADN'T TAKEN ME LONG TO UNDERSTAND WHY AVIS NEVER ENTER-
tained at night. I would present myself at the Metcalfs' in the evening when Avis and I were going on together to the theater or
opera. "Will you pop up for a minute so Harrison can see you?"
Avis would ask; we carried on the conceit that Harrison was devoted to me. We'd go into the den where he was ensconced at that
time of day and have a drink, our first, his tenth. Avis and I would
exchange the latest gossip, light and bright, while Harrison sat in
his chair with his glass in his hand, appearing for most purposes
asleep, except when he belched or scratched himself. From time
to time he'd become animate, lurch to his feet, and make his way
with surprising cunning around his ottoman and past the coffee

table to the bar, where he'd upend the vodka bottle into his glass, then thread the needle back to his chair. Avis never mentioned the situation, unless she had to explain to a new acquaintance why Harrison couldn't accept some kind invitation to dine, in which case she'd say that he "wasn't well."

"You can't invite them to dinner," said one client of mine. "Because what if they both *came?*"

Though she never complained, this was isolating for Avis. One winter she installed Harrison at a beachside house in Hobe Sound with a cook/driver, made sure his friends all knew he was there, and came back to New York to go back to work. Three days later, he was home. "It was all so *sportif*," he said with contempt. "All that blaring sunlight, all that . . . *tennis*. Everyone rushing around half-dressed, looking cooked and chasing balls. No conversation." He couldn't exactly remember how the airline thing worked, so he'd chartered a plane. He said he missed Grace. Avis pretended it was a normal anecdote about a semiretired husband.

When he wanted more drink and wasn't sure he could walk to the bottle, he'd ring for the butler. Did Avis ever tell William not to respond? Since Harrison paid the servants' salaries, I suppose that was a lost cause. Did she ever say a word to Harrison herself? Did she ever try to cut off the vodka supply? I don't know, we never talked about it.

When Grace was little, her birthday parties were at restaurants, because "Harrison wasn't well." At least not after lunch. When they were planning her debut, her father ordered a new tailcoat, determined to waltz with her at the Assemblies. Avis conducted herself as if that were a plausible plan until Grace said that if her father went, she wouldn't.

Grace and Avis were here at the shop when she said it. I imagine she felt safer with witnesses about. Avis gave Grace a look that would have quelled Attila the Hun, not for what she'd said, but because she had said it in public. (Public in that case being me and Mrs. Oba.) It turned out to be a moot point, because early in Grace's senior year at Nightingale, Harrison was found on the floor in the den, bleeding from his eye sockets. He went by ambulance to the hospital, where as soon as he was compos mentis an intervention at last was held, organized by Grace and her half-sisters, with Harrison's doctor assisting and Avis standing by, looking pained. He went from the hospital to a dry-out clinic in Westchester. They thought he was safely sequestered there because he didn't have any street clothes or money. After three weeks, he walked into town in his robe and slippers, got a sympathetic druggist to place a call to a car service in the city where he had a charge account, borrowed money from the driver for a quart of vodka, and was three sheets to the wind by the time he made his way back to the apartment and into his chair in the den.

So Grace had her way about the Assemblies. When the curtseys had been made and the orchestra struck up the fathers' waltz, Grace was in the arms of her uncle Walter. His cutaway looked to me as if he'd had it since Princeton, the pants were too short and the vest and coat barely buttoned, but it was kind of him to come on from Cleveland to do the honors, and he danced very well.

Harrison was to have come so he at least could watch the great moment from the balcony. I was to sit with him, but he never made it out of the den. Catherine and Hilary tried a few more times to talk him into treatment, but Grace was disgusted and everyone else left him to it. There were several more trips to the hospital, but he always resumed drinking as soon as he got home, and early in the morning one Monday in April when Grace was nineteen he was found dead in his chair. Grace happened to be home from Sarah Lawrence for the weekend. No authorities were called until after she had left for the train back to school; Avis told me she didn't think that was a sight a daughter needed to see. Nobody even told Grace her father was dead until she finished her classes that afternoon. Perhaps you can imagine her feelings.

GRACE MUST HAVE BEEN ABOUT THREE WHEN, IN SOME FIT OF misguided hope, I invited Avis and Dinah to lunch together. It was auction season and a particularly busy day for Avis, as I now know, but she had graciously accepted, realizing that I wanted to repay her in some small measure for her generosity to me. I'd spoken of Dinah to Avis, but she didn't seem to remember much about her; the older girls at school rarely do remember the younger ones if they hadn't had a special relationship. It was all the more flattering that Avis had remembered *me* when it was Dinah who was so vivid. I reasoned that we were all New Yorkers now, and both Dinah and Avis were so accomplished in their different ways, and we had shared that boarding school experience that seemed more and more anachronistic with every passing year. Dinah said it was as if we'd all gone to sleep one night in the world of Edith Wharton and awakened the next morning at Woodstock. Surely *that* was the basis for a bond. How wrong could it go?

Dinah and I were already seated when Avis arrived, out of breath, at the brasserie near Beekman Place that I had chosen. I noted with a slightly sinking heart that Avis was wearing a pleated plastic rain hat of a kind that my grandmother kept folded in every purse and raincoat pocket. Dressing like your WASP grandmother was not a thing Dinah was likely to miss or to be kind about. Avis signaled her apologies to us where we sat with our big glasses of beautiful straw-colored wine, looking forward to a long relaxed natter. She wrestled out of her wet coat and rubber rain boots and handed them to the coat check girl.

"I'm incredibly sorry," Avis said when she reached the table. She kissed me and shook the hand Dinah held out to her. "One of those phone calls where you say, 'I really have to go,' and the person says, 'Just one more thing,' and then pins you there for another twenty minutes. And then of course there were no cabs."

"We just got here," I said.

"It's so nice to see you, Dinah. It's been eons."

"Nice to see you too," said Dinah.

"Will Madame have a glass of wine?" said the waiter at her elbow.

"Just water, please. Thank you so much."

I wished she'd ordered wine. There was a brief silence, during which I did not allow Dinah to catch my eye. I began to recall the things I knew about both these women, Dinah's satirical nature and Avis's reserve, to name two, that might have suggested to me in advance that this lunch might not work out the way I had pictured it.

"So," said Dinah. "You're an art dealer."

"Yes. I was at Sotheby's, or Southby's, as people kept telling me. Park Bern-ay." It was pronounced BerNETT: short *e*, hard *t*. It was Avis's attempt at a humorous sally, but Dinah didn't respond. "Now I'm with the Gordon Hall Gallery."

"And what's that like?"

I recognized Dinah going into interview mode, a way of controlling a conversation that gave her complete cover.

"Busy."

"But fun?"

Avis looked for a moment as if she'd never considered whether her work was fun. Dinah got tired of waiting.

"You had an independent study with Mrs. Maffet your senior year," she said.

After a surprised pause, Avis said, "Yes. We did Spanish paintings. How on earth did you know that?"

"You told me."

"I did?"

"Yes. You told me that when you went to the Prado and saw Philip the Fourth you burst into tears."

A pause. I knew Avis *had* burst into tears in one of the Velázquez galleries, but she'd told me it wasn't so much at the paintings as at the thought that she might never get back to the Prado. I could see her wondering why on earth would she have told that to Dinah Kittredge? And when?

"Dinah remembers everything people say," I offered. "It's terrifying."

"Tools of the trade," said Dinah.

"You're a journalist," said Avis, enthusiastically trying to change the subject.

"I write drivel for the occasional shelter rag," said Dinah. Another silence. Is there anything quite as off-putting as insincere self-deprecation?

Gamely, Avis said, "Well, I envy you your memory, mine is terrible."

I protested. "You have an incredible memory for images. And music."

"But words are *so* important," said Avis. Even to me she seemed stiff, as if she couldn't stop being what Dinah expected her to be.

Unexpectedly, Dinah gave a snort of laughter.

"You ladies ready to order?" was a welcome interruption. I

ordered steak frites because it was the most expensive dish on the menu, so they would have whatever they wanted. Dinah ordered steak frites as well, and Avis ordered a lettuce salad.

Avis said, "I read about a woman who died and came back. One of those near-death things? She was looking down at her own body on the operating table."

"And she saw a long white tunnel?" asked Dinah. I could hear the sardonic undertone, meaning, Please, lady, don't be completely predictable.

"Not at all," said Avis. "What she saw were the words people used as they yelled orders at each other. She saw the words themselves as if they had lives of their own, or weight or size. She said that if people understood how powerful words are, they would use them much more carefully."

"I thought sticks and stones would break my bones but names would never hurt me."

"Apparently that's wrong."

"My god, what's next?" said Dinah. "A stitch in time doesn't save nine?"

Dinah the Mean. I'd forgotten that that Dinah might appear. Avis looked down at her silverware. She is incapable of being deliberately rude, and there was no polite way to respond. Three is such an unstable number, I thought unhappily. Why had I thought this would be comfortable for anyone except me?

The food arrived, and I decided, not quite hopeless yet, to launch a change of subject.

"Doesn't it seem a century ago that we were all locked up at Miss Pratt's? To me it seemed like something out of *Jane Eyre*."

"Oh," said Avis gratefully, "that's just what I thought! I was so homesick I wanted to weep, most of the time."

"My home wasn't much to long for, but I certainly badly wanted something else. To be grown up, probably, but I blamed the school."

Avis and I were warming to our topic. She said, "I was used to having the city as my backyard. I missed the Met, I missed the symphony, I missed the art house cinema on weekends."

"I thought the whole thing was kind of a hoot," said Dinah.

I knew perfectly well she had hated every minute of it. Avis, caught up short, didn't seem to know what to do.

"You did not," I said.

"I did. I decided to see if I could break every rule in their pompous little book without getting kicked out, and except for never having a boy in my room, I think I did it."

Avis looked bewildered. "You smoked?"

"Practically every weekend."

"Where?" She seemed actually shocked.

"In the woods, up on the skater's loop."

"You didn't drink," I said.

"Yes, I did. A friend from Yale sent me a cough syrup bottle full of gin. Lollie Ford and I drank it in the bathroom one Sunday while you were all at hymns."

There was a pause.

"Well," I said, "the world has changed so much, it all seems quaint now. Think of life before the Pill, or *Our Bodies, Ourselves*, or *Ms.* magazine. Before women could be doctors and lawyers—"

Avis broke in, "Isn't it true? And it's not just *women* in professions . . . in our parents' world, the professions themselves weren't really acceptable, were they? Somehow gentlemen lawyers were all right, but when you were growing up, did your parents know doctors or schoolteachers socially?"

My heart had sunk into my shoes. I was saying to myself, *Dinah, don't say it, please don't say it*, when Dinah said, "My father is a schoolteacher."

As soon as the dishes were cleared, Avis left us, with apologies.

"Probably late for her Colonial Dames meeting," Dinah said as we watched her leave the restaurant in her wet raincoat and pleated bonnet.

I said, "That's not fair."

There was another stiff silence until the waiter came with our coffees and a crème brûlée for Dinah.

As she dug in, Dinah said, "I'm sorry, but to tell a gossip writer that words are *weapons*? Bombs or something?"

"She was trying to pay you a compliment. You're a writer. She just meant to say she admires what you do."

"My god, if doctors and teachers are 'the help' in her scheme of things, what does that make writers?"

"You know that's not what she meant. She meant that was her parents' world and she's glad that it's dead and gone."

"I doubt it." Dinah laughed her big rattling laugh, but it wasn't warm. "Jeez, I'm sorry I never met her parents. They must have been a treat and a half. Why does she always look as if she just smelled something on your shoe?"

"She doesn't. She's just a little more formal than we are."

"Form follows function."

"Dinah, this woman is a friend of mine," I said, finally showing an annoyance that Dinah rarely saw, since we both knew that I relied on Dinah far more than the other way around. I added, "Besides, I agree with her. Words *are* weapons."

"Okay, I'm sorry. And lunch was delicious, thank you. The rain's stopped. I'll walk you back to work."

Avis had to work quite late that night, I learned the next day, as she had to bid on two different lots for her most important client. There was a Rembrandt portrait in the sale, one that had been lost for centuries, given away to satisfy debts when the artist declared bankruptcy. It had been rediscovered in 1910 when a British dealer spotted it in a bedroom at a country inn near Amsterdam. Since then it had come up for public sale once, and would after that night most likely go to a public collection; there were very few late Rembrandts still in private hands.

With virtually no comparables, it had been tricky to predict what it would fetch, Avis explained when she called to thank me for lunch. If Greenwood hadn't gotten it, there was a Goya he was interested in, and she was also bidding on an altarpiece for a client in Europe. What she didn't say, but I realized with regret, was that the time she had taken for lunch probably meant she hadn't been able to get home to see Grace before the auction began. I hoped she'd at least been able to call to kiss her good night over the phone.

NATURALLY, DINAH AND AVIS CROSSED PATHS FROM TIME TO time, as we all did in the village that is the Upper East Side of Manhattan. There was the odd cocktail party or book fair sponsored by Miss Pratt's, and the Brick Church Christmas carol party that filled its whole block of Park Avenue, or the members' evenings at the Met Museum. There was a period when the only place to get the French sunblock our dermatologists made us wear was at Clyde's Chemist on Madison. But Dinah developed a painfully accurate imitation of Avis's speech patterns after my ill-starred attempt to bring them together, so I stopped mentioning Avis to Dinah.

Sometimes Dinah would ask after my friend Mrs. Gotrocks, although I explained that Avis earned her own keep; Harrison's money was all in trust for his children and grandchildren; he just got an allowance. Avis continued to ask kindly after Dinah and she often praised Dinah's work to me if she'd read a piece of hers in some magazine. Once she even made an introduction for her to a society friend whose apartment Dinah wanted to write up. It wasn't done through me; Dinah called Avis herself and asked her for the favor.

Magazine writing was Dinah's solution to how to work but not make enough money that Richard might petition the court to reduce her alimony. She liked best writing about food, both cooking and eating, and had a biweekly restaurant column in *New York* magazine. She wrote about exotic cuisines and dining out on a budget. Three or four of us would go to deepest Queens or Brooklyn to eat Thai food, or Vietnamese, or Ethiopian, all still quite exotic to New Yorkers in the early 1980s, and order everything on the menu. For years my refrigerator was perpetually crammed with third-world leftovers.

Some people think it's a dream job, but I could never have done what Dinah did. Could you? Eat tripe and brains and big fried ants? Dinah would try anything. And I hate having to eat when I'm not hungry. Dinah is always hungry, it was one of the things that made her so much fun. She did, of course, put on weight. Even after the column was canceled she still worked the beat; she liked to try foods she'd never tasted before and then duplicate them at home. I remember a Chinese sauce she worked on for years before she was sure she'd gotten it right. She claimed that the secret ingredient was mayonnaise.

Dinah enjoyed being the go-to girl when you wanted to know the hottest little undiscovered bistro, but the writing that paid her best was for the house-and-garden crowd. Her apprenticeship in the women's pages ghetto served her well. Dinah is shrewd about knowing what makes a design really sing, finding new words for things that have been described a hundred times before. It's thankless work; you're trying to do with words what is being done better by pictures right there on the same page in living color. Watch women under the dryers at hair salons and try to find someone reading the copy in those magazines. You'll wait a long time. Maybe that's why the magazines have to pay the writers so much.

Few do it as well as Dinah, but she was far more interested in writing a cookbook and even had a contract for a while, though it was canceled when she took too long and the market changed.

She was doing too many things at once. Next she was going to write a life of one of Andy Warhol's Factory Girls, but the woman got annoyed with Dinah's disorganization and withdrew permission for Dinah to use her diaries, and the diaries were pretty much the whole point for the publisher.

Dinah had recovered her balance, however. She had a new beau named Fred, one of the rotating band who went to the restaurants with her. He was an architect doing mostly interiors whom she met when she wrote up a house he designed. He was a bit of a fusspot but devoted to her. They'd been together something like five years when she showed up without him at a new Mexican fusion place we were trying. She was defiant.

"Is Fred coming later?"

"No," said Dinah and ordered enough food for six people.

"Are you two all right?"

"No. I mean yes, we're both fine, but we're not together at the moment."

"Oh Dinah! I'm so sorry!"

"Don't be. He'll be back."

The room was bright, a sunburnt yellow, with loud mariachi music issuing from a speaker right above our heads to convey the impression that the room was full of life, though fairly empty of customers. The waiter brought us enormous margaritas, one pink and one blue.

Dinah looked dubious. "What did we order?"

"One has cassis."

"What's the other one? Antifreeze?"

I tasted it. "Grapefruit."

"Really?" She switched glasses with me and sipped. She

stooped over and rummaged in her bag on the floor. When she had made her surreptitious notes, she sat up again and applied fresh scarlet lipstick.

"I think we should order one of each flavor," she said. There had been about seven on the menu.

"No."

"Wasn't one made with chocolate?"

"Dinah, what happened with Fred?"

"He wants to get married."

"To you."

"Of course to me."

She said it as if it were simply tedious of him. How did people get people to propose to them all the time?

"Why isn't that good?"

A raft of appetizers arrived, and Dinah fell upon them, full of clinical interest. Avoidance patrol.

"Hey. Honey?"

She finished her margarita and started on mine.

"He's never had children. He doesn't relate to the boys."

"Does he *want* children?"

"He says he does."

"And you don't?"

"I have children."

"Lucky you."

She looked at me sharply. I was sorry I'd said it.

She said, "I'm not saying never again. But not right now. And I don't see Fred as a father, frankly."

"That's an awfully big decision to make for somebody else."

"Well, he agrees with you. But he'll be back."

We chewed in silence for a minute; then Dinah disappeared into her purse again. When she resurfaced, she said, "So how are your friends, the Gotrocks?" and I let the subject of Fred drop.

Weeks later I ran into Fred at MoMA. It was an evening preview of an Anselm Kiefer show, and I was waiting for my friend, when I saw a familiar ursine figure planted before a painting with his feet apart and hands clasped behind his back. He was alone. When he turned from the post-Apocalypse landscape he'd been contemplating and saw me perched on a bench in the middle of the room, what interest he'd had in the art evaporated. He took a seat beside me and began talking about Dinah. He was furious. I had to keep reminding him to lower his voice, as all around us artistic women in black costumes of their own devising involving knits and netting and deep black smudges around their eyes, turned to look askance as his torrent of words interrupted the reverent hum of culture being consumed.

"What did she tell you? You were with her that night at the restaurant? I was supposed to go with you, I was at the apartment, we were going together. What did she say?"

"Not very much. She seemed upset."

"Upset? She *should* be upset! You think *she* was upset? What did she tell you, why did she say I wasn't there?"

With my eyes I indicated the art lovers turning to stare, and he said, "Sorry," in a lower tone. "She didn't tell you what happened?"

I shook my head. He plunged onward.

"I got there early. I had a ring in my pocket. A ring! In my pocket! We were going to tell you at dinner!"

"That—you were getting married? You planned that together?"

"No! Not together, I mean that was *my* plan. I'd propose, we'd tell you at dinner, we'd have chiles rellenos and millions of margaritas . . ."

"And?" This really wasn't my business. And yet one wants to know.

"You know," he announced aggressively, as if I were denying it, "Dinah isn't getting any younger. Or thinner. She thinks she can do a lot better than me, she thinks there's always something better around the corner. But I think she was bloody lucky to meet me. It's not every man who wants to take on a fat woman with children."

I said something soothing. It was beginning to be hard to tell if he wanted to marry Dinah or kill her.

"What did she *say*?" he demanded. "I just want to know what words she used."

I thought about it, then said, "She seemed sad, and she said she hoped you'd be back."

"Back! That's a laugh. Why would I come back?"

"Because you had fun together. Because you care for each other."

He stood up suddenly, as if he was going to blow up if he didn't get moving. He put his hands on his hips, looked around the room without seeing it, and sat down again.

"How about because I love her? How about that?"

He now seemed to be arguing for the other side.

I said, "I know you did. I know you do. She's very lovable."

"She is! She's bright, she's funny, she's always interesting. Always. We make a great team! She understands my work, I understand hers . . ." He seemed to realize that he was making Dinah's points, not his own. "We had a great thing. Really great. I thought this is it, this is the rest of my life. But what was I to her? Some sort of hors d'oeuvre? Some sort of dessert? I wanted to be the main course!"

The volume was rising again. I said I understood, and I did. Better than he could possibly know. But he roared on.

"Just tell me, how does she explain turning down a . . . a . . . Me! Turning me down, because she's too pigheaded and angry to let that poor schmuck Richard Wainwright off the hook."

I said, "What?" There we go again. I had heard him all right, but where did that come from?

Finally he'd gotten a reaction he'd been trying for.

"She didn't tell you that, did she? She didn't tell you the reason. What did she tell you?"

"She mentioned your wanting children . . ."

"Children? Me? I don't care if I have children."

I was bewildered.

"She said there was nothing wrong with going on the way we were. But there was for me. I didn't want to be twenty years down the road, with nothing of my own, introducing her as 'the woman I sleep with.' But she's more interested in fucking over Richard Wainwright than in being with me. She says that's the deal breaker. Getting married."

I have to say, I was shocked. She really did care for Fred. They did have a great time together. She *wasn't* getting any younger. And neither was I.

Ten months later, he sought me out at work to introduce me

to his fiancée, a small, smiling olive-skinned girl named Elena with curly dark hair and big yellowish cat's eyes. We had coffee together, and she flattered me by finding the behind-the-scenes workings of the store exciting and glamorous. Together we double-teamed Fred into buying her a beautiful Thai silk suit to be married in. He sat in a spindly chair in the dressing room watching her try things on, and looked like a thoroughly happy man.

THINGS AT WORK HAD GROWN GRADUALLY MORE UNCOMFORTABLE IN these years. Marylin undercut me with clients more than once, but when I went to the manager, he had no patience. You could practically see the word *catfight* forming in the thought bubble above his head. Dismissing me, he said, "I'm sure you girls can work it out."

I came in early from lunch one day soon after and found one of my best customers in a dressing room with Marylin.

I said, "Mrs. Rawson, I'm so sorry—did we have an appointment?"

She looked embarrassed, and her eyes met Marylin's in the mirror. Who said snippily, "She just happened to pop in, Loviah, and you weren't here, so of course I offered to help."

I thanked her and withdrew. I went to check my book immediately to be sure I hadn't forgotten a date with her. Then I went to check Marylin's book, and saw *C. C. Rawson* in ink for the hour I usually take lunch.

I was furious. I did something I never do: called my friend

at his office. He wasn't in and I didn't leave a message, but I was pretty sure his assistant knew my voice, and I was embarrassed I'd done it. One of my appeals for my friend was that I was "always a lady," and a lady does not make her beloved a subject for gossip among his staff. I called Dinah and said I was mad enough to spit hot nails and she said, "Come right over."

She took me to her gym and we swam laps. It was marvelously therapeutic. Then we sat in the steam room like oriental pashas. I kept my towel daintily wrapped around my waist, but Dinah had hers around her beautiful strong dark hair, magnificently at ease with her gleaming naked body in spite of its increasing heft. Where does a person get that kind of confidence?

The steam room was empty except for us, and I fumed about Marylin, her oppressive perfume, her underhandedness, and her smutty jokes, which her ladies seemed to love. "I hope she tells Mrs. Rawson the one about why dogs lick themselves," I said darkly, and Dinah hooted and said, "Why don't we ask her for a sleepover and get her bra wet and put it in the freezer?" One way or another she got me laughing. Then we got giddy and couldn't stop, especially when we discovered what the steam had done to the hair spray in my helmet hair. I might as well have slept in chewing gum.

It was Dinah's idea that I should go out on my own. "You have friends who will back you," she said. "Frankly, I have friends who will back you."

"You do? Why would they?"

"Because you're very good at what you do, you stupid nit. And because not everyone wants to shop at Saks Fifth Avenue. Some people want more privacy. And they don't want to wear all the same labels their friends wear. At a department store you'll always be only as good as the buyer. Why not be your own buyer?"

"Yes, but—"

"Think of the look on Marylin's face when you tell her," she said. Oh, she is so good at knowing people's weaknesses.

"What do I know about running a business?"

"And you're too dumb to learn?"

I remember feeling that Dinah was going to tell me to jump off a cliff and I was going to do it. She likes action. She likes it when things happen and she gets to watch. And I like to please her.

I jumped.

EVEN *I* KNEW HOW BADLY GRACE METCALF WANTED A DOG. OR a cat, but her mother was allergic to cats. Her father loved animals but was certainly going to be no help in taking care of one, and Avis didn't see how a nine-year-old ... ten-year-old ... eleven-year-old could take care of raising and training a puppy and walking it at all hours by herself, even if Grace *was* unusually responsible for her age.

Since she'd become a full partner with Gordon Hall, Avis traveled a great deal. "I'm so sorry, darling. I hate to be away from you," she would say, kissing Grace good-bye as she headed for the airport to fly to Dublin, or Amsterdam, or Basel. It wasn't ideal, but it was challenging work, which she welcomed, and she needed the money, since Harrison had lost the last of his investment clients.

Victor Greenwood was collecting Old Masters with a vengeance by the mid-1980s and talking about founding his own museum, when he wasn't flirting with the Metropolitan in New York, or the Carnegie in Pittsburgh, where he had grown up, or the Art Institute of Chicago, where he had gone to school and made his first units, as he referred to a hundred million dollars. All of these institutions dangled seats on their boards and hoped he would give them his increasingly impressive collections.

The art world was bemused by the obviously congenial relationship that had grown between the famously abrasive collector and diffident and proper Avis Metcalf. Clearly there was something about her that appealed to Greenwood, and he, who had gotten very rich by trusting no one but himself, apparently trusted her. Whether they understood it or not, once that world knew that Victor Greenwood saw something special in Avis, others began to take an interest in what she was interested in, and certain sellers wanted connections to the people who were buying through her.

"I'll be back on Tuesday . . . on Friday . . . for the weekend . . . for your birthday, we'll do something wonderful. What would you like most? Think about it, I'll call you when I get there and we'll make a plan." Grace and her friends spent a lot of time slouching around Bloomingdale's after school, trying on makeup and pretending they were in the market for Judith Leiber handbags. Or she'd take the subway to see Belinda, who would take her to dinner at Serafina or sometimes to the theater even on a school night. On her twelfth birthday, Belinda, airily ignoring Avis's strictures, gave Grace a tiny poodle puppy. Grace named him Jelly.

The whole family fell in love with Jelly. He was noisy but smart and very clownish. Grace paper-trained him in the kitchen, following instructions from a dog-training program she watched on television. When Jelly chewed apart one of her dancing school shoes—she found him in her bedroom lying half on top of it, gnawing on the instep strap and looking up at her with large innocent eyes—she went around the house spraying Bitter Apple on everything he liked sinking his little needle teeth into. Jelly chewed up the legs of two of her mother's antique dining room chairs so that they looked as if they had been attacked by borer worms. Avis just laughed and sent them out to be refinished. And when Jelly lost control of himself after he ate something disgusting on the street and it disagreed with him, Avis patiently followed him around the apartment with a roll of paper towels and a gallon of Nature's Miracle. Because of allergies Avis had never had a pet of her own, and she'd never imagined she would love a dog as much as she did this one. She even let Jelly sleep on Grace's bed; he started the night curled on a towel near her feet but by morning was always up on the pillow beside her head, doing his best to worm his way under the covers.

Avis was in London negotiating with the heirs of a grand collection of Bronzino drawings when Jelly was killed.

He had just been groomed. He'd been washed and fluffed and perfumed, and it was said afterward that that may have been the problem: he didn't smell like a dog. In any case, Grace was walking him home from the groomer's at twilight on his pretty red leather leash when a man approached listening to his Walkman and paying no mind to his Akita strolling untethered behind him. With no warning, the Akita jumped Jelly, and in one garish melee of canine screaming clamped its jaws around the puppy's throat and shook him until his neck broke. It took only seconds, but for Grace it lasted hours; it felt as if it would never stop, and went on feeling like that as it replayed inside her head for hours, then days.

While Grace screamed, a woman ran across the street to them, yelling at the owner of the Akita, "Grab his tail, pull him off!" She gave the bigger dog a kick in the ribs and when it loosened its grip on Jelly as it wheeled to bite *her,* she was able to wrench the tiny body from the Akita's mouth. She held Jelly, limp as a warm bloody plush toy, and looked at the fragile horrified child who stood sobbing before her, still holding the other end of Jelly's leash. She whirled on the Akita man and yelled at him.

"You should face charges, letting that dog off its leash!"

"She's never done anything like this before!"

"I'm calling animal control. This dog should be put down!"

"She's a sweet gentle dog! She's never done anything like this!"

They went on in a furious tangle that resembled the fight that had just finished. Anger was easier for both of them than facing Grace's grief. Grace dropped the leash she still held and took Jelly's body from the yelling woman, sobbing, "I'm sorry, Jelly, I'm sorry, I'm sorry, I'm sorry."

After the woman had extracted the name and address of the Akita man, she walked Grace home.

"You don't have to," Grace muttered between ragged tear-filled breaths.

"Yes, I do. You're more upset than you know, and I want to talk to your mother."

"She's away."

The woman got into the elevator with Grace and her mangled little burden. The woman wore a good gray suit, Belgian loafers, and black tights that had been torn in the fight. Her hair was crisp and short and perfectly cut, an unnatural shade of chestnut. "Is your father home?" she asked Grace.

"Yes."

"Fine."

They entered the apartment together, and Grace led the way to the den where her father slumped in his usual chair. Mozart was on the stereo, and Harrison seemed to be asleep. There was a large glass of clear liquid and melting ice on the table beside him. Grace's crying had left her voice choked and hoarse.

"Daddy," she said loudly, and Harrison shook his head and opened his eyes.

He surveyed the scene before him. Grace. Holding something

black and messy, there were smears on her coat. A lady he'd never seen before.

"This is my father, Harrison Wainwright," Grace said to the lady.

"I'm Casey Leisure, Mr. Wainwright," said the lady briskly. Harrison was struggling to his feet. He managed to get upright and stay that way, then fairly steadily crossed the room to shake hands, saying, "Harrison Wainwright, good to know you."

"Your daughter has just had a horrible experience. Her dog was killed in the street. She needs someone to talk to, she should probably have some Valium and go to bed. And someone needs to deal with. . . ." She took Jelly's body from Grace, who began sobbing again. For a moment it seemed the lady was going to start weeping herself. Grace needed a handkerchief and covered her face with her bloody hands, and now Mrs. Leisure had blood on her coat and hands as well.

Finally Harrison said, "What do you think we ought to do?"

Mrs. Leisure said, "Oh, for heaven's sake. Is there anyone else in the house?" There wasn't. "Is there someone we can call?"

"Belinda," said Grace.

Mrs. Leisure stayed until Belinda arrived, dressed for a dinner party. Belinda thanked Mrs. Leisure, called the vet, canceled her plans, and waited until someone came and took Jelly away. Then she took Grace home with her for supper and the night.

MY FIRST THREE YEARS WITH THE SHOP WERE HARDER THAN I could have imagined. People did back me, but taking money from them worked changes in our friendships. I don't have a natural head for business, and I made a drastic mistake in my first choice of bookkeeper. I seemed to live on airplanes, as I sought out fresh talent in Paris and Milan, then Berlin, Tel Aviv, and Stockholm. Why should the Ladies Who Lunch come to me for designers whose clothes they could buy at Bergdorf Goodman, or whose shows they could go to themselves? I didn't know the answer. At first. More serious was, Why *should* they come to me, only to find I was not in the shop but in Oslo?

That's another story. I learned, and my backers stuck by me, with only one painful exception. And Dinah remained a steadfast booster, though sometimes I wondered if she wouldn't have taken just as much pleasure if I had failed as she took in seeing me succeed.

The first year I was totally in the black and beginning to repay my seed money was 1991, the year Nicholas started high school. His brother, RJ, had gone to Andover, where he played lacrosse and squash. Nicky, however, wanted to stay in the city, and that was fine with Dinah. He had no interest in sports, although he wasn't bad at tennis. If RJ was his father's son, Nicky was Dinah's. Passionate, dramatic, hot-tempered, talented, funny, they were each other's best audience. Like Dinah, he was ambitious. He played Joe in the school's production of *Most Happy Fella,* and we went to every performance; he was like a young Joel Mc-

Crea. He still had those beautiful long eyelashes and deep-set smoky blue eyes. His dancing was deft—Dinah turned to me at one point on opening night with tears in her eyes. "I thought I knew everything about him," she said. "When did he learn to do *that*?" His singing was even better, a shining supple tenor. The second night, Dinah brought a casting director and two producers she knew to the performance. They were warm in their appreciation, and the casting director said afterward that Nicky could talk with her about how to get an agent. I think Dinah was surprised that she didn't instantly offer to cast him in the next Woody Allen movie.

RJ went on to Yale, his grandfather's alma mater. Nicky could have followed him there; he had the grades, but he wanted someplace more focused on the arts. He chose Bennington, a small liberal arts school in Vermont, which delighted Dinah because it famously had the highest tuition in the country.

Richard, along with his parents, his wife, Charlotte, and their three daughters, came to Nicky's high school graduation, and Dinah was perfectly charming to them, inviting everyone back to her apartment for a celebratory lunch along with her own parents and me. The food was Moroccan, as Dinah had recently been sent by *Architectural Digest* to write up a house in Marrakech. None of us had even seen a tagine before. I noticed that Dinah left her diaphragm case in the medicine cabinet in the master bathroom, the one most often used by guests in the dining room, just to be sure that no one on Richard's team thought she was a lonely spinster.

His first three years at Bennington, Nicky's girlfriend was a six-foot-tall Somali dancer named Nala. Dinah loved her. She taught Dinah Somali home cooking; they went on field trips together to the ethnic markets of the outer boroughs, and on one of these, she described to Dinah being "circumcised" when she was six. She taught Nicky African drumming and left him her drums when she graduated and went home. They're still at the apartment, in Nicky's childhood bedroom. Nala is married now and works for a bank in Amsterdam. She often stays with Dinah when she comes to New York.

Nicky was a theater major. He acted, he designed sets and lighting, he studied directing, and he wrote plays. Dinah was always in the audience when a show of his went up, whether he was onstage or had merely designed the posters. His college friends soon used the New York apartment as if they lived there, and Dinah presided with great contentment, as long as they didn't smoke, bought their own beer, and didn't talk to her in the morning until she'd had her coffee. One evening I walked into the apartment to find Nicky at the piano playing and singing the role of Sportin' Life, as a group of his friends sight-read the score of *Porgy and Bess*. It was a happy time.

During his junior year at college, both Nicky and Nala had internships in New York for their work-study term, and lived with Dinah. Nala worked in the office of a city councilman. Nicky was less serious; I believe his job that year was at a talent agency where they can't have had much real use for him. Whatever he did there, it left him plenty of free time to drop in to gossip with me and Mrs. Oba. He liked helping me dress the windows and was very clever at it. He'd stage little dramas. He posed a mannequin in a moss-colored cut-velvet tea gown at a typewriter with a stack of reference books beside her and the entire floor of the window filled with crumpled balls of typing paper. When we saw how interested people were, the mannequin began to write a story. Every few days, Nicky would add a paragraph to the page in the typewriter: *"Michel, you promised!" cried Evangeline, heartbroken. "Consistency is the hobgoblin of little minds," Michel replied, lighting a Gauloises.*

When he couldn't think what would happen next, he'd crumple the paper, throw it on the floor, and begin a new page. I sold three copies of that tea gown, and it wasn't cheap, and so many people were stopping by every day or two to see how the mannequin's novel was going that we even got a mention in Liz Smith.

I remember one evening that winter at Dinah's. Nala had made a fiery stew with chilies and peanuts that had left us gasping. Dinah rushed to the kitchen for beer for all of us. When she could talk, she said, "Beer is full of sugar, it quiets the heat. Julia Child taught me that." And Nicky dropped his fork on the floor.

Recovering my own voice, I said, "Dinah, you're amazing. How on earth do you know Julia Child?"

"Her nephew Jon is a friend of mine. Haven't you ever met him here? Auntie Julia has made mayonnaise in this very kitchen," she said.

Actually, I'd have loved to meet Julia Child, and I think Dinah knew it. Oh well.

The conversation jogged on until Dinah happened to mention something she'd said to Jane recently.

"Jane?" Nala asked politely.

"Oh, sorry," said Dinah. "An American actress. Jane Fonda." Nala and Nicholas dropped their dessert spoons. Nala began to laugh, a delicious rippling giggle.

"All right, what?" said Dinah. She loved being teased by Nicky.

"My brother," said Nala in her charming accent. "At Cambridge, he sang in the choir at his college. If anyone name-dropped during the service, the choristers dropped their pencils. One day a visiting priest said in his homily, 'I was having tea with the queen . . .' and the whole choir dropped their hymnbooks."

She was a joy, Nala. We all took it hard when she moved back to Amsterdam, and we still drop cutlery when Dinah drops names. And it was years before Nicky took up with another girl.

MEANWHILE, RICHARD WAINWRIGHT, BORN WITH A SILVER SPOON, WAS no longer having an easy time of it. Remember all through 1999, the hysteria about the Y2K bug that was going to run riot in cyberspace when the calendar rolled to 2000? Richard had a truly ancient Volkswagen beetle that he restored himself and still drove around the village only partly for reason of style. In 1999 he got it a license plate that said *Y1K,* which even Dinah conceded was witty.

"Year One K Bug." You understand the problem. Nicky said that people in Ardsley kept asking Richard why his license plate said Yick, so he gave it up. What an innocent time that seems now, when a big computer crash was the worst national disaster we could think of.

Anyway, in the fall of 2000 Richard came into the shop. I remember that I'd been up in my flat with the deliveryman, stacking the first bundles of the season's firewood. I came back down to find a tall, slightly stooped man in a knockoff Burberry barn jacket idly studying the costume jewelry in the case that acts as a sales desk. I didn't know him until he turned to face me, smiling.

"Richard!" We embraced. "What brings you here?"

"Are you busy?"

"As you see." We were not.

"You're sure?"

"I have a client coming at two-thirty, but I'm free as air until then. Come upstairs."

We exchanged small talk while I heated a kettle for tea. When we were both seated with our cups in my little sitting room, he said, "Do you think Dinah would see me? Sit down to talk?"

We all *saw* one another at graduations and weddings and such events, and had even had dinner together at Dinah's the year before when RJ and his wife were in town for a theater weekend, so he meant something different.

"Has something happened? Your health? Charlotte or the girls?"

"Everyone's fine."

I waited.

"Dinah's doing pretty well, isn't she?" he asked.

"Her knee is hurting her."

"Oh. I'm sorry."

"Well. We both know she's too heavy."

"Yes. I meant . . . financially?"

I didn't answer, so he went on.

"Someone told me lately what that magazine she writes for pays. I had no idea. I mean, I was impressed."

"She's very good at what she does. Of course they don't all pay as well as that."

"No."

"And freelance is freelance. You never know when your last job may be."

Naturally I knew where this was going.

"Colette and Mary are both in college, as of September."

"Where is Mary going?"

"Wheaton."

Having not had the pleasure myself, that exhausted my supply of conversation on the topic.

"I have to admit, I'm stretched pretty thin," he said.

I said I could imagine.

"Would you mind . . . would you ask Dinah if she'd have lunch with me? She'd take it better if it came from you."

I considered. "You may overestimate my influence, but I'll try. Do you want me to tell her what it's about?"

"I imagine she'll guess, don't you?"

"Yes, I do."

I ASKED HER. SHE SAID, "I CAN GUESS WHAT *THIS* IS ABOUT."

I agreed.

"Do you think I should?" she asked. She clearly didn't want to.

"He says his margins are pretty skimpy, and I believe it. Scary, at our age."

"Not my problem."

"No. But how do the boys see it, do you think?"

She'd come over to have lunch with me in the apartment. I'd bought sushi, and she'd brought a beetroot salad and a tin of homemade lemon squares.

"Do you mean they think I'm mean?"

"I have no idea. But they don't mind Charlotte and they love their sisters, and I'm sure they notice."

"Notice what?"

"If Richard's family is eating chili dogs and cutting their own hair, and you're eating foie gras and renting a house on Martha's Vineyard."

"Richard is cutting his own hair?"

"Looks like it to me."

WE BOTH KNEW THAT SHE COULD AFFORD TO TAKE REDUCED ALIMONY, and the wound to her amour propre of Richard's leaving was decades old; she'd endured others far more recent.

I don't know what went wrong at their lunch, but something did. Richard came to the shop afterward, looking glum. Apparently sentences like "You should have thought of that before you started fucking that popsie" had been uttered. I don't know.

"She got furious because Charlotte doesn't work. But she *does* work, she's got her real estate license and she does the best she can. There's a lot of competition in the suburbs," he said unhappily.

"What did Dinah say to that?"

"Tough."

Well, I knew *that* Dinah. The Dinah who'd grown up on the wrong side of the walls of Canaan Woods, whose mother still bought most of her clothes at what she called Salvation Armani, Dinah whose mother had sold real estate and done it very well, in an era when nobody's mother worked. That she had chosen to marry Richard in spite of and because of what he represented to her had always struck me as touching. But it was far too late to ask Richard to see it that way. Once he told me that she'd started in about his trust fund, I knew he was cooked. He looked sunk.

"How serious is it?" I asked him. The financial situation.

"Well, of course, I can take on more debt."

"Could your parents . . . ?"

He shook his head. "They lived through the Depression. My father gets that pained expression and starts to chew his mustache when he even thinks about debt; he doesn't even approve of mortgages. And they're spending more than they really should themselves these days. My mom needs full-time care, you know."

"I didn't. I'm sorry. Is she still at home?" Richard's mother had to be deep in her nineties.

"Yes, nursing home for one. You can imagine what *that* costs."

I could. And of course, it *was* their money.

"Well," he said, "time to make some changes."

"What will you do?"

"I guess I'll see if I can go back to Wall Street. I've had a call or two from headhunters in the past."

"Oh, Richard." I knew how much he'd come to hate the commute, and how happy he'd been when he had started his own business in Westchester. He ran a family office for eight or ten high rollers he knew, looking after the investments, insurance, estate planning, and such that they didn't have time to attend to themselves. It wasn't sexy, but it required skill, judgment, and absolute integrity, qualities that are not all that easy to find in this wicked world.

"I used to know a lot about securitization. That commands a premium on the Street these days. It won't kill me."

Famous last words. As a minor act of subversion, I sent him home with Dinah's tin of lemon squares.

DINAH HALF-REGRETTED REFUSING TO GIVE HIM A BREAK. I KNEW THIS because she kept justifying herself afterward.

"What if *I* want to retire? I'd like to get a dog. If I didn't have to travel all the time, I could get a dog."

"You want a dog?"

"I'd *love* a dog."

It was the first I'd heard of it. "What kind?"

"A nice clean grateful mutt. I like mutts. I believe in hybrid vigor."

Richard and Charlotte had a Portuguese water dog that had cost a fortune.

Things jogged on. Richard closed his business and took a job way downtown, analyzing something or other, at a decent salary, though what he seemed most grateful for was the gold-plated health insurance.

A WISE MAN TOLD ME ONCE THAT GROWING UP MEANS THE DEATH OF many talents. Nicky's first job out of college was in a touring company of *Les Misérables*. We thought he was on his way, the next Matthew Broderick, but he quit after three months. He said he was bored with the road, and we suspected some affair gone wrong with someone in the company, but he never explained.

He moved back home and started a novel for real. Dinah bought him a fancy computer, but after six months he admitted he wasn't making a great deal more progress than the author of the immortal tale of Michel and Evangeline, and he was really tired of having no spending money. Richard said he was sorry he couldn't help him. He had three daughters to put through school, and Nicky was just going to have to figure it out. His brother, RJ, had now finished business school and taken a job with Alcoa in Pittsburgh. Nicky gave up and took the LSAT, preparing to apply to law school.

While he waited, Dinah got Nicky a job in a literary agency. It was a small office. He read submissions, answered the phones, and gossiped with the bookkeeper, who came in twice a week. At night he sang with a Brooklyn band called Monkeys Have the Bomb. Dinah asked if we could come see them perform, but he said, "Oh no. You'd experience it as punishment." He got overtired working days as well as nights, he got mononucleosis, he lost both jobs and spent two months recovering in his boyhood bedroom. Even Dinah was beginning to see a downside to having such a big apartment. She began to say that Nicky's career plan was to outlive her, inherit the lease, then rent out rooms.

Finally he got another job with the articles editor at a fashion magazine. He loved it, and they loved him. I don't think Richard was awfully pleased. Where he came from, for a man to work in fashion was sort of like joining the circus, bizarre but not in an interesting way. We pointed out that Nicky wasn't really working in fashion, he was in the Magazine World.

"It isn't exactly *Newsweek*, is it?" was Richard's response.

"God, Richard, when did you get so stuffy?" Dinah asked him.

"Well at least he has health insurance," Richard said.

"Health insurance, and he's surrounded by chic, beautiful people, and it's fun!"

"Fun," said Richard. "Is that what work is supposed to be?"

DINAH WENT TO THE VINEYARD FOR TWO MONTHS THAT SUMMER. THE cottage she rented was covered in climbing roses. RJ and his family spent a week in July with her, and Nicky went for a week in August and filled the house with friends. I went up for Labor Day weekend to see what all the fuss was about, and I must say, it was heaven. The rooms were small but bright and fragrant from the roses, and from the deck at the back of the house you could hear the ocean. The kitchen was arrayed with fresh mint, basil, parsley, and dill from the farmers' market in water glasses as if they were bunches of flowers. In the evening there was always a kettle of mussels on the stove, or a bouillabaisse or paella.

I'D BEEN HOME FOR A WEEK—I WAS STILL SUNTANNED—THE MORNING the world blew up.

Uptown we didn't feel the first plane ram the North Tower, or see the dogs in the park come off the ground or the birds knocked out of the trees as they did in Washington Square. What happened to us was the phones started ringing. Gil called me first, to tell me to turn on the television. RJ in Pittsburgh, dressing for work while his wife got the kids' breakfast, called Dinah.

"Good morning, my treasure," she had said happily, because no one but one of her sons would call her at that hour. He told *her* to turn on the television. All networks were showing a live shot of the World Trade Center, where there was a plane-shaped hole in the north face of one building as the smoke poured into the sky and people hung out the windows in the floors above the gash, looking skyward and waving.

"Dad's down there," said RJ in a panicked voice, like someone shouting orders.

For a moment Dinah went blank. Could that be true?

"No, he's—"

"Yes, Mom, he is. His office is in the World Trade Center. I'm looking at my address book."

"What floor?"

"Ninety-fourth."

"Jesus. And what the hell happened? Some asshole in a Cessna, trying to . . ."

"That's Dad's building."

They were watching, trying to count up the floors to see which ones were burning, when the second plane hit.

So was I; I couldn't stop looking. On the screen, the top slumped sideways off the South Tower, and then the whole building was gone. What can that have sounded like? I don't remember hearing anything from the television, just the image. So many souls streaming into heaven at once . . .

I tried to call Gil back—I realized I was hysterical—but either his line was busy or the lines were down. I was standing in my stocking feet staring at the television when my phone rang the second time. Dinah. She told me about Richard.

For a moment—this is the measure of my shock—I wasn't sure who she meant. RJ? Was RJ in New York for business for some reason? Or did she mean Richard Flanagan, the wine expert she'd dated until she figured out he was a pathological liar?

"RJ says his office is in the North Tower. Ninety-fourth floor. He's not answering his cell phone. Charlotte says he left at the usual time, and he's always in the office by eight-thirty."

"Where's Nicky?"

"On his way down there."

"I'll come. Hang up and keep your line free."

Of course we didn't open the shop that day. Mrs. Oba was stuck underground on a train from Brooklyn. When the train finally inched into the East Broadway station, the passengers were released, but by then the subway system was shut down. Everyone feared another attack, maybe on the transit system. In fact, we went on fearing that for months. Years.

Nicky never got below Canal Street, and downtown below Franklin was evacuated, the gas and electric to the buildings cut off. No one knew where the next explosion might be, and they needed all the power they could get at the crime site. Mrs. Oba, I learned later that night, had walked back over the Manhattan Bridge to Brooklyn and all the way home. It took her seven hours.

Nicky reached Dinah's apartment at about noon. He had been standing at Canal and Hudson before the North Tower fell, and he'd seen with naked eyes what looked to him at first like silver coating peeling from the surface of the flaming building until the guy standing next to him said, "Dude—those are people jumping."

He wasn't in such great shape when he got to us. He said he could see right through the building where the plane had hit.

Those two floors, or more, were gone, the space empty except for flames and supporting columns at the corners of the building. On the floors above the breach, people were still waving at helicopters, still apparently thinking they could be rescued. Thinking some-day they'd describe this day to their grandchildren.

He'd tried to get past the cordons, without luck. There were hundreds like him, trying to go toward the site, crying, "My daughter, my husband, my girlfriend . . ." but the police were deaf to it. All the traffic was streaming the other way, thousands of workers and residents walking north in whatever they happened to be wearing when the first tower fell. Some were ghostlike, cov-ered in a sticky chalk layer of gray dust. It didn't do to think about what was in that dust.

It was a beautiful day, I don't know if you remember. Nicky said it was surreal, to walk up Lexington not knowing if his fa-ther was alive or dead and find all the shops open, the restaurants full, people going about their business. Dinah, for once in her life, didn't offer anyone food and didn't eat herself. She just stared at the television, where WTC Seven was burning. During station breaks we obsessively told one another exactly what time it was when normality ended for each of us. Who called. What was said. Where we were. WTC Seven burned all day, because it held the mayor's emergency center, complete with a fuel dump for run-ning generators. Rudy Giuliani strode around. We were learning a whole new vocabulary. Jihad. Osama bin Laden. Was it that day that we started watching the film clip of the man we know now as Mohammed Atta clearing security in the Portland airport that morning? Or was that later?

I know the Portland airport. I've been through that security check. If you had a computer with you, you had to boot it up to prove it was a computer, not a bomb. Such innocent times.

Charlotte called sometime in the afternoon; Dinah had the phone before the first ring was finished.

"He's alive," Charlotte said.

Dinah's eyes cut to Nicky as she slumped against the kitchen counter. Nicky instantly understood. I didn't.

"Where is he?" I heard Dinah say, and I was still thinking hospital . . . morgue . . . until Dinah said in surprise, "*New Jersey?*"

NICKY CALLED CHARLOTTE RIGHT BACK, BUT SHE DIDN'T KNOW ANY more than that Richard had called and said he'd explain when he saw her. She was weeping. Nicky told her he'd call back later, and he did, three or four times, as we waited. In between, RJ called. He said he was coming to New York.

"How?" said Nicky.

All flights were grounded. Of course we knew by then about the crashes in Washington and Pennsylvania. I think trains were stopped as well. I guess there was still driving that day, and now I no longer remember, day by day, how long it was before any of that got normal again, and my diary doesn't say. Meanwhile, where was Richard?

At about four, the doorman called to say Mr. Wainwright was on his way up. We weren't surprised, but only because we'd lost the power to be surprised. We all stood looking at the door. Richard walked in, wearing a suit in a condition I couldn't interpret. He looked as if he'd been through a washer that stopped before the spin cycle.

Nicky walked to his father and wrapped his arms around him. Richard returned the embrace and began to weep. Dinah and I were both in tears as well. When Nicky let Richard go, Dinah went into his arms, and they held each other as they had not done since the terrible Christmas after Richard left the marriage.

Then it was my turn. I, who had never held Richard like that, clung to him and cried for all those souls who were somewhere now, but where? For the horror of the day, for our fear for him and so many others, for the knowledge of the terrible, terrible news that was coming, of who was lost and for the pain and terror in which they died. And Richard wept because he wasn't one of them and there was no reason on earth he shouldn't have been.

When we finally let him go, but still stood close around him, Dinah touched his suit and said, "This smells like wet dog."

"I know," said Richard.

"Are you hungry?"

"Could I have a drink?"

We all agreed that a drink was a good idea. Richard went into Dinah's bedroom to call Charlotte again. When he came back, Dinah had put a towel on the best chair for him to sit on, and handed him a scotch and a Tupperware box of cold curried lamb and a fork. Richard said he had eaten a hot dog on the street somewhere on his way and wasn't hungry, then ate the whole thing without even seeming to know he was doing it.

The scotch steadied us all, although none of us was far from tears for the next few hours as he talked.

He'd gotten to the city late because he'd stopped in Ardsley to vote. He'd come out of the subway and had just bought a coffee from a cart on Fulton Street when he became aware that a plane over the Hudson was flying much too low, the noise much

too loud. Then he saw it, so he knew from the start it was no
Cessna. People on the street were paralyzed, watching. At that
point, after the initial shock, his instinct was to try to get closer.
To see if he could help. Or just to see. They could hear the roar
of the fire above them, and soon, the people trapped above the
crash line hanging out the windows, looking up, looking down.
On the street chaos and ash and debris rained everywhere, but at
that point, he said, there was still a sense that this couldn't really
be happening, or that soon someone would stop it, put the fire out,
'copter in and rescue the people at the top of the building. Sirens
screamed everywhere around them, and fire trucks raced toward
the site from every direction. Richard said he was still thinking
about the work he had to do that day, planning, the way you do,
about where he would do it, since he clearly wouldn't be getting
into his office. He tried calling Charlotte at home in Westchester
to tell her what had happened, but he couldn't get a signal.

Then the second plane hit, and the horror moved inside him
to a different level, although he admitted that, as a spectacle, it
was so overwhelming that you couldn't react with more than as-
tonishment. You stared. Wanted to move but couldn't look away.
Couldn't process emotions, so they went somewhere, and the eyes
and that powerful motor, curiosity, ruled. What would happen
next? When the top of the South Tower with all its human cargo
fell off the building toward the east where they were standing, they
started to run, some of them screaming, and when they looked
back, the whole tower was gone. He said that later he realized he
had felt the earthquake shock of the planes hitting, heard the vast
inhuman roar of the building as it died, but at the time he only
knew running, in a herd, through stinging stinking smothering
pink-gray dust. When the cloud thinned enough for sunlight to

penetrate, they were blocks below where they had been, moving toward Battery Park. They stopped to look back, their eyes and noses full of ash and grit, which wiping made worse. Policemen herded them southward. You could tell who had been closest by the thickness of the dust coating them. Many, who kept looking back like Lot's wife and shaking or crying, had come from the North Tower itself, which was then still standing. "I was on the sixteenth floor."

"I was on the twenty-ninth."

"At first they said not to leave."

" . . . we went down the southwest fire stairs . . ."

" . . . so she tried to go back up, I don't know . . ."

They ended up in the park at the tip of the island with no place to go but the water. They went to the harbor's edge and stood like puzzled horses. Police boats arrived, Harbor Police or something, little motorboats with swollen rubber bumpers along the gunwales, which was lucky because there was no place to land. No pier or dock or place to tie up. They just nosed the boats up beside the seawall and held them there with the engines running, amazing seamanship really, while dazed hysterical people climbed or dropped or fell over the seawall into the boat. It was hard on the women in their business suits. (*Pencil skirts,* I thought, *you'd have to just pull them up to your hips, and no one wears slips anymore.*) One woman took off her heels and threw them into the boat before her, but one went into the water. She must have had to walk the whole way home in her stocking feet. When a boat was full it took off across the river mouth to New Jersey. The refugees climbed out, and the boat zipped back to the New York side for more people.

Richard found himself on a pier at the edge of a New Jersey park he'd never heard of, on a sparkling September morning, looking back across the river at a tower of black smoke, and flames and a hole in the sky where the buildings had been. He understood what he was looking at much less than we did, because he hadn't heard the radio or seen a television. Rumors spread among the refugees: there were other planes, the White House had been hit. The word *terrorists, terrorists* buzzed through the group but was not well understood. Their mental processing units were pretty much shattered. After a while two men in hazmat suits approached Richard and asked him what the stuff was all over his face and hair and clothes. He told them, and they turned a fire hose on him.

I've forgotten now exactly how they got back across the river. A cadre of them who had been together from the park onward chose without discussion to stay together. Those who had cell phones lent them, and sometimes they worked. One young man had a Walkman with a radio in it; he was in charge of reporting what the news was saying. A half dozen of the women who had escaped the North Tower had no money, keys, or ID, having left their handbags at their desks. The others bought them bagels or water or whatever they came across as they walked. By the time they reached the Upper East Side, Richard was walking with just one young lawyer named Thomas who should have been in the North Tower on the hundredth floor, but a fight with his girlfriend had delayed his leaving for work. Thomas didn't know where he would spend the night, and Richard said his ex-wife would find room for him, but Thomas said he thought he'd go find his alcohol support group and headed for a bar on Third Avenue.

RICHARD'S COMPANY REOPENED QUICKLY IN RENTED OFFICES IN JERSEY City. Richard tried to go back to work, but the subway terrified him. He wasn't sleeping and was afraid of everything. Sirens, smoke, even dogs. He tried driving to work, but crossing the bridge was worse than the tunnels, and he developed a panicky fear that the trucks on the highway on the Jersey side were going to topple sideways onto him and crush him. He was so tense and erratic that Nicky told me he thought his father's marriage was in trouble.

Dinah invited Richard to her apartment for lunch. They sat at the dining room table all afternoon, with Dinah's tax records for years back, her statements from Social Security and her retirement account, crunching numbers and projecting income, if she continued to work at her current rate for such and so many years. They agreed that she could afford to reduce his payment to her by two-thirds; in return he would oversee her investments, renegotiate fees with her broker, make sure her insurance and will were in order. All the things he used to do for his private clients he would now do for Dinah, for free, for life. He resigned from his job, went back to Westchester, and reopened his family office. Within five months, he had his old clients back, and at least one new one: me. To have him take over the job of fighting with the monsters who provide, or rather do everything they can to avoid providing, my health insurance was worth the fee by itself. Dinah claimed it was the best deal she ever made, but then, she's like that.

NICKY STARTED LAW SCHOOL THAT JANUARY. HE WAS twenty-six. He took student loans to cover tuition and went on living at home to save room and board money. It must have been that winter, too, that Dinah called me about our high school reunion. Hoping for big reunion gifts, the school started promoting a year in advance.

"Are you even *thinking* of going?" she demanded. It was to be our fortieth, if you can believe it. Well, why shouldn't you believe it? But *we* found it hard. Inside I felt as young as I ever had, and it was hard to reconcile my inner reality with the face that now looked out at me from my mirror topped with increasingly improbable auburn hair.

"Why?" I asked. "Are you *not* thinking of it?" As I had had no Bright College Years, Miss Pratt's had remained important to me, if only for the lifelong friends I'd made there.

"The only people from our class I really want to see are you and Nanny Townsend and Leonora, and I can see you all here, and the food will be better." She invited us to dinner (we brought the wine) and she was right. After that we met every six weeks or so to catch up with one another.

The four of us were finishing dinner one October night at Dinah's when a key turned in the front door lock, and Nicky appeared, wearing a broad-shouldered suit from the 1940s and a becoming fedora. Behind him was a slight and arty blond boy, now sporting round tortoiseshell glasses, whom I dimly remembered from Nicky's high school crowd.

"Good evening, ladies," Nick said. "I am Clark Kent."

"Well, of course you are," said Dinah. "We've all suspected that."

"You look very dashing, Nicky," said Leonora.

"Thank you. I've got a lot invested in this suit. Mom, you remember Toby?"

"Of course, darling, how are you." She kissed them both. "Where did you get it?"

"Opera Guild Thrift Shop. I had to have the pants taken in about a foot. We're having our class reunion at Paula Donnelley's, but Toby didn't know it was a costume party. Can he go as you?" he asked Dinah.

"He doesn't have to wear my underwear, does he?"

Nicky took that as a yes. They started toward her bedroom.

The interruption had had the happy effect of shortening Nanny's detailed explanation of how well she had been feeling on hormone replacement therapy and how sorry she was to have to give it up, because now she wasn't sleeping and sometimes had to get up and change her drenched pajamas in the middle of the night. Not that we didn't care; we did. In fact I had a breathlessly interesting contribution to make to the topic regarding evening primrose oil. Still, having a boister of youthful high spirits sweep through the room was a welcome treat. We could hear the boys laughing in Dinah's bedroom.

The young returned, and we gasped. Toby was uncanny as the Full Dinah. He was wearing a long dark skirt and Dinah's wide black wool jacket with the huge bone buttons, perhaps the most characteristic item from her winter uniform, and her long cherry-colored scarf double-looped around his neck in the way my age group does when we haven't had any work done on our many-pleated necks. His eyes were dramatized with a graphite shadow and lines of kohl at the lashes, and he wore a bright slash of familiar crimson lipstick and one of Dinah's berets.

"Oh. My. God," said Leonora.

"If you've wrecked my favorite lipstick I'm going to kill you, you know that," said Dinah.

"Toby, you look divine. Who did your makeup?" I asked.

"Nicky," said Toby, appearing pleased.

"My goodness, you *do* pay attention," I said to my godson.

Leonora said, "I would know you were Dinah Wainwright *anywhere,* Toby. It's quite frightening."

"The shoes aren't perfect," said Dinah. Toby was still wearing his own high-top sneakers. "I kind of like the look, though."

"Thanks, Ma," said Nicky.

"Good-bye, louts. Have fun," said Dinah.

As they went out the door I saw Nanny and Leonora exchange a look.

Dinah called the next morning to say that Toby had been a succès fou. Cries of "Oh my god, it's Nick's mother!" had been heard all over the party. Nicky didn't get nearly as much attention as Toby did until midnight, when he'd shed his suit and revealed his Superman costume.

THERE WAS NO QUESTION THAT NICKY WAS DOING WELL AND HAVING fun, but I think you can imagine his mother's pleasure when he asked if he could come for dinner and bring a girl.

As I heard the story, they met when Nicholas stopped in a bookstore in Carnegie Hill one evening to browse the art books and schmooze with the owner. He noticed a fine-boned blonde standing on the mahogany library stairs shelving oversize stock, and couldn't help but notice her delicate ankles and quiet but very good clothes.

"Who is *that?*" he asked.

"She's called Grace Metcalf," said Clifford. "We're trying each other out."

Grace was just back from three years in France to which she'd fled after her father died. She accepted Nicky's invitation to walk in the park after the shop closed, and they were still together six hours later, leaning their glossy heads together over guttering candles in a trattoria on Third Avenue as the last waiter piled chairs on the tabletops and leaned sarcastically against the cash register, feigning sleep.

It had been a wind-haunted autumn night in the city, chilly but not yet bitter, with wood smoke in the air and yellow leaves still clinging here and there among bare branches, turning over in the wind, or giving up at last and falling to where they crunched underfoot. Grace remembered Nicky from their teenage years; although they had gone to different schools they had moved in the same circles, but Nick belonged to a glamorous older crowd and hadn't notice her at the Hols and Cols and Mets and Gets where she and her not yet sleek or stylish friends had sat in clumps at dances. They walked to her old school, then to his, telling each other stories of what had happened on this block, in that shop, in the apartment right up there on the eighth floor where someone had had an amazing party one Thanksgiving. They described the Halloween costumes they'd worn as children, the buildings where they been allowed to trick-or-treat. Grace confessed that her friend had had a crush on Nicky and dragged everyone to see him in *Most Happy Fella*. Everything amazed them, everything made them laugh. The streets were luminous, enchanted places where each of them had walked alone, becoming themselves, until it was time to discover each other.

They talked about the songs they had loved, what they'd danced to, books they'd read for English class. All their memories were happy, all their luck seemed to have been good. He said he didn't want to call her Grace; it didn't suit her, he declared. By the time I was invited into the romance, a month or two later, they were calling each other "pup."

Dinah was the first to learn they were an item, but I believe I was the second. Nicky telephoned. "Lovie, may I take you to lunch? There's someone I want you to meet." We agreed on Sette Mezzo on Lex in the seventies. I arrived first and was at my usual table in the back when Nicky walked in with his "someone." My Grace. It was an ugly winter day, with a sky like wet concrete, and a bitter wind, but as they shook off their heavy coats and followed the maître d' toward me, they both seemed to shine with happiness. People turned to look at them as they passed.

I was on my feet to embrace them both.

"Grace Holland Metcalf! Look at you! Nicky, you sly dog, is *this* your girl?"

They both laughed and wriggled with pleasure at their surprise.

"I don't believe it, it's too wonderful!" It was so wonderful I started to laugh.

Grace had lost weight while she was in France, making her always trim figure positively elegant, and today she was wearing her silky wheat-colored hair in a loose bun with a red lacquered chopstick through it. She seemed to be made of cashmere, small and entirely feminine, except for an elaborately carved gold and onyx sealing ring that I recognized as her father's. She smelled of citrus.

"Tell me everything! How did you find each other?" They told the story of their meeting, in alternating versions. And then about their first date.

"He took me bowling! I'd never been bowling!"

"How was she?" I asked Nicky, amused.

"Very good," said Nicky at the same moment Grace cried, "Terrible!"

When they got to the moment about halfway through their first dinner when they realized they had me in common, they both said, "There really are only six people in the world."

I said that was true, by which I meant that to live in a vast, mean, and dangerous world but feel that in fact it's a trustworthy lacework of lucky coincidence is to feel richly blessed.

When our food came, they turned to musing how, with so much in common, they hadn't found each other before.

"Avis and Dinah must have been at boarding school together too, weren't they, Lovie?" I explained that we had overlapped, but Avis had been two years ahead of us.

They wanted to know how I happened to know Avis as well as I did now, and I told them. "She's a remarkable woman," I said, and Grace agreed, without elaboration. Nicky glanced at her.

When I got back to the shop, the phone was ringing. Dinah crowed, "Did you *ever*?"

"You are going to have to stop calling Avis Mrs. Gotrocks now."

"I don't see why."

"You must admit, Grace is a lovely human being."

"Adorable," said Dinah.

"How long have you known?"

"Since Sunday. I've been dying to call, but they so much wanted to tell you themselves."

We settled down to a good long chin-wag about how serious they were, what might happen next, and what Avis was going to think.

As I already knew, there was a reason Grace had gone to Paris to finish college and not come back until now. Harrison's death had let a genie out of a bottle in that little family. It was Harrison who had abandoned Grace in so many ways, but it was her mother she was furious with. She was angry that Avis had let her father drink himself to death. She was angry that Avis traveled so much. She was angry that in emotionally confusing circumstances, Avis reacted with good manners rather than with some passion or wisdom of the heart Grace longed for, which would have been messier but felt real. I once suggested to her that we are charged, in this life, with loving each other, but not necessarily with interfering with each other's choices. She asked me, if she decided to hang herself, would I stand by and let her? Things seemed a good deal simpler to her at the time than they did to me. As is often the case with the young.

YOU KNOW HOW, WHEN YOU ASK ABOUT YOUR FRIENDS' CHILDREN AND all is well, you get a happy story? When I asked Avis about Grace in those years, all she said was, "She's fine." I knew that it made her very sad to be so distant from Grace, but she didn't know what she had done that couldn't be forgiven, and I certainly wasn't going to be the one to tell her. I did try to tell her that it was good that Grace felt sure enough of her love to dare to be angry with her, but Avis found that pretty cold comfort.

Meanwhile, Grace was a girl in the market for a mother, and that was not the kind of thing Dinah ever missed.

"My friends always love my mother more than they do me," Nicky said cheerfully. In addition to Nala, two of his high school girlfriends had stayed in touch with Dinah years after Nicky broke up with them. But from the beginning, with Grace and Dinah it was something more.

Dinah made time for the young, and they always knew that her pleasure in their company was unfeigned. They were welcome at her table, she didn't mind changes of plan at the last minute, she loved their jokes and the rush of ever-evolving private languages they brought into the house. She saw movies none of the rest of us saw, she knew the new bands and got the point of hip-hop when the rest of us didn't even want to. She could do the moonwalk, she knew what vogueing was, she was always in demand to demonstrate the Mashed Potato, which the young found blissfully funny. She was sexy.

It might be true to say that she didn't recognize a difference between herself and them. It might have had to do with the fact that Richard had supported her for so long, a little as if he were the daddy and she were still and forever a not quite adult, or maybe that's just me. Maybe I make too much of the difference money makes, whom you take it from, or don't. I'm sure she would say of me that I'm incomplete because I never had children of my own. Perhaps she'd be right. Being complete is not a condition given to many of us.

I had always tried to be a safe haven for Grace. I loved to read to her when she was little, and I brought her stylish presents, always something a little more grown-up than the age she was. When she was seven I noticed that no one had troubled to teach her to ride a two-wheeler and suggested to Avis that it was time. Grace didn't know that. I didn't especially want her to; I wanted to make Avis look good. If I had known that Avis was going to buy Grace a bike and have the nanny teach her to ride it, I'd have taught her myself. Just thinking about that little face makes me sad.

Dinah was under no such restraint as trying to make Avis look good. One night when Nicky was working late we went to see *The Hours* with Grace, and out for a bowl of pasta afterward. Dinah got off on the subject of being the first in her class to get her period.

"I thought I was dying," she crowed. "I'd never heard of bleeding that didn't mean something terrible had happened. I cried all night, thinking how sad my parents would be that I had a fatal disease. That and trying to decide what to wear on my deathbed."

As an oldest child, I had my own story to tell. Then Dinah said to Grace, "I suppose *your* mother had you all kitted out with supplies and instructions?"

Grace said, "Are you joking? My mother hasn't noticed I'm out of grade school. She'd still be having those fucking yellow ducks embroidered on my socks if the Women's Exchange hadn't gone out of business."

I was thinking of some way to say how well Avis meant, without sounding mealymouthed. Dinah wasn't. She roared her great gravelly laugh. "Ducks? On your socks? You *must* be kidding." It was like a romance, what had sprung up between Grace and Dinah. They couldn't get enough of each other. I wasn't sure myself how Dinah had come to be so important to Grace so quickly, so much more than I had ever been to her, but it happens like that sometimes. I could adduce reasons, so could you, but it wasn't reasonable, it really was a matter of the heart. People were always falling in love with Dinah.

MRS. OBA'S NIECE, STEPHANIE, HAD COME TO WORK FOR ME, TO learn the business. She handled the walk-ins, and she could run the shop on her own if necessary, which left me free to get away for more than a long weekend now and again, a welcome development. One afternoon in early spring I came downstairs to take a break from a new inventory program I was wrestling with to find Stephanie with a tall, rather strongly built redhead whom I had never expected to meet in the flesh. She was wearing a periwinkle blue strapless sheath with a sexy kick pleat and a matching stole, appraising herself in the mirrored back wall of the showroom. On her feet she still wore a pair of ballet flats. She turned from her reflection to me as soon as I entered the room.

"Good afternoon," I said, taking her in every bit as carefully as she was regarding me. "That's a marvelous color on you."

For some seconds, she just looked at me. Finally she said, "Of course, the shoes don't help."

"Would you like to borrow a pair of heels?" We were now

standing side by side, reflected in the mirror. She was younger than I, but not by as much as a decade. Her haircut and color were dramatic for my taste, the shade a dark russet not found in nature, and the cut severe, but well done; Frédéric Fekkai, I would guess.

"Do you have a pair? I'm a nine."

"Certainly."

Stephanie, who had been hovering, disappeared and returned with some silver evening sandals.

"Are you shopping for a special occasion?" I asked.

"Oh, no, I was just . . ."

"Yes," I said.

She turned her figure sideways to appraise the effect in the mirror while my reflection watched. Her belly was going a little soft; otherwise, she was admirably trim. Normally at this point in the proceedings I flatter a little, if the dress really suits the customer, or if it doesn't, suggest something else. In this case, I stayed quiet.

Eventually she said, "I like the built-in . . ." She put her hands on her ribs, indicating the foundation garment upon which the bodice was constructed. I nodded. "And the price?"

I mentioned a number that was not small. She didn't react, a sign that either she wasn't seriously considering a purchase or that money was no object, and I didn't think it was the latter.

"Well," she said at last, "I'll think about it."

She turned to look at me directly. Then she turned to the dressing room, and Stephanie followed her, carrying her flats. As she drew back the curtain, I saw that there were at least five cocktail dresses on the peg inside.

"Is Madame still considering any of these?" Stephanie asked, very correctly.

"I liked this one." She took it and held it up, as if she were asking what I thought of it, though she wasn't.

I said, "That's a new designer for us. I think he's going to work out very well."

"American?"

"Yes. From Seattle, oddly enough."

"Why oddly?"

Oh God. Why had I said anything? I'd been doing so well.

"I don't know, I just hadn't thought of Seattle as a fashion hub."

"Oh."

"I guess now it's an everything hub. What with Starbucks. And Bill Gates." Shut up, Loviah.

"I haven't been there."

"I haven't either. This designer came to me."

She stopped in the door of the dressing room. "Really? That's interesting."

Was it? Why? I wanted her to go in and put her own clothes back on before I said anything dumber.

Eventually she did. She emerged, wearing a pair of jeans and a jacket off the rack from Armani Ex. We showed her out.

Then I went upstairs and called Gil.

"Guess who was just here?"

He said, "Who?"

"Meredith." His oldest daughter.

WE'D ALWAYS WONDERED HOW MUCH ALTHEA KNEW ABOUT US, OR IF she knew everything and didn't care. Either was possible. The children were a different matter. They hero-worshipped their dad, Meredith especially. As did I. Meredith's relationship with Althea was often strained, but in spite of being what any statistician would have to call middle-aged, she was Daddy's Little Girl.

I described Meredith's visit, how she had seemed prepared to try on everything in the store to kill time until I showed up. How we had circled each other, tails erect, sniffing.

"No wagging?" he asked. He used to tease me about my little Norwich terrier, Hannah. It's a cliché, I suppose, the childless woman and her pet, but there are reasons for clichés.

Some helpful soul had told Meredith about me, that much was sure. The question was, what would she do about it? There'd been a time when I'd pictured having her as my stepdaughter. Someone to protect and laugh with, someone to take to Elizabeth Arden for massages and manicures. But that was always a dream I dreamed alone. Althea didn't believe in divorce. She was Catholic, but that wasn't why: she just thought it was common. "So undisciplined," she was known to say. Althea gained no weight she didn't mean to gain, barely ever was ill, never complained and never explained. It had to be like being married to the queen of England.

We talked it over that weekend at our place in Connecticut. Sitting with his long thin frame collapsed like a stork's into the wing chair by the fireplace, Gil looked hardy and content, still with thick dark hair, barely silvered, still with the muscular grace of the athlete he was. It was hard to believe he was nearly eighty. He wore an old tweed jacket and a pair of thick socks with slippers; the only sign of age I could see in him was that his feet were always cold.

Hannah, the traitor, abandoned her spot beside me on the sofa

and stood before him, wiggling and making a little imploring
noise in her throat until he picked her up and settled her on his
lap. I brought him his silver bullet, a very dry gin martini with
three olives. He sipped his drink slowly, and at the end ate two
of the olives and fed the third to me. He delivered this to me on
the end of a toothpick, as if he were feeding a baby bird. To this
day, the scent of a gin-soaked olive is enough to transport me to a
happier time.

"Do you think she just learned about me? Did she come to see
what a Scarlet Woman looks like?"

Gil was quiet, pondering. We both looked out the window at
my rose garden, which was filled with color although it was early
in the season.

"Something must have happened. Something's changed."

Gil didn't like to talk about Althea with me. We were separate
things to him. He'd chosen to stay in the marriage, and so had
she, and I had to respect the privacy of that. So it was unusual that
he said now, "Althea is coming home for the summer."

"Home. To New York?" I tried not to show the shock I felt.
She had spent the summers in Provence for as long as I'd been in
the picture.

"I've taken a house in Easthampton for her. She wants to have
the grandchildren out to stay with her." Meredith had two children; George, the youngest, had one and another on the way.
Clara, the classic middle child, claimed to be married to her career, which so far consisted of big parts in very small dark foreign
films and a series of seriously unsuitable boyfriends.

After a pause, I said, "Is this the new pattern? Or an experiment?"

"Experiment, I think. She lost two old friends in France this winter. One had been ill, but the other just died in her sleep. Those were body blows. She may give up the Paris house."

We looked at each other. I couldn't imagine what that would mean for us if it happened.

"Is she likely to enjoy playing Go Fish with four-year-olds?"

"You never know. She's a surprising person." I got up and took his glass into the pantry to pour him his dividend.

"She comes from a line of long-lived women," Gil said after I was resettled on my sofa. "When the husbands in that family die at ninety-five, the obituary always reads 'survived by his wife and his mother.'"

I understood. If she wanted to be closer to her family as these inevitable losses mounted, anyone would understand.

And what did Meredith's visit mean? There seemed nothing to do but wait and see.

AT A DINNER PARTY ON GRAMERCY PARK THAT SPRING, THE GUESTS were talking about their summer plans. Some people called Delafield were divorcing; my hostess's house was right next to theirs on Georgica Pond. "It's heartbreaking, really. They just finished the guesthouse."

"What happened?"

"He has depression. But he's been much better lately. New pills or something."

"I don't think I know them."

"Yes you do—Paul and Elsa, second marriage, she's from Oslo, he's in publishing? They go to Brick Church?"

"Is she leaving him *because* he's better and now she can?"

"That really is sad, if true."

"It might be Paul who's leaving. I heard there was a handsome tennis pro involved."

"Who gets the house?"

"She's in the apartment, with the children. The house in Easthampton is rented."

"Lucky renters. Do you know them?"

"Gil and Althea Flood. They're older. The Realtor says they're lovely."

"I thought she lived in Paris."

"Does she?"

"You know, I have a friend who would be perfect for Paul."

I stopped listening.

MY SAD AND DIGNIFIED FRIEND AVIS, KNOWING NEW YORK would hold nothing for me that summer of 2003, invited me to come visit her in Maine, where she'd been spending each August on an island since Harrison died. Her cottage was modest, two bedrooms only, with a kitchen that hadn't been changed since the 1950s. A lady came from the village to clean once a week; otherwise she was alone. It took me two days to get there.

As we approached it on the ferry from Northeast Harbor, the island, soft with summer grasses, appeared golden in the sun, studded randomly with austere white houses and looking altogether like an Andrew Wyeth painting. The day was gorgeous, with a high pure sky, and the bay shimmering.

Half the population seemed to be waiting at the dock for visitors, packages from FedEx or UPS, or in our case, the crabmeat Avis had ordered for our lunch. Hefting my bags down the gangplank, I spotted her chatting happily with a short man in a navy mechanic's jumpsuit that had TOM embroidered over the pocket. He was tanned like leather except for the white seams around his mouth and eyes. The nails on his hands were so deeply edged with black grease, it seemed they couldn't have been clean in years. Avis was wearing a pair of baggy sun-faded pinkish shorts, espadrilles that no longer had a color, and a man's white shirt, open at the neck. On her head was a wide-brimmed straw hat, its edges coming unwoven in places where something had chewed it over the winter. "Tom" accepted a large gray canvas sack stamped

U.S. MAIL from one of the deckhands and started off up the hill, pushing his sack before him in a wheelbarrow. Avis put her hands on my shoulders and kissed the air beside my ear. It was a warm greeting; touching people is hard for Avis. She took my smaller bag, although I warned her it was the heaviest.

"You weren't kidding," she said. Carrying it made her walk with a hitch in her gait, but she wouldn't give it back. "What's in here?"

"Books. Laptop. A bottle of champagne."

"Oh how nice! We'll have more use for the champagne than the laptop, though."

Uh-oh. No Internet? I hadn't thought of that.

"We have dial-up. Sometimes. But don't worry, if it's impor-tant we can go over to the main and use the computers in the library." No silent nightly exchange of the day's news with East-hampton, then, no wishing one's absent loved one peaceful sleep and sweet dreams.

She was putting my bags into the trunk of a battered gray Karmann Ghia that had to be fifty years old.

"Oh my goodness" is all I could think of to say when I saw the car.

"This is Betty," she said. "Belinda gave her to me when I turned eighteen. I can't put her top up anymore, so we have to walk if it rains, but otherwise she's doing well for an old bag."

Betty's engine started with a gruff rumble that reminded me of something, a sound from when I was young, bringing a shock of pleasure.

"I used to know someone who had one of these," I said, remem-bering a shy blond young man who had courted me for about five minutes during my debutante summer. With the memory came the scent of honeysuckle in Canaan Woods and the warm green smell of June lawns. We turned onto the main road that ran along the ridge of the island.

"She isn't legal, of course," Avis said. "None of the island cars are. There's no one to inspect them, unless you take them to the main, and why would we do that?"

"How do you keep them running?"

"The man I was waiting with at the ferry does it somehow."

"Tom?"

"Brian. He got that jumpsuit on eBay. He has a brother with an auto graveyard on the main, where he gets the parts."

We drove past a weedy pair of clay tennis courts, past the tiny library and the post office and down to Avis's little house. My room, the guest room, was upstairs, papered with old-fashioned wallpaper, with pale blue ribbons twining against a white background. There were gauzy white voile curtains and a view out to open sea. I had my own widow's walk, although Avis was the actual widow. Her bedroom was downstairs with a slightly more modern bathroom than mine, which had a claw-foot tub and no shower. There was plenty of hot water, though, and the towels and bed linens were fresh and new, and the mattress was excellent. I unpacked my clothes and books, sat for a moment appreciating the heart-stopping sweep of the meadow and the bay and the thoughtfulness of fresh sweet peas in a little vase on my bedside table. I wished Gil could see it. I wished I could see the room he was in at that moment. I hoped that Althea was hating the Hamptons and wished briefly that she would fall down a hole and break her neck.

Then I went down to join Avis on the porch, where she was waiting with crab salad, a bowl of cherry tomatoes, and homemade lemonade.

After lunch we walked down to the post office, a white clapboard two-room building with a small wall of ancient mailboxes in the entryway and a cheerful young woman in a flowered summer dress who got up from her chair behind the counter to greet us.

"Good afternoon, Audrey."

"Afternoon, Avis. Is this your company? Up from the big city?"

I introduced myself.

"How long will you be staying?"

"Two weeks. Her mail will come care of me," said Avis.

"I'll pop 'em in your box then. You have a package, do you want it now?"

"How big is it?"

Audrey approximated with her hands.

"We'll come back for it with Betty. We're taking our constitutional at the moment."

We walked out to the end of the island, stopping to chat with people we met, accepting an offer to tour an ambitious garden with a yellow climbing rose that interested me particularly. It belonged to a young couple from Philadelphia who were expecting a group from the Garden Club of America the next week. They were anxious that their clematis make a good show. The lady from Philadelphia was the only person on the island who didn't call Avis by her first name.

Out past the village, we picked warm blueberries and ate

them in the sun. They had a lovely tartness and felt slightly grainy on the tongue. We made some plans for how to spend the time of my visit. I offered to cook dinner that evening or to take her out to eat, if there was anywhere to take her, but she said she was going to make her world-famous chicken burgers. I was allowed to shell the peas, which had come from the garden minutes before, and her neighbor Caroline had baked a raspberry pie.

It wasn't until we were seated over our supper, with candles and a bottle of rosé, that Avis mentioned Grace. In the evening light her strong narrow face looked surprisingly young. She reminded me of the girl I had first known at school, all legs and angular bones, with the regal bearing that sent a different message from the rather anxious expression in her eyes.

"She's decided to take a degree so she can teach. She got into Columbia," Avis told me, doing her imitation of a mother with a normal bond with her daughter.

I knew that already but didn't say so.

"Will she come up to visit while you're here?"

"Oh yes, she's coming next week."

I was puzzled, since I myself was occupying the only guest room.

"Not here," said Avis. "She'll go to visit Belinda in Dundee, on the main. I thought we'd get Brian to run us over for a day, if you'd like to."

"I'd love it. I haven't been there in years."

"It's absolutely charming. Belinda found a house there that suits her perfectly when Nantucket got too overrun for her."

I wondered, if it was so charming, why Avis was here instead of there, but didn't ask. It was easy enough to see that this island life suited her.

"Were you sorry about Nantucket?"

"No, it was always too much of a scrum for me. I went because Grace loved it."

I thought of Gil, saying fondly that Avis was an odd duck. Nantucket was my idea of heaven. I wished I'd had a mother with a house there, instead of a mosquito-infested campsite in the Rangeley Lakes, which was our childhood summer vacation if we were lucky.

"Grace is much more like Belinda than she is like me," Avis said. "They both love hubbub."

"Is there hubbub in Dundee?"

"Apparently. Have you seen much of her this spring?"

"Belinda?"

"Grace. I'm told she has a beau coming with her this visit."

I had a moment of feeling extremely cross with Grace. She was angry with Avis, I understood that, but that was not an excuse to be unkind. There were manners that should be observed, no matter what one was feeling.

Then I remembered how little my own mother knew about my private life.

"Have you met him?" Avis asked, carefully attending to getting peas onto her fork. She was hungry to know but surely understood that any answer would hurt her feelings. There was nothing to do but ignore the unkindness.

"Wait till you hear—it's my godson Nicky Wainwright. Dinah's son!" I said, light and bright and feeling as if I had slapped her.

There was not a moment's hesitation in Avis's response. A huge smile lit her face.

"How absolutely wonderful!" she cried. "The younger one, the actor?"

I wished Nick and Grace were there that minute so I could paddle them both. Avis had remembered all that I'd told her about Nicky because he was important to me. "Yes, Nicky, the actor-law student."

"Do you think they're serious?" she asked, marveling.

"I think *they* think they are . . ."

"Isn't this wonderful? Wouldn't it be *fun*?"

"It would be," I said, with all the heart I could, knowing it was already fun for Dinah. We sat together in the darkening evening looking out at the fireflies in the meadow.

"Let's have the champagne," said Avis. That was a motion I could second.

OUR DAYS PASSED EASILY AND HAPPILY. AVIS MADE IT EASY. ONE DAY we went over to the main to hike in Acadia and explore Mount Desert. We picked blueberries and made muffins, most of which Avis put into the freezer so I could take them with me when the visit was over. We spent long hours reading on the porch. We wrote letters. One evening when a thunderstorm knocked out our power, we played Russian Bank all evening by candle-light. At first, in the blackness that had fallen so suddenly, along with the eerie silence of no humming refrigerator, no cranky water pump in the cellar groaning on and off, no anything living in the house except us, we couldn't find the candles in the kitchen, and the flashlight wasn't on the hook inside the cellar door where it was supposed to be. We felt our way around in inky dark, the storm having blanked out the moon. Avis rummaged in the tool closet, hoping to find hurricane lamps and dropping things on her feet. I finally found my purse hung on a coat hook. Avis thought I was a genius to realize that the screen of my cell phone could be used as a flashlight.

The next morning, with power restored, we woke to find all the living room lights on, and the kitchen faucet running. "Thank heaven," said Avis. "I was afraid we'd have to make our tea with gin." That afternoon we took Betty to the island grocery to stock up on batteries and lamp oil.

We played some desultory tennis on the clay courts, which apparently belonged to everybody. Avis was surprisingly good, and yet I, who never practice, always seemed to beat her in the end. Over the course of the visit, I figured out that Avis doesn't like to win. I don't know if it frightens her or makes her sad to take something that someone else wants. It raised the question: what in this life *did* she want badly enough to try to take it from another person?

THE DAY OF OUR VISIT TO DUNDEE DAWNED HOT AND CLOUDLESS. Brian was taking us over in his extremely aromatic work boat, the *Carol Ann*. He had put his lobster pots out around dawn that morning, then come into the town wharf to pick us up. Once we were out on the bay it seemed this was a day the lord had made just to remind us that into every life come moments of perfection.

We skimmed around the Bass Harbor light and up Great Spruce Bay, *Carol Ann* making a cheerful racket, and arrived at Belinda's dock at about ten in the morning. One had a sense of being flooded through the eyes with the blue of sky and sea, the light, the sheer beauty of it. If it had been ink it would have spread through one's soul, tinting everything with glory.

Grace and Nicky, hand in hand, came down the lawn to meet us. Nicky held his big hand out to Avis, introducing himself, while Grace embraced me and kissed me. Then Avis and Grace kissed the air beside each other's ears.

"Sweetheart," said Avis warmly.

"Mother," said Grace.

We walked up to the sun porch where Belinda was waiting for us, her white hair perfectly coiffed, wearing a shirtwaist dress printed with nautical flags and a big necklace of white plastic beads.

"You're both just brown as berries," she said to us. The children began to chatter about what we should do with ourselves until lunch. Tour the village? Climb Butter Hill? Go out in kayaks?

"I've never been in a kayak," said Avis.

"It's great," said Nicky. "You skim along like a water bug. Even I can do it."

"Now don't make poor Lovie go out and paddle around like a duck," said Belinda. I had never been in a kayak myself and longed to try it, but of course I said, "That's right. You go. I need a catch-up with my pal here."

So I watched from the porch as the other three went down toward the stone beach where four kayaks lay upside down on the grass above the tide line. They fitted themselves with life jackets and spray skirts. Avis looked a little like a water bug even before she entered the boat, with her long bare arms and legs punctuated by knobby joints, struggling to fold herself into the hollow kazoo shape of the boat. Nicky briskly tucked her spray skirt into place all around the cabin hole so that the boat seemed to replace her lower limbs. Grace gave the boat a shove from behind, and Avis glided off onto the water with a cry of surprise. A maid brought me a glass of sweet iced tea.

BELINDA, FOR ALL SHE WAS PERFECTLY TURNED OUT, WASN'T FEELING well. I told her all the news I could think of from New York, and even had the rare pleasure of being able to talk about Gil and Althea. Her interest and sympathy were balm to my soul.

When the paddlers came back, Avis was glowing with pleasure. They had gone over to the yacht club moorings and peered at the visiting boats. Lunch was vintage grandmother food: clam chowder with oyster crackers, tomato sandwiches, and applesauce with ginger snaps for dessert, cooked and served by a chatty village woman named Ella. We ate at a glass table on the porch looking up the bay toward the Bass Harbor light.

Avis noticed how little Belinda ate; I watched her eyes. When we had finished, Avis asked Grace if she would take us to visit an old friend from Miss Pratt's who had a summer place nearby. I didn't know the woman, as she had graduated before I'd arrived, so suggested a game of Honeymoon Bridge with Belinda. But Belinda wanted a rest. I went along to the house on the Salt Pond, where Avis and I sat in lawn chairs with our hostess, Eleanor Applegate, kibitzing and talking about old school friends while Grace and Nick played a jolly game of croquet with the children of the house.

It meant the world to Avis to be with Grace and Nicky, watching them, laughing with them. But I knew that Dinah would have been out on the lawn with them, whacking away with her own croquet mallet, challenging the rules and playing to win. And when we were back at The Elms, saying our good-byes, with the *Carol Ann* waiting down at the dock, the formality between Grace and Avis was unchanged by any apparent warmth shared during the visit.

Avis was made very happy by the day, though, and Brian had had a fine time as well, shooting the breeze at Olive's Lunch, stocking up on fishing gear and automotive supplies. The bay had gone glassy and there was a tinge of pink on the water as the afternoon sun moved toward the wooded horizon. We waved to yachtsmen who waved back as they slipped silently along on the bay, sails almost limp, making for Dundee Harbor. When we rounded Bass Harbor Head into Brian's home waters, we helped him pull his lobster pots. I took the helm and did whatever I was told while Avis and Brian, in heavy rubber gloves, pulled the traps up onto the stern. Brian extracted the lobsters, measured them, threw back the undersized and the roe-bearing females, and pegged the claws of the keepers. Avis meanwhile rebaited the traps and threw them back into the water, keeping the buoys and toggles well away from the propeller. By the time we got back to the village wharf, Avis smelled as fishy as Brian did. The icing on the cake was that when Brian put us down at the wharf before going out to his mooring, we found ourselves surrounded by the matrons of the Garden Club of America, all decked out in their summer finest, waiting to board the ferry. *This* Avis was a person Grace didn't even know.

AFTER I LEFT AVIS, I STOPPED IN ELLSWORTH TO SPEND A NIGHT WITH my parents before catching my plane in Bangor. My father's luck, which had never been great, had run out some time before, and after a year of increasingly erratic behavior he had been diagnosed with dementia the previous winter. I'd been in touch, of course, and though at a distance had made some arrangements that helped with his care, but it was my two youngest siblings who lived close to home and did all the heavy lifting, especially my sister April and my younger brother's wife, June. (You can imagine for yourself the calendar jokes they get. They're fond of each other and often together, so they've heard them all.) My brother Tim is a fisherman, and June is a hairdresser, absolutely salt of the earth and extremely bright, but that didn't stop my mother making fun of her Down East accent.

Getting my father to stop driving had been the hardest part. June had been with him one day when he'd tried to turn off the ignition with the radio knob, yet the great State of Maine had allowed him to renew his driver's license. For a week, first my sister Sally from Portland, then Tim, then June, had wrested his keys from him, explaining to him that he had Alzheimer's disease, and that if he continued to drive with a diagnosis like that and he hurt someone, he could be sued for everything he had, right down to his underpants. The light of understanding would dawn, he'd begin to weep, then shocked and exhausted he'd have a nap, and when he woke up remember no word of the conversation. It was shattering. They had to go on breaking his heart at least once a day, for weeks.

I cooked supper for my parents and put the blueberry muffins into their freezer. They like to eat supper about 5:00 P.M., as most of their neighbors do. Dad went up to bed before it was dark, and Mother and I sat on the back porch in the twilight looking out over the unmown grass in the yard at the half-built catboat that had sat in a cradle there under a tarp since before I left for boarding school, waiting for my father to find time to finish it. The car was parked outside because the garage/shed was filled with a half-finished dollhouse, a bench strewn with tools for making picture frames he never got around to, a wooden canoe with a gash in it he'd bought but never mended, a riding mower with its engine in pieces, two no-longer-functional washing machines, and a lot of equipment for doing automotive bodywork, from a business he had half-finished starting.

I tried to talk with my mother about her trying to take all the care of my father herself, making the house a jail for both of them, and she, annoyed, made condescending remarks about my bone-dry spinster existence and how little I understood of the things in life that really matter. I thanked her for her interest and went up to bed.

Belinda invited Avis and me to a literary luncheon at the Town Club that September. Avis and I both belonged to the Colony Club and enjoyed a gentle feigned rivalry with our Town Club friends, including Belinda. As you can imagine, this sort of thing was no part of my upbringing in Ellsworth, though I understood the Grange and the Odd Fellows. When I was young, clubs seemed to me to belong to the world of English novels, but with time one gets used to many things one never expected to. A club is a great organizing principle, a place where you have at least one thing in common with everyone you meet. It's a haven for those of us who sometimes have too much time on our hands, a party you don't have to plan. Not a home, but still a place where, when you go there, they have to take you in.

I think Belinda had put together a table for this particular program more than anything else to please me, as the speaker was an author I revered. Having a half-hour gap between a medical appointment near the club and the time of the luncheon, I threw myself on the mercy of the door staff, who know me well. They allowed me to wait for Belinda upstairs where I could find a quiet corner to read my book instead of sitting in the little holding pen by the door where nonmembers are normally sequestered.

I chose a tall wing chair next to a window with my back to most of the room, thinking to be most private there. Instead, I found myself in earshot of a conversation that was certainly none of my business and was, besides, destructive of concentration. Two ladies I didn't know, who had apparently come from a club meeting of some sort, were discussing candidates for membership. Rising to change seats seemed wrong, as the talk was sufficiently indiscreet that we all would have been embarrassed, so I did my best instead to pay attention to the words on the page. I lost the battle, though, when I heard Dinah's name.

"Her proposer is a great friend of mine; believe me, I'm damned if I do and damned if I don't."

"Well, you have to say more than that—the committee can't just table a nomination without a reason."

"We can't say why in open meeting."

"Why not?"

"Because it's hearsay. I can't *prove* anything."

"Then tell *me*. If I take your point I'll vote with the rest of you, and you'll have a majority, no discussion needed."

There was a silence.

"You have to swear you won't tell. And you can't ever say you heard it from me."

"All right."

"Were you in New York when she was writing that column, 'Dinah Might'?"

"I loved that column."

"Yes. But remember how suddenly it disappeared?"

A pause. "Did it?"

"Overnight. Yanked out of the paper by the roots."

"All right. And . . . ? Now wait, she was going on maternity leave. My friend Elise knows her pretty well. Elise adores her."

"She was caught extorting money from people in exchange for keeping their secrets out of the paper."

"*Black*mail?"

Another pause.

Finally the shocked second speaker added, "*God,* that's ugly."

"You see the point. If even here you had to worry that something you say is going to wind up in the paper or that she'd come asking to be paid not to . . ."

"Yes, but wait. Why isn't she in jail?"

"She made a deal. She's very well connected."

"God."

"Yes."

I BARELY HEARD THE AUTHOR'S TALK AND WAS NOT GOOD COMPANY AT lunch. I was reeling and couldn't think what to do with what I'd heard. Should I speak to Belinda? How could I? It was so wrong of me to eavesdrop, and besides, it wasn't my club. Should I write an anonymous letter to the admissions committee? Of course not, only a bully or a coward writes an unsigned letter. I couldn't confide in Avis, in this case. It leaves such a taint in the mind to hear something like that about someone, confirmation *or* denial. Where was this coming from? Ultimately from Simon Snyder, of course. One should have expected it, though one hadn't. But how to counter such malignancy once it gets loose? No matter what, there will always be errant cells full of damage, lodged in unexpected places, not poisoning their hosts, innocent or not, but which will certainly poison *someone* as they spring unexpectedly to life and resume multiplying.

Simon had taken his time, but the trap he'd devised for Dinah was brilliant. She'd done a good thing for principled reasons, and she'd paid a high price at the time—she lost a job she really loved. If she tried to defend herself now, the only way to do it would be to expose the only people who knew for sure what had really happened. The gossip press would be on Serena Tate and the others like flies on a fresh kill, undoing the good thing she'd done in the first place. You can't get into an ink fight with the people who own the inkwell; it was Dinah who first told me that. I couldn't tell her, or anyone. By which, of course, I mean I told only Gil.

THAT WAS A TERRIBLE WEEK, IN SPITE OF 2003 BEING ONE OF the mildest and loveliest New York falls on record. The trees turned their leaves yellow and flipped them gently so they sparkled in the autumn sun, which delighted the eye and warmed the spirit. It stayed almost shirtsleeve weather, wonderful walking weather in a city of walkers, until deep into October. Central Park was in glory and I managed to have almost daily rambles there with Gil, in spite of the fact that Althea had not returned to Paris but instead had resumed residence in the Fifth Avenue apartment she had not shared with her husband since George left for boarding school. It was reckless of us to be so much together in public, virtually in Althea's front yard, but I was busy in the shop during business hours, and Gil was out escorting his wife in the evenings, so combining our constitutionals seemed the only way to manage. We could always claim to have fallen in together by chance.

We were so accustomed to talk over everything, to debrief each other on the mundane events of our days, that neither of us felt we could think clearly or quite fill our lungs if we were deprived of it. The summer had been a desert in that regard, and it had changed something in Gil. He was no longer willing to be hostage to appearances. What were the consequences at home, and there surely were some, we didn't discuss. Althea had the part of Gil she wanted, and I had the part I wanted. Not enough of it, but still. So many people have nothing.

There are few unmixed blessings in this wicked world, and

the deep sorrow of that gorgeous fall, in addition to the ugly cloud of rumor shadowing Dinah, was that I finally understood that Belinda was beginning to die. We had grown close over the years, sharing talk about books and friends, Gil and Avis, and now Grace and Nicky. A mother is one thing, but a true friend of your parents' generation is something else, rare and enriching. I admired her and enjoyed her and felt privileged more than anything else when she called on me as if I were family. But I knew it boded ill.

Though she never telephoned me at the shop except to make or change an appointment, she called one morning in October on a cell phone, an appliance she had always deplored. She must have borrowed one from a nurse. She said, "Oh, Lovie, I am so sorry to bother you at work." She talked as if my being at work was the same as it was for the head of a Fortune 500 company. "I'm not interrupting? I know how busy you are."

"Things are very quiet this morning. How are you?"

"Well, that's the thing." She paused, and in that gap I could hear how little she liked making this call. "I had a little procedure this morning, quite unexpectedly. It was nothing much, but they gave me quite a lot of"—here I heard her asking a question of someone else, then she resumed—"Demerol, it's called, and now they won't just hail a taxi and send me home to Ursula. They say I must have someone go with me."

"I'd be delighted to see you home," I said.

"Oh, Lovie. Really? I'm sure your schedule is chockablock."

"There's nothing at all that Stephanie can't handle. Are you ready to leave now?"

There was another conference before she said, "They're just

waiting for some blessed event in my lower intestines it seems, but they think I'll be ready in an hour."

"An hour will be perfect. Are you sure you don't want me to come now, to keep you company?"

"No, it really is so good of you. Are you *sure* this isn't a terrible imposition?"

"Absolutely sure. Are you at New York Hospital?" I knew her internist practiced there, because he was mine as well.

"No, MSK. It's right across the street . . ."

I knew where it was, and my heart went cold. Memorial Sloan-Kettering. Cancer, of course. Belinda was giving me her room number.

"Mrs. Binney's care partner is here," said the nurse at the desk to another, who showed me to the curtained cubicle where Belinda, half upright in her hospital bed, was dozing. She looked beautiful in spite of wearing no makeup, but how had I failed to notice how thin she was? I took a chair by her side and removed my book from my handbag. Beside Belinda a screen monitored things I didn't want to think about. She woke when a nurse came in to check her readings and ask if she'd like something to eat. She wouldn't.

When the nurse had gone, Belinda said, "She's the most amazing woman. She's in the new production of *La Sonnambula* at the Met, which everyone is going to hate, very stark and modern. She's in the chorus. I can't wait to see it, she's going to take me backstage. Show me what you're reading."

I showed her my book, a memoir by Mina Curtiss I'd tracked down with some difficulty. "I haven't read that in donkey's years," she exclaimed, making it clear that she approved, and then somewhat inevitably, "Of course I knew Mina. They don't make them like that anymore."

I helped her to gather her belongings and get her shoes on. She was wearing slacks, a surprise. I didn't know she owned any. In her tote bag she had books, a shawl, her makeup case, and her needlepoint, as if she'd grown accustomed to finding herself suddenly trapped here for days. As we walked gingerly to the elevator, three people we passed in the hall greeted her by name. "Good-bye, be good—we don't want to see you back here!" they cried affectionately.

Trust Belinda.

IN THE TAXI, I WAS TONGUE-TIED. I WANTED TO KNOW WHAT WAS wrong, how long she'd known, what the prognosis was. Did Avis know she was ill? I couldn't think of a way to ask any of this, a sure sign that Belinda didn't want to have that conversation.

"Hasn't it been the most marvelous weather," she said, looking out the window with a kind of joy, and what could I do but agree? We talked about the golden light, about how we wished we could paint so we could capture it. Photographs of beauty are somehow *too* real; the more beautiful they are, the more they seemed clichéd or sentimental. "There was a book I used to read to Grace when she was small, about a squirrel who was scolded for not storing nuts in the fall like all the others. He just sat solemnly looking at the world, saying he was storing all the colors. And, of course, in the dead of winter, that turned out to be what was needed most."

I insisted on seeing her up to her apartment, to be sure Ursula was ready for her. Then I went back to my own flat to call Avis. She was relieved that I knew at last.

AVIS ASKED ME TO TALK TO GRACE. "YOU'LL KNOW WHAT NOTE TO strike. I always get it wrong with her," she said and seemed only to be expressing gratitude that I was willing, though she must have felt more than that. What could it be like to know you were the one person who couldn't seem to communicate with your only child, whom everyone else found so easy?

Grace met me at the zoo in Central Park, in the penguin house. Delight at the comedy and innocence of the world seemed the right base coat to lay down before the picture I had to paint for her. As we stood on the darkened walkway, looking into the lighted water world behind the glass, I couldn't help noticing that Grace took as much notice of the little boy beside her on his father's hip as she did of the animals. How well I remembered that time of life, when all strollers filled me with longing. I waited until we were out in the sun and walking toward the boat basin to ask her if she remembered the book about storing the colors.

"I *loved* that book," she said. "I always wanted to take it home, but Belinda said it was important to have treasures you could only visit. Maybe she'll give it to me when *I* have children."

"And will that be anytime soon?"

We walked in silence until she said, "That's the question, isn't it?"

"And what is the answer?"

"Well . . . your godson."

"My godson. Yes?"

She bent to pick up a perfect yellow maple leaf that had been lying on the path like an upturned palm. "He's a bit of a Peter Pan, isn't he?"

"Nobody does it better."

"True. But is he planning on making a career of it?"

"You tell me."

"We love being together. We adore being together. We love all the same things, we make each other laugh, there's hardly ever a cross word between us."

The way she said this last made me suddenly doubt that was quite the truth. That and the fact that only Dinah might have denied that Nicky's temper could take you by surprise.

"Hardly ever?"

We walked in quiet for a bit.

"What's the worst fight you ever had?" I asked her.

She didn't have to think very hard. "I threw out his old moccasins because I'd bought him new ones." She didn't look as if it was an experience she wished to repeat.

"He said I shouldn't try to change him. He was enraged. But I wasn't trying to change him, I was trying to please him!"

"He's always hated change," I said carefully. "It's why his parents' breakup was so hard on him." Which it had been, much more than for RJ, who had his sports and his cheerful mob of friends who were somehow less complicated than the people and things that interested Nicky. I once had quite a quarrel with Nick myself about whether or not divorce should be illegal. I couldn't get him to see it from any point of view except his own. He was about fourteen at the time.

"I don't care if he goes around in tatters if he wants to. Lovie, he even gets along with my mother!"

"I hear a 'but' coming."

"But we don't seem to be going anywhere."

"You mean he doesn't talk about marriage."

That was what she meant. "It's not just that he doesn't propose, we don't even talk about it. If I say anything about the future, a future together, children, where we might like to live, he changes the subject. He tickles me or takes my hat and makes me chase him." It was true, they were like a pair of puppies together, tumbling and playing. It looked adorable, but even puppies grow up.

Grace asked, "There isn't anything I don't know, is there?"

I sincerely hoped not. "Like what?"

"Some old flame he isn't really over?"

I said I didn't think so.

"Is he one of those dread 'fear of commitment' types, then?"

"I'd put it another way. Nicky has always been committed to the way things are. A capacity to be content with what is, rather than always wanting something else, is not all bad. At least he's loving. There are worse things."

She agreed.

"However, change is sometimes thrust upon us," I said, and began to explain why time was entering the equation.

There had been a tumor. There had been surgery, completely successful, three years ago, followed by radiation. Belinda had been free of disease since then, but it was back now with a vengeance. Chemotherapy was an option if she could recover her strength, but for now she was subject to infections that were at least as likely to kill her as the cancer was. Grace's first reaction was to cry. But her second, predictably, was to be angry at Avis.

"Why didn't Mother tell me?"

"Belinda asked her not to."

"She should have told me anyway!"

I thought Avis had been right to respect Belinda's wishes, but I wished she had told me as well, so I sympathized with Grace without agreeing.

"The point now though is, if you and Nicky are going to do something, wouldn't it be nice for Belinda to be able to share it?"

She agreed. It would.

NICKY MUST HAVE TAKEN IT WELL, BECAUSE TWO DAYS LATER, HE ASKED Dinah for the engagement ring his father had given her, which had been in a safe-deposit box since the divorce. On the weekend, in the gondola in Central Park, he asked Grace to marry him. They arrived at Dinah's apartment on foot afterward, flushed and happy, to tell their news. Finding us both there with a celebratory dinner waiting, Grace said to Nicky, "Oh, you mean thing, you told your mother before you told me?"

Nicky laughed, and Dinah opened champagne.

As we settled around the fire after dinner, I finally said, "Darling girl, you really have to call your mother."

Grace made a face. "I know, but you know what she'll be like."

"No, I don't."

"She'll say how wonderful and then get out her calendar and want to set dates and call caterers."

"If she does, you know it's only because she wants to make it perfect for you."

"But why doesn't she just say she's happy for me, and let Nicky and me decide what *we* want?"

"She might. Give her a chance."

Grace and Nicky were sitting together in the huge overstuffed chair by the fireplace, with Grace's legs across Nicky's and her head on his shoulder. Dinah sat across from them in her own big chair filled with pillows, and I sat beside her on a leather ottoman. It may actually have been a tuffet. I got up and brought the cordless phone from the kitchen and handed it to Grace.

Grace and Nicky looked at each other. He kissed her on the nose, and she started laughing. "Oh, all *right*," she said.

"No, let me!" said Nicky. Grace punched in the number and handed him the phone.

"Hello, Mrs. Metcalf? This is Nicholas Wainwright . . . Yes. I'm sorry to call so late . . . Good. I would like to ask you for your daughter's hand in marriage. And her foot. All of her, really." There was a longish pause, during which Nicky listened and beamed. Then he covered the receiver and said to us solemnly, "She says yes." On the other end Avis was speaking again. "Yes, Mrs. Metcalf . . . well then yes, thank you, Avis. You've made me a very happy man. Yes, she's right here." He handed the receiver to Grace.

"Hello, Mother," she said. "This afternoon, in the park . . . In the gondola . . . Yes, very romantic . . . No, there was water in the bottom and he's wearing his good pants . . . yes . . . No. We have no idea, spring sounds lovely, or possibly winter. Or fall."

"Or summer," said Nicky.

"We haven't had a chance to discuss it . . . I don't think we *were* thinking of a church wedding, were we?" She looked at Nicky, who just laughed. Avis was talking, and Grace looked at Dinah and rolled her eyes. "Yes, I know the nicest dates get taken, but . . . all right . . . All right . . . Yes . . . Good idea, find out when the moon is full in June. And May . . . Yes, I'll go tell Belinda tomorrow. We'll both go. Yes. Yes. Thank you so much, I am too. 'Bye." She pushed the off button and looked at me, making an exasperated growl between clenched teeth.

After the children left, Dinah and I sat by the fire and talked it all over. "I'd love to give them an engagement party," she said. "But if you count just my family, and Richard's and the Metcalfs, this apartment is already too small. I could do it at the Town Club, but I'm not in yet." She looked into the fire. "I wonder what's happening with that."

THE NEXT DAY, SUNDAY, WAS COLD AND RAW. GIL HAD A STANDING TENnis match on Sunday afternoons when we were in town, and he came to me afterward for Sunday night supper by the fire. My cooking was simple but a relief to him, since the chef de cuisine Althea had brought from France had left abruptly, claiming that it was impossible to find proper ingredients and that no one in New York speaks French. Althea was in theory interviewing replacements but in the meantime was content for them to dine in restaurants every night that they were not otherwise engaged. Gil said sadly that he'd reached a point where he opened a menu and could not find a single thing he could bear to order. I gave him creamed chipped beef on toast and homemade applesauce. He ate with relish.

"Dinah wants to give an engagement party, but . . ." The Town Club business.

Gil said, "Why don't we give the party? You're Nicky's godmother."

"We? You mean together?" The idea thrilled me.

"At your club. But I'll help if you'll let me. I'd like to. I'd like to for Belinda's sake." He smiled. "And for my own reasons."

"And would you come to the party?"

"Of course, if you invite me. Belinda is one of my oldest friends."

It was something I never dreamed I'd be able to do. Give a party to celebrate the engagement of a beloved child. Two beloved children. With Gil. It was rather wicked of him, and he enjoyed it immensely.

THE PARTY WAS A TRIUMPH. THE SOCIAL PRESS COVERED IT IN GLITTER-ing fashion; there were six pictures in New York Social Diary on the Web the next day and elaborate coverage in that month's issue of *Avenue*. We even got a mention on "Page Six," since one of Nicky's high school friends was now a famous rapper and had a supermodel girlfriend, and one of Grace's had her own cable TV talk show. There was attention in the fashion press for the clothes (excellent for the shop, as I had dressed the bride-to-be, her mother, and, of course, myself) and the *Social Register Observer* eventually carried a large engagement picture of Grace and Nick, with details of the party, of their pedigrees, and, embarrassingly, of mine. Though my grandmother would have been pleased. (My mother pretended to be scornful, but I notice she's still listed in the stud book herself.) Dinah for once seemed to love doing the establishment thing in the establishment way. Her whole family attended, as did Richard with his wife and daughters, and of course RJ with his wife and sons. Bill Cunningham, the *New York Times* photographer, came as a guest, not a member of the press, but got a marvelous picture of Belinda in an Oscar de la Renta cocktail dress, dripping with diamonds and carrying a cane painted to look like leopard skin. He worked it into a collage of people sporting animal prints on the street the following Sunday.

Nicky's and Grace's friends were beautiful, lively, and noisy. The radiant fabric of the evening snagged only a couple of times. The first was Althea's arrival. I saw her pause in the doorway, framed. She was wearing Saint Laurent, predictably, one of the best pieces from his last collection. Her honey-colored hair was huge and sculpted so that she looked like a lion, and I don't mean lioness. She scanned the room with her head raised, scenting the air for wildebeests. Her eyes skimmed over me without a pause, as if I were flora, not fauna. Finally she strode into the room on course for Belinda. They greeted each other with double cheek kisses and every appearance of delight.

The other surprise was the appearance of Serena Tate. I knew Leo Tate had died some years ago, and that she lived in Washington most of the time these days, where she was the constant and much-photographed hostess and companion of one of the giants of the Senate. Who had invited her? She greeted Belinda, who knew everybody, then made her way to Dinah, managing to reach her just as the Society Diary fellow asked them to smile for the camera. Then I understood: Gil. He'd invited her to support Dinah in a battle Dinah didn't even know was being waged. There was no way of knowing if Simon had malignly linked her name with Serena's, but if he had, the picture might be worth a thousand words. Though a thousand hardly seemed like enough.

I'M AFRAID AVIS DID EVERYTHING GRACE FEARED SHE WOULD WHEN IT came to the wedding. Given that sooner was much better than later for Belinda, the full moon in June was abandoned and we moved right along to planning the perfect winter extravaganza. A high service at St. Thomas on Fifth Avenue in early February, followed by dinner and dancing at the Plaza. Winter white was her plan; she was thinking lilies, white roses, and white freesia. I can't tell you how Grace hated it.

"I'm assuming Belinda is paying," said Dinah.

"No, Avis is doing it."

"She must be doing better than I thought, peddling pictures," said Dinah, as if the news weren't especially welcome.

"Why don't you tell her it's not what you want?" I asked Grace.

"Because *she's* wanted it all my life."

"But she's a reasonable person. It's your wedding."

"No, it isn't."

"Grace."

However, unlike Grace, Nicky was quite enjoying himself. He agreed with Avis that it should be an evening wedding, formal, and that he and his groomsmen would wear white tie.

"He'll look like Fred Astaire," said Grace.

"He'll look like an Adonis, and he knows it and so do you."

Dinah was strangely cool about the whole thing, except to laugh subversively with Grace whenever Avis came up with a new item of wretched excess. There were to be potted trees trucked in and tied all over with white silk blossoms. Peter Duchin's band would play, with Peter himself at the piano. The dean of the Cathedral of St. John the Divine would perform the ceremony.

Grace said, "Of course, I'm disappointed that she couldn't get the pope."

Dinah viewed me, I think, as Avis's henchman in all things to do with the wedding, though it wasn't true. As it was, I was a little miffed not to be doing the bridal dress, which Avis was having made in Paris. She'd asked if I minded, and I'd said that of course I did not, but what else *could* I say? And I had hoped she would use a talented young friend of mine for the flowers, but she felt that in midwinter, a newcomer might have trouble finding the right plant materials. My friend would not have, and she's a brilliant designer. But.

Dinah was having trouble with her knee, the first of her joints to begin to fail under the extra weight she'd carried for too long. "It would have been nice to be able to dance at my own son's wedding," she said bitterly, as if her discomfort were Avis's fault. It was she who had put off having the knee replaced, though she knew it was inevitable. "You know what they call it? Amputation! That's what it is, they amputate your goddam leg and then hook it up again with a bionic knee in the middle." Everyone said that the pain was excruciating and you should wait as long as you can, but the timing couldn't have been worse for her. Her choice now was to have the surgery at once and be in rehab during all the planning leading up to the Great Event, as she called it, or to wait until afterward and be in agony on the day.

What happened next, I learned only long after the fact.

In December, Grace's half-sisters gave her a bridal shower. It was in Hilary's apartment in the Apthorp, on the West Side, and the theme was kitchen and bath. Belinda sent a set of mono-grammed towels from Porthault that cost so much the hostess said Grace would have to have them dry-cleaned. I gave her a blender wand for pureeing soups right in the pot. I got the impression that pureed soups were not at the top of Grace's list of foods she looked forward to serving, but several people exclaimed loyally that they couldn't live without *their* blender wands. As the presents were opened the living room seemed knee-high in ribbons and bright tissues and Grace was soon surrounded by measuring cups and spoons, Silpat cookie sheets, muffin pans, mango pitters, knives, and cookware, Jo Malone bath oils, and two fluffy bathrobes, one of them monogrammed. Her maid of honor had given a frothy nightgown and some lacy thong underwear, which made Grace blush. Nicky sat, handsome and enjoying himself, while people draped ribbons over him and Grace's friends, I suspected, envied Grace her catch. All the while, Avis sat in the chair beside Grace's seat of honor on the sofa and diligently recorded the gifts and the giver's names in a white leather book. Now and then she would say, "Wait, who was that from? Could you give me the card?"

and Grace would hunt through the wrappings for the gift tag. I would have loved to have a mother who would care and help with those kinds of social niceties, but Grace was another generation, and for Avis, there was no getting it right with her daughter.

When Grace came to a box wrapped in a pink shade one could only call lubricious, with a logo even I recognized as belonging to a sex toy store in SoHo, there was a roar of nervous delight and laughter. A former colleague of Nicky's from the magazine, a dapper bachelor named Ned, went straight to Avis, saying, "Now, Mrs. Metcalf, you wouldn't understand this one, so I'll take over while you avert your eyes." Avis handed him her book and pencil and covered her eyes with her hands, looking like the See-No-Evil monkey, but with considerably more nose. "You'll have to give me the play-by-play," she said to Ned. He complied.

"She's got the box on her knees, and she's engaging the ribbon. The ribbon is fighting back, wait, I think she's got it. Yes! The ribbon is off. The titty-pink paper is off, it was wrapped without tape of any kind, a virtuoso performance . . . the lid is open, she's got her hand in the tissue paper, and now, Yes! It's out! It's pink, it's . . . I couldn't possibly tell you what that is, Mrs. Metcalf, I recommend you count to ten and think of England." There were roars of laughter, and Nicky took a great ribbing and blushed deeply. Grace returned the object to the box while Ned said, "She's got it back in the nest, she's closing the top . . . there! Quite safe now, you may open your eyes. Grace, did it come with batteries?"

Avis, who was now laughing, seized the white book to see what he had written. "What's this?" she asked him.

"It's my phone number. When Grace writes her thank-you

notes she can call me up and I'll tell her what it is and who gave it to her." Avis loved it, and she and Ned teased each other for the rest of the party. It became quite a friendship.

However, the most startling aspect of the afternoon was that Dinah never appeared. I knew she'd been making Grace a book of her favorite recipes as a present. Nicky left the room once to telephone, and Grace's look of concern followed him. When he came back he mouthed to her "no answer." Grace frowned but reached for another box. Her job was to be gracious and happy.

When the last guests had said their good-byes, I helped Avis load half the presents into a cab and followed her in another with the rest of the loot. Off we drove with them to Fifth Avenue where the boxes would wait until Nicky and Grace set up housekeeping together. Nicky and Grace hurried to Dinah's.

What they found was that the elevator in Dinah's building was stalled somewhere between floors, and this being Sunday, the super was unreachable, at home in New Jersey with his beeper off. Nick and Grace ran up the eight flights, greatly alarmed to find Dinah's present to Grace with the wrapping torn lying on the landing halfway between six and seven. They found Dinah at home, in tears of pain and humiliation. She had tried to walk down the stairs but her knee had given out. She fell. (Not very far, she insisted, but she banged her mouth on the railing and loosened a tooth.) She yelled for help, but nobody heard her. "This building is a morgue on weekends; everyone goes to their yuppie country houses except me and Mrs. Missirlian on the second floor, and she's deaf."

Finally, laboriously, she had dragged herself back up a flight and a half, on hands and knee, with her skirt hiked up to her waist because otherwise she kept kneeling on it. She tried to make it sound comic, but failed. The children were appalled. What if they hadn't been expecting her? What if she'd hit her head or broken something? She might have lain there till morning.

"Why didn't you call me? Or 911?"

"I didn't have my phone. It wasn't charged, and what did I need it for?" said Dinah.

Black humor aside, she was very upset, and so was Nick. "Mom. Look. From now on you never, ever, leave the house without a phone. Charged. Promise me."

"'Help, I've fallen and I can't get up.' Next you'll want me to wear one of those buttons on a rope around my neck."

"Yes! I will! Promise, or I'll tell RJ."

"Not that! Not the dread RJ!" Poor RJ, he *was* a tiny bit humorless and prone to lecture.

"Mom, I'm serious. Grace, tell her."

"Mom, we're serious!"

Dinah promised. They brought her tea, a bag of ice for the knee and her knee brace, and Nicky laid the fire and lit it for her.

Grace asked as she drank her tea, "Tell the truth, Dinah. Can you walk?"

"I'd like my cane," she admitted, and Nicky went to find the one she'd gotten after surgery on her torn meniscus. (When you're young you never even hear such words; then suddenly you reach an age when you can't have a conversation without them. Gil says getting old is like going to medical school one course at a time.)

They told her about the party. Grace did her entirely too apt imitation of Avis primly writing down the names of the givers and the details of the gifts while all about her people were drinking wine and tying ribbons around each other. But Dinah didn't really cheer up. After a while she began to cry again, and both children were dumbstruck. Dinah was never blue. Often cross or loud or out of patience but never this purely sad.

"What is it? What *is* it?" Grace asked.

"Mom, please," said Nicky. At last she came out with it.

"I'm dreading this wedding. Just *dreading* it. I know Avis has dreamed of this since you were born, Grace, but I've looked forward to Nicky's wedding day too. Of course RJ would want the whole suburban country club thing, and he had it and it was fine, but I thought planning this with Nick was going to be fun. That we'd do it on top of a mountain with a punk klezmer accordion band. Or that we'd do it right here, you'd write your own vows and be married by Reverend Billy, and we'd all wear blue jeans and then have a feast. Instead, it's like planning a wedding with Lizzie Windsor." (This was how Dinah referred to the British monarch.) "I won't be able to dance at your wedding, I'll be lucky if I can walk down the aisle without crutches. And the only evening dress we could find that I can afford makes me look like a giant eggplant."

This hurt when I heard it, I can tell you. I went to no small trouble over that dress; it had to be made from scratch, and she never knew that I had only charged her for materials. She had chosen the fabric herself, and the color was very becoming.

Nicky and Grace were upset. Was there no way out of this? How could they go through with Avis's wedding knowing Dinah was so unhappy?

"I know," said Grace. "We'll elope."

"You can't," said Dinah. "It would kill Belinda, and I like *her*.

And my parents would be sad as well." It would also have disappointed Nicky, but she luckily didn't have to say that.

"All right," said Grace. "We'll get married twice. We'll get married here, in secret, with a punk klezmer band and Reverend Billy, and only our best friends standing up with us. Then we'll go through Avis's wingding, and no one will know it's just a performance. And if you don't get through it or don't want to stay, or even don't want to *come,* you won't miss anything real!"

At this point, you're thinking what I'm thinking. Dinah has to say no. She has to say it isn't fair and it isn't right; it's mean-spirited. To let Avis go to all that trouble, and incredible expense, and not know the whole thing is a charade? It's *too* bad.

But Dinah apparently said yes. Well not apparently, she did. She said yes. I don't know, maybe that's why now we're all dressing for a funeral.

I'LL TELL YOU WHAT IT WAS LIKE, NOT THAT I WAS THERE, SINCE APPAR-ently I couldn't be trusted not to tell Avis. They were married in Dinah's apartment right after Thanksgiving. Sebastian, Grace's little poodle, was the bride's attendant; he wore a red velvet ruff for the occasion. Nicky's friend Toby got himself ordained by some site on the Internet so he could perform the service. Dinah's sisters were there, and RJ and Laura, and about twenty young people, many of whom I had considered my friends. Dinah read a poem; Grace and Nicky recited vows they had written themselves, then they faced each other in front of the fireplace, holding hands, and sang to each other. Grace sang "A Wonderful Guy";

Nicky sang "The Most Beautiful Girl in the World." They were pronounced husband and wife by the power vested in Toby by the State of New York, and then everyone had champagne and blinis with caviar. I have no idea what anybody wore, except the dog—gym clothes, probably. Avis still doesn't know it happened, and I hope she never finds out.

IF NOTHING ELSE, THE OFFICIAL WEDDING WAS A BONANZA FOR HAIR salons, dress shops, and the social press. Though it wasn't that long ago, in these days of failed banks and financial disaster at every hand, it seems like an event from the last days of Pompeii, but at the human level it was a complete success in the one way that mattered most, at least to me: Belinda loved every minute of it.

We made a new dress for her in navy satin that was actually in two pieces, to allow for the tubes from her side that were permanently draining into a pair of sacs she called Harold and Maude. Mrs. Oba made a matching bag for them held with a broad satin strap that crossed her now tiny rib cage diagonally like a military sash. It was decorated with large grosgrain roses that concealed almost perfectly its actual function. Belinda walked up the aisle to her seat on the arm of Nicky's friend Toby, resplendent in his swallowtail coat, with her cane swathed in ribbons that matched her dress, her well-coiffed head bobbing with effort on her long neck while she smiled proudly at beaming friends on both sides of the aisle. It was the last time she walked in public. After the ceremony she allowed herself to be moved into a wheelchair, but from it she enjoyed the dinner, the toasts, the couple's "first dance," and the cutting of the seven-tier wedding cake covered with marzipan doves.

Belinda did not leave her bed again for days afterward. Then she seemed to recover, and we eased into foolish hope. But in March she had a terrifying bout of rigor shakes—do you know the term? It rhymes with *tiger* and it's shattering, caused by the kind of infection you get when your immune system is on the mat and about to be counted out. That put her back in the hospital for weeks, after which, though she lived almost to the end of the year, she was in the hospital more than she was out of it.

One morning in early April, Belinda's housekeeper, who was Peruvian and took care of her with as much slavish devotion as if Belinda were the Great Inca, called me at the shop. Her English was not good, so this was an act of particular courage for her.

"Missus Lovie . . ." Ursula always sounded as if she might burst into tears if she had to attract personal notice to herself in any way.

"Good morning, Ursula. Is Mrs. Binney all right?"

"Yes, missus. No, missus. She is in the slammer, Missus Lovie." She uttered this without irony, as it was the way Belinda referred to the hospital. "She wants a banana smoothie, missus, and I don't know, and Missus Avis is not at home . . ."

"Thank you so much for telling me, Ursula. I can take that right to her now."

"Oh, thank you, Missus Lovie!" You'd have thought I had personally averted the death of the sun, or the need for her to cut her own heart out on some high stone altar. I bustled uptown in foul raw weather and waited in the lunch rush line at the shop near the hospital that Belinda favored. When I placed my order, the counterman said that he had no bananas and was annoyed when I wouldn't order something else. I struck back out into the drizzle and wind and walked until I found a bodega, bought a bunch of bananas, went back, and handed them to the counterman. It was worth it: Belinda in her high narrow room was delighted with the story and sang to me, "Yes, we have no bananas . . ." a song that she claimed had greatly amused her father. It was a good day for her, and I stayed quite a while as she told me stories of her childhood in Dover, Ohio, where her parents had owned a hardware store.

It is my observation that the people who enjoy money the most are the ones who weren't born with it. For the congenitally rich, money creates a kind of cage, a structure of manners and expectations they don't dare question, because if they do they might discover they don't know who they are. For our classmates at school it was the water they swam in, isolating them in ways they sometimes never understand. But the money she'd married, then cleverly managed into a sizable pile, changed Belinda from a quietly pretty girl in rural Ohio to the Great Inca of New York City, and she enjoyed every cent of it because she never lost the memory of what it was not to have it. Not that she hadn't enjoyed her simple childhood; she had, very much. That was her true distinction, not the money. The capacity to enjoy and appreciate what she had, whatever it was.

What she had now was time, measured no longer in vats or even gallons but teaspoons. Her response to her death sentence was to resolve to live every moment she had left impeccably. Never to rage or blame, never to feel that her minutes mattered more than other people's, never to presume that her needs and wishes weighed more than theirs did. A hospital like MSK is filled with patients so frightened and angry at their fates that they attack even those trying hardest to help them. No wonder Belinda was a favorite there. I saw her undone only once in all the time I spent with her in the hospital; we were downstairs in Imaging, where she was waiting for some kind of test for which they were dripping fluid into an internal organ—we didn't discuss which one. She sat in her wheelchair in the hallway with her metal tree beside her hung with bags attached to tubes attached to Belinda at various points on her body. I sat beside her, telling her some tale I had heard at the shop. Her face was gradually clouding with distress, and I didn't know what to do. Go on chattering? Scream for help? At last she interrupted me. When I got back to her with a nurse in tow, he blanched to see how much liquid had left whichever bag it was, blowing up something inside Belinda to the point of unbearable pressure on some, I suppose, sphincter. I rolled the intravenous tree behind her as he rushed the wheelchair down the hall, knocking on doors to bathrooms. I thought he might burst into one and pull whoever was in there off the can, but he found an empty one, and the two of them disappeared inside.

When she was returned to me, Belinda's lashes were wet with tears. She looked at me with a face for once empty of cheer and said in a tiny voice, "You can't imagine the indignities." It was true, I couldn't. Though I was learning to fear them deeply in the small hours of the night. The next moment she pulled herself together like one gathering up a failed house of cards, and said, "Now tell me the gossip." This became my purpose, the thing I could do for her, bring in news about life outside to surround her. She wasn't prepared to leave what she had loved, although it belonged to others now, a moment before her time.

BELINDA HAD WANTED TO GIVE NICK AND GRACE A TRIP TO EUROPE AS a wedding present. They told her they couldn't go because of their jobs, but the truth, I'm glad to say, was that they wouldn't have anyway. This was no time, Grace said, to be leaving Belinda or Dinah, who was finally having her knee rebuilt. For a wedding trip, they took a long weekend and went to California.

"California!" said Belinda happily. "Oh, I *love* San Francisco! We used to go out and stay at The Clift. The light on the bay at twilight, all green and violet, is too beautiful to bear!" She would never see that light again, or see anything more than half an hour from the hospital. Grace and Nicky stayed at the Huntington, on the top of Nob Hill, at a cost that even Avis found hard to believe, and spent their time, as near as we could make out, at the zoo.

"Nicky *loves* zoos," Grace reported, apparently finding this deeply charming. "He loves animals. When I wake up in the night and he's not in bed, he's always in the den, watching the Nature Channel." He had wanted to take Sebastian on the honeymoon, but wisdom prevailed, and Sebastian was residing instead in Dinah's kitchen.

After San Francisco, they drove down the coast to Monterey, where they spent half a day watching the sea horses at the aquarium. They spent a night at a paradise for sybarites set into the sere hills above Big Sur. They had a romantic dinner and a naked soak under the stars in the coed Japanese baths. "Ooh la la!" said Belinda. The next day they hiked in Los Padres National Forest, and afterward had side-by-side massages in their room.

They spent a night in Santa Barbara, and two nights in L.A.

"I never cared for Los Angeles," said Belinda. "What did they find to do?"

"They spent one day at the Getty Museum and one at Disneyland."

"Well, they are a pair," Belinda said. And then, thoughtfully, "But what kind of a newlywed twenty-eight-year-old is up in the middle of the night watching the Nature Channel?"

NICKY, AS IT TURNS OUT, LOVED L.A. HE LOVED THE CLIMATE, HE loved the cars, he loved the beach at Malibu. We learned this when, about a month after the wedding trip, he was offered a part in a television pilot by one of his college pals, now a Hollywood hyphenate, writer-producer. I was keeping Dinah company as she pedaled resentfully on her recumbent bike machine, under orders from the P.T., whom she called her Physical Terrorist, when Nicky arrived with the news. (Grace had given Dinah an iPod already loaded with "Mom music" for her recuperation, but she hated exercise so much that mere music was not enough of a distraction or incentive. I came over a couple of times a week to crack the whip.)

"It's a comedy/drama about a marriage license bureau," said Nicky.

"Set in L.A.?"

"Keep pedaling, Mom. No, set in New York."

Dinah grudgingly resumed her labors. "That's good at least," she said. "So you'll film here?"

"Only the exteriors. If it goes, we'd be here a couple of days a month."

Dinah stopped again.

"Keep pedaling, Mom."

"Stuff it," she said, hauling herself to her feet and making for her big chair by the fireplace. "Get me a Diet Coke, will you?"

Nicky came back with one for each of us.

"I'm playing the upper-class twit whose girlfriend leaves him at the altar, and he winds up working there. Alvin wrote the part for me."

"Wait, Nick. I'm thrilled for you," said Dinah. "But could I just point out that you have a wife and she lives in New York?"

"Gosh," he said, slapping his forehead. "Is that who that girl is who's always at my apartment when I get home? You must be right!"

"Not to mention your tragic old mother, whiling away her sunset years eating cat food by herself."

"Grace loves Alvin's work, and she knew I was an actor when she married me."

"She did not. She thought you were going to be a lawyer. So did I. How are you going to pay your student loans if you quit?"

"She knew I was an actor first, and this job pays three times as much as I'd make as a starting lawyer."

"Really?" said Dinah. "Three times?"

I said, "Alvin's work?"

He named a couple of movies I had heard of but not followed closely, being fairly much opposed to entertainments with the word *jackass* in the title.

"What happens if the show doesn't go?" I asked.

"I'll finish school and be a lawyer." Knowing how way leads on to way, I doubted that, but maybe he'd be a hit as an actor. Stranger things have happened.

"What's the pilot about?" Dinah asked.

"There's me and my girlfriend, Petula, a flower child who shows up with her new fiancé, some hedge fund monster, and she tells me she'll always love me like a brother and asks me to give her away."

"Give her away! How about throw her out a window?"

"I hope you don't do it," I said.

"I give her away. Weeping. Then for the rest of the show, just at the happiest moments, I wander through again, with tears streaming."

"I guess that's funny."

"There's the pink-haired punker who's marrying a guy who needs a green card. They can't understand a word of each other's language. Then there's a guy who wants a license to marry his cat, because she was his girlfriend in a former life."

"That's funny," said Dinah.

"Then a guy who works in the bureau becomes hysterical and begins ranting about his lonely hovel and his Fiestaware, and trying to make his mother's recipe for pot roast for one, and they take him away, and there I am, still weeping in the corner, so I get his job."

Dinah and I look at each other. "For this we sent you to college?"

"I knew you'd be pleased," said Nicky.

The pilot took four weeks to shoot. Grace, who'd begun student teaching, was exhausted, but she and Sebastian flew out for two of the weekends. Her friends all thought it was way cool.

DINAH'S COOKING CLASSES STARTED THIS WAY, THAT SAME spring of 2004. Dinah met a man at the rehab place where she went after she had her knee rebuilt. His name was Mike Allison. They passed each other several times in the hall before Dinah called to him, "I'm a knee, what are you?" He has one of those faces that looks sad or sullen in repose, but changes entirely when he smiles, which he did as he said, "I'm a hip."

"Lucky you," said Dinah as they stumped past each other on their walkers. Mike was a widower, a finance guy who had recently moved back to the city from the suburbs. He seemed lonely. "Two major crises: he lost his wife, then he lost his context," Dinah told me.

"Then his hip."

"Yes, but let the record show, knees are much worse than hips."

"I'll take your word for it."

The first time I saw Mike, he was walking ahead of me toward Dinah's building with a bottle of wine and two bunches of tulips. I thought he well might be Dinah's new friend and had a moment of disappointment at the silver hair, the round bald spot at the back of the head, the slight stoutness on what had the look of a once-athletic body. I hadn't expected him to be old. When we were properly introduced and I saw him in the light, I realized he was younger than we are. This happens more and more, and it is quite disorienting. You'll understand in about twenty years.

Dinah had invited me and Grace and two of Grace's friends

to a dinner that night to meet her new buddy, the hip. It was early May but still chilly weather. She had planned short ribs with horseradish sauce, a soup to start and panna cotta with caramel to finish, then she realized she couldn't possibly stand long enough to cook it. I urged her to let me bring soup and buy dessert, but she said, "Grown men have been known to faint at my panna cotta." Grace volunteered to be her sous chef so Dinah could sit and give orders.

By the time Mike and I arrived for that first dinner, the kitchen was an unholy mess but the apartment was filled with delicious smells. I set the table and showed Grace how to clean and arrange the tulips while Dinah and the hip man sat by the fire with their drinks and set about getting to know each other.

Everything about that evening clicked from the start. Grace's young friends were freshly scrubbed and attractive and wildly appreciative of everything. Grace was in that heightened state that comes sometimes with the pleasure of mastering something you never thought you'd understand, and Mike—it had been years since I'd seen Dinah with a man who got her sense of humor so immediately and completely. I found myself wishing Gil could be there instead of wherever he was—in Aruba, I think it was—but I suppose that had its charms as well.

I was bringing in the salad—a simple green salad of butter lettuce with spiced walnuts and pomegranate seeds, if that's your idea of simple—when I heard Grace say, "All right, come clean—what do you mean by your 'misspent youth'?"

Mike's face was pleasantly flushed, and he'd loosened his tie. "You promise not to laugh?"

We all promised.

He said, "I was an opera singer."

"Shut *up!*" said Grace's waiflike friend.

"Prove it," said Dinah.

Mike straightened his posture and launched into "Una furtiva lagrima." By the time he was done, I was in love if Dinah wasn't. He told the rest of the story, how he started, why he stopped, while I was unmolding the panna cotta, so I missed much of it. But by the time the evening was over, the group was planning a rematch. Dinah had promised that she would teach all of them how to make chicken with forty garlic cloves the next week, and everyone was lobbying about what kind of dessert soufflés to make with it.

Thus began Dinah's third career. Travel was no longer the pleasure it had been for her; climbing stairs or hills was a problem, and airline seats had come to feel unreasonably confining. Lately she'd been accepting only assignments close enough to home to drive to or reach by train or subway, and how many times can you find new ways of describing another chrome-and-leather bachelor loft in the meatpacking district for yet another Goldman Sachs billionaire? Actually, if I'd been a writer, I'd probably have been able to carry it on for quite a while, since I really care about how things look. But Dinah has always wanted to know what they mean beneath the surface, and in her view, these private palaces didn't mean anything underneath, except that the owners were much richer than she would ever be.

At first the classes were held every Saturday, and Grace's friends began coming. Grace and Dinah were more and more in each other's pockets, working smoothly together, sharing private jokes, almost as it had been with her and Simon Snyder. Dinah added weekday classes, and *New York* magazine wrote her up, followed soon after by a feature on her savory cocktail cookies in Oprah's magazine. Her knee was healed and forgotten as she acquired new devotees, explored new cuisines, and sat for more interviews. During the second summer she moved out to Water Mill with Mike while her kitchen was remade for teaching large classes. She did a before-and-after article on the renovation, and with the fee was able to buy a huge Sub-Zero refrigerator and a restaurant-size freezer.

People pointed out that pouring money like that into an apartment you don't own was a poor investment, but she said it was cheap insurance, protecting her from murder by landlord. And Mike was like the Man Who Came to Dinner and never went home. He helped with the prep work for the classes and paid for a helper to clean up after the meal was eaten and the students had gone. He and Dinah sang Sondheim together in the kitchen. The students ate the food they all prepared, course by course, perched on stools around the work island, made friends and started romances. Dinah hadn't been so happy since before Richard met Charlotte.

And was Mike in love? I certainly thought so. If Dinah's size was going to be a problem, that would have been apparent from the first, and it clearly wasn't. There are more men than you think who prefer their ladies heavy, maybe because they feel it protects them from competition. If there are also erotic aspects to the phenomenon, and I suspect there are, I draw the veil. But I know at least one size eighteen wife of a real estate tycoon whose husband left her for a woman even larger, and it's an interesting part of my business, finding really good clothes to fit them both.

Nicky's pilot didn't sweep the ratings, but it did well enough for the network to order six shows. When those did well enough, the bosses ordered six more, a full season. Avis was sweetly proud of him. She told all her friends about the show and stopped going out on Tuesday evenings so she could watch it. Grace rolled her eyes and said, "You *could* TiVo it, Mother," but Avis said, "That wouldn't be any fun," meaning she didn't know how. "Besides, doesn't it help the ratings if I watch it when it's broadcast?"

"No," said Grace.

At a dinner Grace and I attended, Avis told her guests about Nicky's show. "You should watch, you really should, they are perfectly charming. They're directed by that young man Albert Grable, who makes those movies."

"Writer-producer, Mother," said Grace. "And it's Alvin."

Avis paused. "What did I say?"

"You said director."

"Oh," said Avis, and looked a little sad.

Grace had only joined us that evening because she was restless and lonely. Nicky hadn't been home for three weeks.

One afternoon in late fall of that year, on a last day of Indian summer, I closed the shop early and walked, wearing only a light wool jacket, all the way to Belinda's apartment, relishing the sun on my face, and the last gold leaves still clinging to naked branches. Althea Flood had gone to Venice with friends, and Gil and I were to have a whole week together, the first good stretch in what seemed like eons. I couldn't wait to get up to Connecticut, to be sure my gardens were properly covered in pine boughs and ready for winter.

Ursula opened the door to me and exclaimed, "Missus Lovie!"

"How are you, dear, on this beautiful day?" I handed her my jacket.

"Fine, missus! . . . Missus Avis is here, missus!"

"How nice. Upstairs?"

"In the study, missus."

I went in to find mother and daughter just beginning a Great Inca tea, with cookies and hot cinnamon toast and the whole silver tea service on a table before Avis. The teapot had an incongruous tea cozy over it, printed with blueberries. I kissed both my friends and took a seat on the sofa with Avis, who poured.

"We were just talking about Iraq," said Belinda. She was sitting in a chair carefully fitted with just the right pillows, in reach of the radio. The metal tree from which her bags hung was behind her, and Harold and Maude in their day bag were tucked into the chair beside her. I didn't like the color of the fluid in the tubes snaking out from under Belinda's bed jacket, but she herself looked lovely, with her hair done and her makeup in place. I noticed she barely ate anything, except to nibble from time to time on a piece of naked ginger from the bowl on the tea tray. Avis had it sent up from the club because it settled her stomach.

"You look lovely," I said to Belinda as I accepted my cup.

"Don't I? Ursula is just a whiz. She insisted on going with me the last time I had my hair done, and she studied everything, the shampoo, the blowout, and now she can do it all. She blows me out every morning."

"You're not letting her cut it, are you?" Avis asked, sounding alarmed.

"No, Lance comes up if I can't go to him. But I have no doubt she could do it if she had to. I don't know how I got so lucky." She beamed. Avis and I managed not to look at each other. I wished I could have Belinda's temperament transplanted into me like a cornea or a kidney when she no longer needed it . . . but no. Spiritual attainments come to you only one way.

Then just as everything seemed perfect in our world, except that one of us was dying a painful and relentless death, Grace blew in.

She was excited, and her cheek still smelled of the fresh fall air as she kissed us in turn.

"What brings you here, darling?" asked Belinda. "Have some tea, it's still hot."

"First I need the loo." She took her handbag and dashed off. Ursula rushed in and took away our teapot to refill it with smoky lapsang souchong, Miss Grace's special favorite.

When Grace came back, very excited, she was carrying something not unlike a Popsicle stick. She showed it to me and demanded, "Lovie, isn't that pink? Right there, that line?"

Although I would have loved to be the final arbiter, I had to say, "But really, I'm not the one to ask . . ."

Belinda said "What *have* you got there?"

Grace rushed back to the bathroom to throw the stick away and wash her hands, and when she came back, she sat down and drummed her feet on the floor in an ecstatic tattoo. "Granny, I'm pregnant!"

Avis clapped her hands and cried, "Oh Grace!"

Belinda said in amazement, "You *are*? Have you been to the doctor?"

"No, but this morning I suddenly realized how late I was, and I'm never late, *never,* so I got a home test on the way to school, but then I couldn't do it at school, in the bathroom with the little girls going in and out . . . I've been going crazy all day, waiting to get out, and it was faster to come here than to go home, so . . . I'm pregnant!"

Belinda radiated joy and held out her arms. Grace flew into them. Then Grace kissed her mother again, and me, and then she did another jig of joy on the carpet.

THE END CAME FOR BELINDA LESS THAN A WEEK LATER. IT SEEMED shockingly sudden, because it began as had so many other crises that she had survived. Just the day before, I had ridden downtown with her on a mission to Grace's apartment, to see the plans for turning the den into a nursery. That was a lovely afternoon. She wheeled around the apartment in her chair, admiring everything. She got tired a little before I realized she was done, but she dozed in the car on the way back, and we got her upstairs and into bed for a good nap before supper. Avis saw her in the evening and said she was crowing about her outing.

The next morning, though, something went wrong with Harold and Maude, and she was back in MSK to have them re-plumbed. Ursula was with her, clutching the bag with Belinda's hospital shawl, her books, and the cell phone Avis had insisted she carry so her friends could find her without having to know where she was. Avis was there all morning as well, since a hospital is no place to leave a loved one alone. When she was still in lockdown by the afternoon, Avis called me to take over; she wanted to explain in person to Gordon Hall why she couldn't fly to Ireland that night to look at a picture that might or might not be a Ribera.

They let me take her home at about five that evening. I'd sent Ursula ahead to get ready. Belinda seemed fine, if weary. Once she was in bed, and finally shaking off the last of the sedative, she wasn't quite ready for me to go.

"They want me to think about hospice care," she said. "But it's too soon."

I said enthusiastically that of course it was. I was still working on whether she could manage a trip to see the skaters at Rockefeller Center, if we wrapped her up carefully and the driver lifted her into and out of the car. Belinda looked at me quizzically and said, "You *do* know this story only ends one way, don't you?"

She was back in the slammer the next day; the drains were leaking again. They let her go home once more; Friday she was back yet again. This time they kept her overnight, and on Saturday morning, Avis called me in tears of anger. A young doctor had looked at Belinda's chart and said to her brutally, "Why are you here? There is nothing more we can do for you."

Soon one of the doctors who had cared for Belinda with such humanity appeared. She apologized. She grieved with Avis. She said they were willing to keep trying the temporary fixes that had bought Belinda days, then hours. But they couldn't rescind the message. It was always going to end only one way.

Belinda said, "I want to go home, but I don't want to die in my own bed. I don't want to make that kind of mess for Ursula."

We ordered a hospital bed and called hospice. Avis sent word to an e-mail list of friends that Belinda would love to see cards or flowers but please, not to visit, as the family wanted her last energy, her last consciousness for themselves. I stayed away until Avis called to say the message didn't apply to me. Nicky took the red-eye home. Grace's stepsisters left their families and came. Two or three of us were always with Belinda from that time forward. Ursula continued to do her hair, which annoyed the nurses and pleased Belinda. She had said to all of us, "Don't let me die without lipstick." That became the final act of fealty Ursula could show to the Great Inca. The nurses wiped Belinda's face and took the lipstick off. Ursula, ever vigilant, darted in and reapplied it. I still can't speak of it without wanting to cry.

Very early on the fourth morning, Belinda opened her eyes, looked straight at Avis, said "Thank you," and died. And not a day goes by that I don't want to call her, to tell her something only she would understand, to ask her something only she would know.

At the funeral, I sat in front with Dinah. When almost all the pews were full, the family appeared from wherever they'd been huddled. Avis and Grace walked up the aisle together, their arms around each other, between two banks in the sea of mourners. Nicky came behind them, escorting a desolate Ursula, and then came Hilary and Catherine with their husbands and children. Gil was across the aisle, about halfway back, alone. Althea was still in Venice.

Our grief was deep and pure, and I thought at the time, un-utterably painful. Now I know the difference between a grieving heart and a heart both grieving and outraged. If you want to talk about pain.

DINAH WAS JUST THE SLIGHTEST BIT SATIRICAL ABOUT GRACE ASKING me, the childless spinster, to help her interpret her pregnancy test. She said she understood perfectly why she was not the first to know that Grace was pregnant, as she'd assumed she would be. Belinda's apartment was right across the park from Grace's school. And Belinda, after all, had been dying at the time.

Still.

AND LIFE WENT ON. AS IT WILL.

The winter and spring of 2005 passed quietly for Gil and me. We spent long weekends in Connecticut, where my lilacs, when they finally came, were spectacular, followed by irises as lovely as any I've seen. But I know now that things were not so happy for Grace. Now that she had her degree and a full-time teaching job, she had her evenings and weekends back and no one to share them with, and she missed Belinda. She'd gone out to California a number of times during the summer and fall, but if Nicky was working, it was a bore to be on the set—the cast was a team, and she wasn't part of it, no matter how often Nicky told us how much his friends loved her. If she didn't go to the set, she had nothing to do. Nicky's apartment was tiny, and he was a surprisingly careful housekeeper. There was no particular use in her shopping for dish towels or rearranging the kitchen drawers. She rambled alone around Santa Monica, or went window-shopping on Rodeo Drive, or cooked him elaborate meals he didn't want when he got home, since the craft services food suited him fine. When she was there, she missed her friends and her New York world. And one weekend in January she'd flown out to surprise him and found that he wasn't working at all; he could have come home but just didn't feel like it. It was slushy and cold in New York, and Malibu was eighty degrees and sunny. (Avis told me this only very recently. I guess Grace felt she couldn't complain to either me or Dinah. She had told her mother.)

The winter weather had finally given way to spring the afternoon I sat down with a cup of chai and a newspaper, turned to the gossip page, and stopped. The headline for the lead story was "Divorce at the Marriage Bureau?" It was accompanied by a picture of Alvin Grable and Nicky on the set of the show, laughing. The copy read, "Sources tell us that Nick Wainwright, a star of Alvin Grable's struggling sitcom, *The Marriage Bureau,* punched his boss at an after-hours club called The Situation Room, on Melrose, after an altercation. Apparently Wainwright took issue with a remark Grable made to a cocktail waitress and was defending the damsel, but police aren't buying it. Wainwright and Grable, friends since college days, refused to comment."

Dinah was blasé about it. "No such thing as bad publicity," she said. She and Mike were getting ready to leave for London for a week of theater. Grace was more upset.

"It seems so unlike him," she said when I called her.

"What does Nicky say?"

"He says that Alvin was drunk and being a jerk and the papers blew it all out of proportion."

There were follow-up stories the next day. "Insiders" were saying that tensions had been building on the set for some time. One source claimed the two had had words over an episode for which Nicky felt he deserved a writing credit. Reps for Grable and Wainwright said the story was ridiculous, and police confirmed that Oscar-nominated Grable was not pressing charges. That night Grable went on Letterman with his head swathed in bandages and swore he was unhurt, there had been no assault, he had bumped into a door in the dark during a midnight visit to an elderly aunt.

The Marriage Bureau's ratings were up two weeks in a row, and the network ordered six new episodes. The celebrating had barely subsided when Nicky was written out of the show.

THE CHILDREN'S APARTMENT, WHICH I SUSPECTED AVIS PAID FOR, WAS in a new building on the edge of the East Village. It had two bedrooms and two full baths, but the apartments were designed like dorm suites, with the bedrooms on opposite sides of the common space, the better to share with someone you didn't really want to be that close to.

By Easter the second bedroom had been fully converted from a den to a nursery. Since Grace had elected not to be told the sex of the baby, Avis had bought a crib with flannel bumpers decorated with gender-neutral bunnies; Grace had filled the dresser with bibs and onesies, flannel sheets and blankets, tiny socks and hats. A padded changing table was equipped with wipes and Q-tips, disposable diapers, and a smell-proof pail. "Although," said Avis, surprising us both, "as long as you nurse, the caca smells very sweet." Grace looked surprised that her mother had any opinion on baby shit, let alone actually liked it.

Grace was sitting in this room alone at about ten o'clock one June night, reading a parenting magazine and rocking in the nursing chair Avis had sent her, when she heard the apartment door open.

Her heart lurched. No one had buzzed from downstairs to be let in. Lately some of their neighbors had buzzed in strangers, two of whom had been found smoking pot on the roof, and there had been fussing about deliverymen who dropped off their kung pao chicken, then illegally roamed through the halls shoving menus under doors. One, when confronted, had menaced a teenage boy on the fourth floor. There had been a tenants' meeting.

She sat still, listening. She hadn't heard the door close. She called, "Hello?"

Oh shit, oh shit . . . wrong thing to do. Footsteps started toward her. She pictured a psycho delivery guy pacing the halls, trying doors. She'd left the front door unlocked. Had she? She must have. Where was her phone? On the counter in the kitchen. She was a mother. Almost a mother. She was clumsy and enormous; no one would attack a woman this pregnant. If she were killed, the baby could live outside her. Would the attacker cut the baby out, like the Manson Family killers? She looked around for something to protect herself with. Shit!

She wrapped her arms around her huge belly as the footsteps

approached the door. She'd defend this baby with nails and teeth if she had to. She wished she could kickbox. She wished she were wearing high heels instead of fuzzy slippers. They call those heels stilettos for a reason. She sat in the yellow light of the baby's circus lamp, with painted clowns dancing around the rim, and stared at the open door, waiting for her fate.

Nicky appeared in the doorway. He was wearing a beer hat, a transparent inflated plastic mug of beer with foam on top. Grace screamed, and the baby seemed to somersault.

"Nicky! You monster! Why didn't you call?"

She was in his arms, halfway between laughing and crying.

"Hey," he said, "it kicked me!"

The baby, under her rapidly pounding heart, was doing gymnastics. Was it frightened too? Was this bad for it? Nicky laid his head against her stomach. She removed his beer hat and buried both hands in his thick dark hair. The useless Sebastian, sound asleep up to now, was at last prancing around Nicky's feet, barking excitement.

"I could have died of fright! Why didn't you call?"

"I thought it would be fun to catch you in flagrante with your lover."

She swatted him, then followed him to the front door, asking questions. The door was propped open with a suitcase, and two more were in the hall.

"I got done faster than I expected. Found a tenant for the apartment, sold the guy my furniture, packed, went to the airport, and got a seat on standby. They even upgraded me to middle class because I'm a famous actor!"

Later she found his ticket on the dresser and noticed he had actually bought a full-price ticket in business class. Well, she thought, he'd had a nasty couple of weeks, and he deserved a little comfort. And he could afford it.

GRACE WENT INTO LABOR TWO WEEKS LATER. AVIS WAS ALREADY AT THE hospital when Dinah arrived with a bag full of magazines, lollipops for the mother, and food. A nurse alerted Nicky that the grandmothers were in waiting, and he came out to take the lollipops.

Dinah said, "In my day, they only let you have ice chips after the enema," rather hoping, if I know Dinah, that talk of enemas would discomfit Avis.

"How well I remember," said Avis.

"You do?" Dinah assumed that Avis would have had herself rendered insensible, or somehow delegated the labor to staff.

"Yes, and Grace took twenty-three hours to present herself. I was absolutely starving."

"My first one was six hours, but Nicky was practically born in the taxi."

"Well done," said Avis.

"Peasant hips," said Dinah. She offered Avis a spicy chicken wing, and Avis accepted. The waiting room was a mess of crumpled wax paper, napkins, and crumbs by the time the baby arrived.

WHY DO BABIES ALL SEEM TO BE BORN AT THREE IN THE MORNING? I was deep asleep when they called me. Neither grandmother had quit the field. Nicky grinned ecstatically, they said, when he came to announce the most beautiful baby ever born, and that she had Dinah's hair.

"How is Grace?" Avis asked.

"Insanely great. One of the nurses said she had never seen anyone smile like that."

"Can we see her?" both asked. Dinah meant the baby. Avis meant Grace.

Soon Grace, cleaned up and still smiling, was rolled out of the delivery room on the way to a room of her own. Her pale hair was dark with sweat, and there were deep bluish crescents under her eyes. Avis touched her daughter's cheek, and said, "I'm proud of you, darling." It had never been easy for Avis to say things like that, and she'd chosen a good moment.

The baby was taken to the nursery so the new mother could get some sleep. Avis and Dinah admired their grandchild through the nursery window, and Nicky went home to send an e-mail to everyone in the world to say that the baby was twenty-seven inches long and they were calling her Rainbow Raisin.

"Avis has hired a baby nurse for them," Dinah informed me, as if she had just learned that the baby was to be raised by Nurse Ratched. She was calling to tell me the baby would be called Belinda, not Brooke for her own mother, as Dinah had hoped.

"Grace loved Belinda. So did Nicky, and they're still in mourning for her."

"Nicky loves Brooke too, and Brooke's still alive to appreciate it."

I happened to know that they had never seriously considered it; Nicky said if they named the baby Brooke everyone would think they were hoping for a bequest from Mrs. Astor. "Is the nurse going to live in?" I asked, thinking a change of subject would be wise.

"That was the plan, but Nicky hit the roof."

I had thought that new parents normally wept with gratitude at having experienced help in the first weeks of a baby's life.

"If they wanted another human being in a cramped apartment 24/7 they'd want *me*," Dinah informed me. "Nicky wants to raise his baby with his wife. He's home, he's a night owl, he couldn't have a stranger in the house."

She had called me from the kids' apartment, where she had just finished cleaning the bathrooms, getting everything ready for the homecoming. I agreed that I would meet her there, after I closed the shop, and bring flowers.

Dinah was on the floor in the kitchen editing the lower shelves of the refrigerator when I arrived.

"Remember that first flat you had where I used to come and stay?" Dinah greeted me.

"Do I!"

"Up seven flights of stairs?"

"Four. My legs were like iron in those days."

"Oh God, what do you suppose this was?"

The container she had just found behind three nearly empty jars of pickles had hillocks of gray-green mold, like a blanket of lichen, covering the contents. "They can't have cleaned out this reefer since the Coolidge administration. Who *raised* these people?"

The buzzer rang. I checked the video cam and soon we had a UPS man at the door with an enormous box from Bloomingdale's addressed to Mr. and Mrs. Wainwright.

"Well, I'm Mrs. Wainwright," said Dinah, and she set about cutting the packing tape with a steak knife when no scissors could be found. Inside the packing carton was another box with a gift card and tied with satin ribbon. Dinah opened the card and read, "'Granny Dinah told me you needed one of these. Love to all three of you from Nona.' *Granny* Dinah? Gag me with a spoon." The inner box held a professional-size food processor. Dinah said, "Oh, for Christ sake. I told her they needed a little tiny one, like a blender, for making baby food." There were now Styrofoam packing peanuts all over the floor, and I was looking at the extremely minimal counter space in what passed for a kitchen. "Even *I* don't have one this big," said Dinah.

"Then you take this one and give them yours."

"Lady Gotrocks will come to visit and notice."

"Don't be mean. We'll explain. She'll be pleased."

"To be giving alms to poor Mother Courage here?"

"She isn't like that. At all. She admires you. She'll laugh at herself, and be embarrassed, and then pleased that you can use it."

"No." Dinah started repacking the box. "We'll return it and get a credit, and I'll help Grace choose what she really needs."

For a little stretch I was quite cross with Dinah, who seemed to me pointlessly disdainful and competitive toward Avis, so I left her to work in silence while I arranged the flowers. Fortunately I don't think she noticed I was annoyed. I think to her I had never stopped being the public school urchin from Ellsworth, Maine, to whom she was teaching the ways of the world.

When the refrigerator was finally clean to Dinah's standards and we'd done two loads of wash, trekking down to the basement laundry room and back, we took ourselves out for Ethiopian food, Dinah's latest passion.

She ordered. We ate from the same dishes, picking up gobbets of spicy meat and vegetable with swatches of a spongy bread that was more like a warm wet towel than a loaf, but utterly succulent.

"What do *you* want the baby to call you?" I finally asked her, when we'd said all there was to say about the food.

"RJ's boys just call me Dinah."

"I think Granny Dinah is rather charming."

"What do Althea's grands call her?"

I said, "Your Majesty," and Dinah laughed. Oh, it was a pleasure, that deep-throated laugh.

"Do we need more beer?"

"Always."

Dinah signaled the waiter. When he had brought the bottles and poured, Dinah said, "What if I told you I'm thinking of marrying Mike?"

"Oh my god! I'd say, 'Oh my god!' Dinah! *Are* you?"

"I am."

I started to laugh. "Oh my god. I am absolutely thrilled!"

She smiled broadly. "Are you?"

"Thrilled! He's a *great* guy, Dinah. I thought this day would never come, what's gotten into you?"

She shrugged, happy. "I don't know. He's got a good track record as a husband. We have a wonderful time together." Her deep blue eyes seemed lit with hope.

I raised my glass to her, and we clinked and drank.

"Has he asked you?"

"Not exactly. Everything but, though. We've had the money conversation. The where-would-we-live conversation. The what-would-retirement-look-like conversation."

"The Florida/not Florida conversation?"

"Even that." She looked deeply content and also excited, pleased. Young. Like a person with a second chance. I felt suddenly sad that this would never happen for me.

"I am so happy for you, I could weep," I said.

AVIS ALSO THOUGHT THAT THE CHILDREN SHOULD COME HOME TO A clean apartment. She sent Ursula downtown to see to it. Ursula was waiting when the little family arrived home from the hospital, bowing shyly when Grace and Nicky exclaimed at how fresh and sparkling everything was. She had made Grace's favorite foods for dinner, and she tried to get Grace to go to bed and have supper on a tray, but Grace wouldn't. Ursula served them at the table, fussing every bit as much as she had for the Great Inca, although their flatware was stainless and they'd never unpacked the cloth napkins. The baby slept in her carrier on the other end of the table throughout the meal, like some marvelous dish they were saving for later.

Late that night, pottering in the kitchen, Grace exclaimed, "Ursula's thrown out all the sponges!"

"Ursula? That sounds more like the fine Italian hand of my mother," Nicky said. Dinah used dish towels tucked into the pockets of her aprons for everything in the kitchen and washed them in hottest water every night, not trusting that sponges were ever clean enough. But Grace, sleep-deprived from nursing every three hours, and so besotted with the baby that not much else penetrated the fog, forgot he had said it and forgot that she'd agreed. She fervently thanked Avis for sending Ursula to clean so beautifully. Nicky, being Nicky, didn't thank anyone.

I THINK IT WAS IN SEPTEMBER THAT A CLIENT INVITED ME TO A luncheon to benefit refugee women. She had taken a table. I'm fond of the client and was further pleased because Gil was on the board of the organization. The luncheon was at a new hotel at the top of an office tower near Central Park with spectacular views of treetops still in the full green splendor of late summer. At the table, my neighbor on my left was my classmate Nanny Townsend. We got caught up with each other, but the seat at my right was empty until well into the main course, so I sat silently when we changed conversational partners after the appetizer. I didn't mind, as it gave me a chance to watch Gil at his table near the dais. I liked seeing him smile as he talked; I liked admiring his large handsome silver head. Once he looked over at me and our eyes met. My old sweetheart. He'd been my love for well over half my life.

Then the seat on my right was suddenly filled by a woman who arrived talking and never stopped; her mouth was still in motion when I left the ballroom an hour later. Her name was Casey. She was wearing a Prada suit and a little too much jewelry for daytime. She apologized for her lateness, told us in detail what important thing had detained her, in minutes had filled me in on whom she was married to first, whom she is married to now, how long she had lived in Los Angeles and how long in Bermuda, why she stopped going to Fishers Island in the summers, whom she had lately met in Provence, and how well and how long she had known our hostess. She didn't even stop when the speeches began, except that when the philanthropist Victor Greenwood was thanked from the podium, she looked around saying, "Oh, is Victor here?" She had a delightful smile, but a mind like a bat, swooping down on things that looked nourishing to her, then swooping off again. Nanny murmured to me, "Casey's friends say they should take out a full-page ad in the *Times* saying 'Casey Leisure knows these people, list in formation,' and then list everyone in the world.

I was listening to an honoree from South Sudan when I heard Casey say, "Of course, I knew Mary Allison well, and Mike is simply devastated without her. Out of his mind, really. Did you hear, he's gotten mixed up with Dinah Wainwright? His friends don't know what to do."

I joined the conversation. "Do you know Dinah Wainwright?"

"Oh, I've known her for donkey's years from the Vineyard."

The woman on her other side said, "I remember her column 'Dinah Might.'"

"Well," said Casey, "but did you know she didn't really write it?"

Surprise was expressed.

"She can't write her way out of a paper bag."

I said, "I'm quite a fan of her work for *Art and Design*."

"I know the woman she pays to write it for her," said Casey. "Really, I do. Well, my friend knows her. And once I shared a cab with Dinah, coming home from some dreary dinner in Chelsea, and I said, 'I'm a great friend of so-and-so, her ghostwriter, and she just looked at me and said, 'Who?' It was *too* funny."

"It must be expensive for her," I said.

"Oh, don't worry, she's got plenty of dough. The point, though, is sweet Mike Allison. Do you know him?"

I said, "A little."

"He seems nuts about her, so no one says a thing to him. He and Mary were so devoted, there are things he doesn't know about women. I suppose it can't hurt him to have some fun as long as he doesn't marry her."

"I always loved that column, 'Dinah Might,' " said the woman on the other side. "It was really clever."

"Yes. Well," said Casey.

I stayed in my seat until the coffee was poured. Then I blew a kiss to my hostess and slipped away. I sent her a note that afternoon, saying how sorry I was to leave, but such was the life of the working girl.

THANKSGIVING THAT YEAR WAS PERHAPS THE HAPPIEST I CAN REMEMBER. Althea was planning to spend the winter in the south of France, so I would soon have my love nearly to myself again for three lovely months. Dinah invited Avis to Thanksgiving dinner, and Avis gratefully accepted. Mike and Dinah's intention to marry was now known to the family and a source of rejoicing on our side; on Mike's, too, this seemed to be happy news.

Mike's son Barry was short but had his father's muscular build. He worked as the tech expert at a charter school in New Jersey. Barry's wife, Tia, pixieish and very pregnant, carried her expectation as if it were a bowling ball surprisingly attached to her slender body.

Do you think Tolstoy is wrong about happy families? I think he's wrong in at least one respect; some happy families sing. For grace, Mike and Barry sang a canon based on those verses of Matthew: Seek first the kingdom of heaven, and all of it shall come to you. Ask and you will receive; seek and you will find; knock and the door will be opened.

Avis knew the hymn and joined in. Mike said to her, "You have a lovely voice. A very pure sound," and Avis blushed, not a thing she did often.

"Did you sing at school, Avis?" Dinah asked. I remembered quite clearly that Avis did not, and gave Dinah a look.

"No, I botched all my tryouts," Avis said. "Awful stage fright." To Mike, she said, "Dinah's the one with the voice. You should have heard her singing 'Hard-hearted Hannah, the vamp of Savannah, G-A.'"

Dinah was surprised. "How on earth did you remember that?"

"You sang so well, and were *so* funny!"

Grace said, "Dinah, I think you should sing it right now."

"I don't remember the words."

"Was this a variety show or something?" Mike asked.

"No, on Saturday nights we had our one meal of the week without the faculty. Claques would bang on glasses and start chanting 'We want Nan-cy Dew-ey,' someone they liked who could really sing, and whoever it was would stand up and let 'er rip."

"Was this like a convent school?" asked Tia.

Mike asked, "A cappella?"

"No. Yes, a cappella. Dinah was a phenomenon."

"And she still is," said Mike, raising his glass. We all agreed and drank to the chef.

Nicky said, "You know, Sebastian sings opera."

Avis said "Really?"

Barry and Tia began ringing their spoons against the glasses and chanting "We want Sebas-tian, We want Sebas-tian!" I had no idea what was coming. Sebastian did, though. He woke up and rushed to Grace when he heard his name. She picked him up and held him. Nicky brought a jar of peanut butter from the kitchen and fed him a knob of it. As the dog struggled to eat, his little tongue and jaws working madly, Mike sang "La donna è mobile." It looked exactly as if Sebastian were lip-synching. Avis was literally weeping with laughter.

After dessert and coffee, we called for Mike, who gave us "Nessun dorma," and then at last Dinah did get up and sing "Hardhearted Hannah," accompanied by a wicked shimmy. When we cheered and clapped, she said, "I couldn't let myself be outdone by a dog."

When the kitchen was clean, and the young had gone home, Mike and Dinah stood with their arms around each other as Avis and I said good night. In the elevator, Avis said, "I really don't think I ever had a better time in my life."

ASK AND IT SHALL BE GIVEN. SEEK AND YOU SHALL FIND. KNOCK AND the door shall be opened unto you. What would the world be like if we believed that and it was true?

After Christmas, Gil and I spent ten blissful days on St. Martin, on the French side, a place he'd never been with Althea. We played a lot of tennis. We swam in the surf and walked on the beach, and sat in the shade and read stacks of books. The staff addressed me as Madame Flood, and on our last night, Gil gave me a ring, a large perfect pearl set in white gold, with matching earrings. What people call a dinner ring. He'd given me many presents over the years, but never the ring I wanted. I cried for all sorts of reasons, and touchingly, so did he. We were outdoors, on a terrace lit with torches, in velvet warm night air; I'd had a little too much sun that afternoon and had that delicious feeling of being hot and chilled at the same time that one associates with summer nights when young.

IT WASN'T LONG AFTER WE GOT BACK THAT THE AXE FELL.

I had discovered a little lump somewhere it didn't belong—it's not important—that my internist said was either a cyst or it wasn't. He sent me to a specialist. The office was on the ground floor of one of those massive apartment palaces on Fifth, quite near the Met. I was nervous about the lump, so I couldn't keep my mind on what I was trying to read. I studied the carpet, the rather tired blue-striped wallpaper that was starting to come unstuck in an upper corner, the framed wall posters of art shows one had missed by several decades. The only other person waiting was a well-groomed but heavyset brunette in her early fifties with thick-ish features, just the tiniest bit bovine, and a heavy jaw that her too-short haircut did nothing to counterbalance. She had a honking great emerald-cut diamond on her left hand, though, so one supposed she had more to offer than her looks. She was immersed in a copy of *Town & Country*.

The receptionist buzzed in a very attractive blonde in a vintage Joan Vass overcoat, which got my attention. When she had disentangled herself from her iPod, hung her dripping coat and umbrella, and stowed her scarf and hat, she looked around and cried "Betsy!"

Betsy and the blonde, whose name was Carol or Cheryl, knew each other well. I occupied myself by working out how in this great city made up of so many interlocking villages they had become connected. Childhood friends? Their children were friends? Professional colleagues? Wives of colleagues? Ah! The Town Club.

The one with the jaw had a rather wicked wit, just showing you can't ever judge a book. The pretty one was computer dating. When last seen, she had been off to Mohonk with a man who had seemed perfect for her. How had it gone? Not well. They had shared a love of Brahms all right, but alone with Carol he was far less interested in sex than he was in trying on her underwear. Even I had to smile, although of course I was pretending not to listen.

"It's not all bleak, though," said Carol. "I had dinner last week with a guy I met two years ago and really liked. He called me out of the blue."

"Well, you go, girl!" said the jaw. "What's the story?"

"I don't really know much. He's a widower. Very musical, very sweet and funny . . ."

"But you haven't slept with him."

"Not yet."

"So you could still have the underwear problem."

"Two in a row would seem like awfully bad management, wouldn't it?"

"Yes. What's his name?"

"Mike. The wife was a member of the club too. Mary Allison."

At that moment, a nurse came in and asked me to follow her to a treatment room.

ONE MORE PROOF THAT WE ARE ALWAYS WORRYING ABOUT THE WRONG disaster in this life. My lump was a cyst. However, three weeks later, Mike e-mailed Dinah that he thought they should take some time off from each other. He'd met someone else. Sorry, sorry, sorry, he typed as he bowed himself backward out the door and then cut off all communication.

The e-mail was three days old by the evening she finally forwarded it to me, and when I dropped everything and called her, she was slurring her words. I have something of a horror of that condition, and was not sure she would forgive me for seeing her like that, so I didn't go to her until the next day. I went at lunchtime, so I could use the shop as an excuse if I needed to get away.

The blinds were drawn in the living room. A heavy crystal vase Mike had given her, celebrating some private anniversary, was on the floor in pieces, as it must have been for days. The water it had contained had been left to dry on the floor, and the flowers lay withered like dead fish on a riverbank. Clearly Dinah had been walking on them as if they weren't there.

I said, "I'm surprised that Baccarat broke on a wood floor. It's pretty heavy."

"It didn't. I had to hit it with a hammer."

Apparently that had been an experience so satisfactory it called for repetition. In the kitchen there was quite a lot of smashed crockery Mike had had nothing to do with.

There was a half-finished bottle of rum on the counter, but I didn't think she'd been drinking. The apartment smelled richly of marijuana. I wonder where she got it.

I made tea. We talked for hours. There were a lot of tears. "Met someone. Met someone. Do you fucking believe that? I've loved—really loved—two men in my life, and they both 'met someone.' Lovie, what is *wrong* with me? Is it my karma or something? Am I terrible in bed? Is there something written on my back? This doesn't happen to you, does it?"

I didn't answer.

"Well, *does* it?"

"No."

"*I* should have fallen for someone in his eighties. They can't fuck around if they can't fuck at all, is that your secret?"

Since this was both inaccurate and cruel, I began to collect my things to go, but Dinah said, "The problem is, I don't believe it. Oh, he may be seeing someone *now,* in fact I know he is, but that's not what happened. Something else happened. Something fucking changed, and it wasn't me. I felt it, but I couldn't tell what it was. He denied there was anything. And then he *met* someone."

"How do you know he's seeing someone else?"

"I called Barry."

This seemed to me so desperate and undignified that I didn't know what to say.

"Barry's met the Someone. Barry met her before his fucking father was good enough to clue *me* in. Men are such cowards. He had to have something else lined up before he left. They're just like frogs hopping from lily pad to lily pad, and if they happen to shove you into a bottomless pit as they bound off to skim along the surface, well, isn't that too fucking bad for you?"

We sat silently for a while before I said, "I know it isn't your style, but this is too much for you to carry alone. Don't you think you ought to talk to somebody?"

"You mean a *shrink*? Like every other fat lonely angry single woman in New York?"

That is of course what I meant, and since she knew very well that I and half the people we knew had not thought ourselves above such recourse, I chose not to answer.

I SAW LESS OF DINAH FOR SOME MONTHS AFTER THAT. PARTLY THIS WAS because I was able to spend most of my time with Gil, and because I was gradually beginning to accept that he and I had many more good years behind us than lay ahead. He was in most ways like a man twenty years younger than his chronological age, but not in all. I wanted to make the most of the time we had left, and whatever my fears in the small hours, Dinah was not my choice of confidante about them.

She rallied, of course, in time. A friend who writes for "On the Town," the Web-based social blat read by everyone between Carnegie Hill and Bloomingdale's, did a column on Dinah's cooking classes with lots of pictures of Dinah tasting a sauce, Dinah spreading meringue, and attractive young people in SOMEONE'S IN THE KITCHEN WITH DINAH aprons chopping and stirring. She came into the shop one afternoon to crow that she had just signed a book contract. She even bought some large onyx earrings while she was there, at full price.

The nights she was not cooking, she seemed to be out On the Town herself a good deal, a fact I followed on the Web site along with everyone else. She was invited to gallery openings and press events of all sorts, and I began to think I recognized her touch in blind items and captions that ran with unflattering pictures of people at glamorous events. The photographer would catch someone with a mouthful of scalding hors d'oeuvre, or beaming for the camera unaware there was sauce on his nose, or a woman in an expensive dress whose corsetry was not what it should have been. The taglines that ran with these pictures became conversational shorthand all over town. OH, THE GLAMOUR OF IT ALL! was one, and TOWN CLUB DOWAGER was another.

I remember my grandmother, back in the 1970s, in a huff because a coed group of Princeton students had had a romp in the snow one night wearing only their ski boots. A jolly dustup about the whole thing had made its way to the national press. Working for Mme. Philomena and living on gruel while all my classmates were in college, I thought it sounded heavenly. Not my grandmother. "Something has gone wrong with the morals of your generation," she declaimed, as if she were Walter Cronkite reporting the My Lai massacre. I ventured that it had nothing to do with morals—they hadn't robbed a bank or started a war, they simply had a new attitude about nakedness. As if I hadn't spoken she repeated her original sentence, and added witheringly, "Students at the Ivies and Seven Sisters used to be ladies and gentlemen."

I'm a great deal more sympathetic now. I wanted to express my displeasure at the meanness of these items by ceasing to read the column, but of course I can't do that. I have to know who's out and about and what they are wearing.

GRACE AND AVIS MADE AN APPOINTMENT AND CAME INTO THE SHOP together. This would have been around Lindy's second birthday. It was June. They had had lunch together at a sidewalk table on Madison, celebrating Grace's new teaching job.

"Look how little and cute she is!" said Avis. "She's been doing yoga. Buckram."

"Bikram. You do it in a sweltering room, I am now strong like ox. You should try it, Mummy." I hadn't heard her call Avis that since she was in Mary Janes.

"It sounds so daunting," said Avis. But she was pleased.

It was a most successful afternoon for me. Grace was once again a perfect size four, and I had some dresses that looked better on her than they had on the showroom models. They took three of them. Then they thought Grace had better try a jacket or two. I showed them a beautiful boyfriend jacket, worn slightly long at the wrists and broad at the shoulders, in a dove-gray herringbone cashmere. Grace stood looking at her reflection as Mrs. Oba showed her how to turn back the cuffs to show the striped silk lining. She had a chic new gamine haircut, and the color of the jacket brought out the blue-slate shade of her eyes.

"It's really very practical," said Avis, doing my job for me. "You can wear it with trousers or over the charcoal dress. It will wear, won't it, Lovie?"

"Like iron," I said. Nothing as soft as that jacket wears like iron, but Avis knew that. They bought it, and also a slouchy little boiled wool blazer with midriff pockets.

"You will *live* in that," said Avis. If all my customers had been like her, I wouldn't be spending half my life closeted with accountants these days.

Grace said, "Lovie, what size is that taffeta shirt in the window?"

"I think it's an eight—do you want to try it?"

"I want my mother to try it."

"What taffeta shirt?" said Avis.

It was a double-breasted evening blouse in a burnt orange undershot with something slightly iridescent that made it gleam. It had a diagonal closing that hugged the rib cage, one of Avis's best features, and a wide collar that would hold whatever shape you put it in. Frankly, I had pictured Belinda in it; that's why I put it in the window. I miss her.

"I'd have to wear it closed across the chest," said Avis, as if I'd forgotten her scars. You can hardly see them anymore, but *she* sees them.

All four of us were in the dressing room now. Mrs. Oba fastened the hidden closings at the midriff while I sculpted the collar so that it stood up framing her face, revealing just a slit of skin from collarbone to chest. Not a scar to be seen. She looked positively regal.

"If you don't buy that I'll never forgive you," said Grace.

THAT WAS THE SUMMER OF NICKY'S NEXT VOCATION, THE BAR ON Planet Ludlow. It was Toby's idea. He had found a former auto body shop next to a carver of Hebrew gravestones down in the Lower East Side neighborhood of Stanton, Orchard, and Ludlow streets, once home to Old Law tenements filled with refugees from the ghettos of Eastern Europe, now the haunt of recent graduates of Wesleyan and Vassar. The space seemed to Toby to cry out to be a watering hole cum literary salon, and Nicky seemed to him the perfect attraction to run the front of the house. He would make it the clubhouse for his Hollywood friends when they were in town, perhaps even convince them to make fools of themselves at the mike in back, where Toby would curate a slate of readings by their young literary pals, paired with monologists, a stand-up comic, or the occasional singer-songwriter.

Together they convinced a bunch of their old high school gang to put in sweat equity or money. Someone had an uncle who helped with the liquor license. Two of the girls reupholstered old car seats in red velvet to use as sofas, and they hung auto body parts like sculptures along the walls. Someone else donated bar stools found at a flea market upstate. Well over half the group had worked waiting tables or trained as chefs or both.

I was deeply skeptical. It takes a lot of attention and some very specific skills to manage employees and run a business, as I had learned myself the hard way. However, it appeared I had misjudged them, because the place opened with skillfully managed fanfare and was a hit almost immediately.

Dinah was all over it, of course. She'd consulted on the menu, a sort of tapas assortment of cleverly reimagined bar food. Nicky hired a bartender who made really delicious pear martinis. Toby's literary choices were rarely my taste, but of course I was not the target audience, and the demographic they were seeking, young bankers and hedge fund hoglets and others making fortunes in the booming markets, came in droves.

Nicky was as happy as a pig in a wallow. I went with Dinah to a couple of programs early on, but they tended to start about the time I needed to be in bed. The same was true for Grace. On weekends she sometimes got a sitter and went to have dinner at the bar with Nicky, but once again they were living in different time zones. Most nights after closing, Nicky and Toby played liar's poker at the bar with the staff until three or four in the morning, while Grace went to bed at ten and was up with Lindy at six. .

At Christmastime that year, RJ's wife called from Pittsburgh to say she was coming to town and wanted to take me to lunch. She's a nice woman, very even tempered and loyal, but when we sat down together at the overpriced bôite she had chosen because some writer on a travel junket had written it up in the Pittsburgh paper, she had a head of steam up.

RJ, she said, was really hurt this time. He claimed he understood why he had had to go to boarding school but Nicky was allowed to stay home. Why he was never offered the engagement ring that Dinah had saved for Nicky to give to his bride. Why Dinah was always babysitting for Lindy when she had declined to take on that particular duty for RJ's boys.

I could have said that RJ could afford his own ring. That two active little boys are different from one tiny girl. But I knew what her point was, and knew she was right.

"He's really upset, though, about her putting all that money into Nicky's bar. Do you know what she gives RJ for his birthday? Fruit of the Month Club! The boys get gift cards to Barnes & Noble, not very big ones either! She's *their* grandmother too!"

"Laura, I really don't think she's put money into the bar. She's helped with the food and the PR . . ."

"Have you asked her?"

Of course I hadn't. And Richard would have to know if she'd taken substantial money from her accounts, and if it worried him, he would have told RJ.

"Would you talk to her?" Laura was saying.

"Me?"

"Yes. RJ won't. But she should know how it makes him feel!"

My smoked salmon omelet wasn't very good either. I should have known to dodge this invitation in the first place. But I'd been curious.

IN THE END, I DID TALK WITH DINAH ABOUT IT. PROBABLY NOT THE smartest thing I ever did. It let me in for a good grilling about what Richard had said, what Laura had said, and how I'd gotten in the middle of it in the first place.

Finally she said, "Of course I put money in. It's a loan, and he's paying me back."

"But, Dinah, you can't afford to lose that kind of money."

"I'm not going to lose it."

"But you could have. Nicky's a grown-up . . ."

"Exactly. That's exactly why it was the right thing to do."

It was so obvious that borrowing money from your mother for a crapshoot is not exactly grown-up that I didn't even answer. Dinah wouldn't have listened anyway. The fact that the bar was succeeding completely justified her.

And the bar was succeeding. Unfortunately, Nicky wasn't.

None of us really knows what happened. One rumor was that he and Toby quarreled over Nicky grandly giving away the most expensive bottles of red in the cellar, or drinking them himself. Another was that the bartender was dealing coke from behind the bar and that Nicky knew it and didn't stop it. What we do know is that the bartender was fired, Nicky and Toby don't speak anymore, and Toby paid back all but a few thousand of Dinah's loan before the economy tanked and the bar closed.

Avis took a house on Nantucket for August that year so she could have Grace and Nicky and the baby with her. If she mourned the loss of her quiet island life in Maine, she didn't say so. The Nantucket house she rented was a huge shingled affair, with gables, on Hulbert Avenue right on the sound where you could watch the ferry come and go. There was even a little cottage out back, originally for the staff, that she offered to me, and which I gratefully accepted, since Gil was with Althea for the month.

I tried to remember how long it had been since I had visited the island, as I stood on the sunny top deck of the ferry going over from Woods Hole. Decades. The ferry was full of day-trippers with their bicycles, and young families going to the island for the weekend, the week, or the month. On my first visit, I remember thinking that someday I too would be making this crossing with my husband and our happy children, eager for the warm surf and glowing beaches. I watched the seagulls following our wake, screaming and diving into the white froth when someone threw a bread crust or a handful of Cracker Jacks for them. Sunlight flashed on their gray wings, and someone near me was using sunscreen that smelled of coconut oil. Summer.

Oddly, what it made me think of most was my grandfather, describing the overnight trip on the coasting packet ship from Boston to Maine when he was a boy and the family moved bag and baggage from Philadelphia to Great Spruce Bay in the summers. He and his brother Calvin would tie two chunks of bread together with string and throw it for the gulls. He used to laugh to tears at the mirthful thought of how the birds struggled once they ate the bread and then found themselves soaring but shackled. He urged me to try it. And my grandfather was a complete gentleman. I would have said otherwise that he hadn't a mean bone in his body.

Maybe the peanut butter dog opera wasn't funny either, however much the dog seemed to enjoy it. Maybe none of us recognize cruelty in ourselves.

What a thing to be thinking about under a blazing blue sky on a glorious day of creation. Houseguests have to sing for their suppers more cheerfully than that.

The men on the ferry who wished to declare themselves old Nantucket hands wore baseball hats or shorts in a color that looks weather-beaten even when new, called Nantucket red. The tourists would all have hats in this color by the time they made the return trip. We all want either to belong somewhere or for others to think we do. I myself possess a Nantucket lightship basket handbag with a scrimshaw ivory whale on the lid. It was my grandmother's; they cost a fortune now. None of my siblings knew what it was or cared about it, so I preempted it from the sale of her belongings. I even had it with me on this trip, but only because I needed to have the hinge repaired.

Nicky and Lindy met me at the ferry. I saw them both waving as I made my way onto the wharf along with the pedestrian throng and the babble of greetings, instructions, questions, and warnings to children not to fall or get lost that went with disembarkation. As we jostled along, cars were streaming one by one from the belly of the ship through its gaping mouth onto the sunlit wharf like a herd of four-wheeled Jonahs.

"Here she is, Lindy-hop! Here's Auntie Lovie!" Nicky hopped each time he said her name, and she tried to hop too, tucked firmly against his hip, with her little legs clutching him around the waist. Nicky put her down and took my luggage. Confidingly, Lindy took my hand.

He led us proudly to a vintage Saab convertible that apparently came with the house. I held Lindy while he drove.

"Is this safe, Nicky? Shouldn't she be in a car seat?"

"You are her car seat," he said. I thought he drove rather fast as well, but he always did like to startle the bourgeoisie. Lindy stood on my lap and held on to my hair, playing at butting my cheek with her nose.

The house was practically on the beach. Avis had hired a young graduate of the Culinary Institute to cook, a slim homely girl in a long white apron and green plastic chef's clogs who came in by the day. She served us a delicious lunch on the porch. Grace was nowhere to be seen; she was sailing with childhood friends. After lunch, Lindy went down for her nap. I offered to stay with her so that Nicky could get out and enjoy the day, but he said he wanted to work. He was writing a screenplay.

Avis said she herself was dying to read it. Nicky told me, with a wicked smile, that he had talked to Alvin Grable's agent about it, and she wanted to represent him. Off he went upstairs with his laptop. Avis and I took a long walk on the beach.

Five o'clock came, and still Grace wasn't home. Lindy was a sunny child but had been asking for Mummy for over an hour and was finally querulous. Avis looked weary, and I could have done with a nap myself. I'd forgotten how much sheer boredom there is in looking after young children.

We were sitting with Lindy in the airy living room, the rattan rug strewn with puzzle pieces and toy barnyard creatures. Nicky was still upstairs. I had read what seemed like stacks of picture books aloud, we'd had a tea party on the grass with dandelion cookies, and we'd found all the broken shells worth finding on the beach beyond the narrow lawn. Avis was singing "Kookaburra sits on the old gum tree," to Lindy. When they got to "Laugh, kookaburra," Avis would put her hands in the air and pretend to laugh, her nose and her long narrow teeth making her look fleetingly like an elegant horse. Lindy imitated her, lost her balance, and sat down hard on a plastic cow.

She started to howl. Avis scooped her up and went on singing, but Lindy would not be soothed. She went from wailing with surprise and pain to screaming. Avis kissed her and jiggled her helplessly. Nicky came down the stairs two at a time in bare feet, stepped painfully on a Lego block and swore as he crossed the floor, seized Lindy from Avis, and left the room. The screaming grew wilder and more bereft as it traveled up the stairs and into the bedroom over our heads.

"He won't spank her, will he?" He had looked to me as angry as Lindy.

"Oh, I don't think so," said Avis uncertainly.

The screaming upstairs was unabated when Nicky rejoined us in the living room. He sat, stormily pretending to ignore the sound. I thought she couldn't possibly keep it up for more than a minute or two, but the noise raged on for five, then ten, then twenty. Then she'd been at it for almost half an hour.

It was excruciating. I busied myself on the floor, collecting wooden and plastic pieces of things, and wondered if it was too early to ask for a drink. Avis sat with her hands clasped over her bony knees.

She said, "I'll just run up and be sure she doesn't have a pin in her or—"

"She doesn't," Nicky snapped. "She has to learn to comfort herself. Please leave her." Of course, she couldn't have a pin in her, there are no such things as diaper pins anymore, but I agreed with Avis. Surely there might be something really wrong?

But he was the father. Avis stayed where she was and I did too, and the shrieking continued.

Grace came into the house, running. "What's happened? You can hear her out on the road!"

"Nothing happened! She was crying for you and now she's having a tantrum." Nicky looked as if he was holding on to the chair arms to keep himself still. Husband and wife stared at each other, locked in an argument we could see but not hear.

The sound from upstairs, now coming in hoarse waves, battered the walls and beat at our ears like bird wings. Their eyes held each other's.

"She's almost asleep," Nicky declared, though I doubted it. Grace's skin was sun-gold. She was still wearing a salt-stained visor over her hair.

Grace left the room, heading for the stairs.

Like a cat, Nicky was out of his chair and after her. Her footsteps quickened; so did his. From the stairway landing, where their footsteps stopped, we heard a thump, as if a body had slammed against a wall, and a single cry of anger and surprise.

Avis and I stared at each other.

For a long moment nothing could be heard except the baby's wail. Then one set of footsteps hurried up from the landing and into Lindy's room. There was a last shuddering sob from the baby, and then silence.

Silence. It took several seconds to remember that this state, which seemed at first shot through with comforting colors, like water after great thirst, was our normal state.

Nicky came back into the room. His face was red and wore a closed, congested expression. Briefly he looked at me, as if he thought I should take his side. His dark hair stood up a little on one side, as if when the baby started to cry he had been napping, not writing.

I said, "I think I'd like a gin and tonic. Can I get anyone anything?"

No one answered me, so I went into the kitchen to make myself a drink. When I came back, Nicky had a magazine in his lap, and Avis was gone.

Some time passed. Out on the sound, the ferry was crossing the broad blue water that formed our view, lumbering back toward the mainland, its belly full of SUVs and its back thronged with tired and sunburned people. A large gull strutted along our beach with its chest puffed out like a comic-book plutocrat, pausing now and then to peck at the sand. Then it took off, out toward the ferry.

Grace came in holding Lindy, who burrowed against her, face still red and wet, clinging to her like a marsupial baby whose mother's body is still its home. Grace had been crying too, but was no longer.

Nicky looked up and stared at her. Ignoring him, she came to sit in a chair close to me.

"She'd have been asleep in another minute," said Nicky.

"I couldn't stand it," she said.

"Apparently." He got up and walked out of the room, off the porch and down to the beach.

Avis came in from the kitchen with a glass in her hand. She had combed her hair and put on lipstick. "Can I get you anything, darling?" she said to Grace. Grace shook her head.

Nicky didn't come back until after sunset, when we were half finished with dinner.

The next morning, Avis hired a babysitter for the duration. The sitter was a big patient girl with huge bosoms, poor thing, only fourteen but the oldest in her family, and wonderful with the baby. She came at nine in the morning and went home after Lindy had had her supper. I thought maybe now Nicky would spend some time with Grace and her friends. Thought he should, in fact, but he said they all worked for investment banks and kept asking him things like "So, what are you up to now, guy?" Also, he was almost through his second act and couldn't waste the momentum.

Grace played tennis and went sailing, and Avis and I rode bikes to distant beaches, often with the sitter and Lindy along. In the evenings, groups of attractive young people came to eat lobster and corn on the cob, drink stunning amounts of jug wine, and talk and laugh. Most nights they played charades, at which Nicky excelled. A halcyon time, I would have said, apart from the start.

Dinah, however, was not so pleased. I proposed to stop on the Vineyard and pay her a visit on my way home, but she said tartly that she was too busy and her house was full. I didn't see her until September in New York, and she was in a sour mood.

"Now that Grace's back at work, Nicky is just frantic. He's trying to work too, you know."

I said that I did know, and that he'd had a good stretch of work time when he was on Nantucket.

"Not as much as he would have if Grace ever helped."

"Wait. That's not fair. Grace did the early mornings and breakfast so Nicky could sleep in, and the rest of the time there was a sitter."

"I know about the sitter. Trust Avis to think you can have your children raised by the help."

"Dinah. You had a nanny for RJ!"

"I was *working*. And I never liked it. Now Nicky's either got to give up his work to take care of the baby, or have a nanny in the house all day, and he can't get anything done with people in the house. You don't know what it's like, being a writer."

"Why doesn't he join Writers Room? Or the Society Library?"

"It's *hardly* in the neighborhood," she said, as if it were the stupidest suggestion she'd ever heard. Last time I checked there were subways that made it possible for New Yorkers to work in neighborhoods they don't live in, but I didn't want a quarrel. We shifted the conversation to the clothes she should wear on camera for her tryout for a show on the Food Channel. I know some things about colors under the lights, and I had a makeup person my clients work with whom I thought she should meet. She remembered to ask about Gil and about business. Which was still booming in 2007, those were the days. I still missed my little dog, Hannah, who had died in July, and Dinah was reasonably sympathetic.

As I was leaving, she said, "You know, Nicky and Grace spent four days with me in August, and Grace still hasn't written me a thank-you note."

It's a good thing I didn't laugh. A thank-you note? Dinah expected a thank-you note from Grace? Did Nicky write her thank-you notes? Grace was practically her daughter. Had Dinah ever written *me* a thank-you note for all the discounts, all the . . . oh, never mind. Dinah said, "And she never thanked me for cleaning her grotty apartment before she came home with the baby! Remember that?"

I did, and I explained about Ursula.

Dinah put her hands on her hips. "Well, that's just ducky. She and Mumsy seem to be hitting it off these days. Have they started wearing mother-daughter outfits yet?"

So *that* was it.

I said that I must be going.

WHEN YOUR LOVE IS A GREAT DEAL OLDER THAN YOU, YOU have to face the fact that one of you is going to be left behind, and it will probably be you. You might think that since I had been without Gil so much during the years we shared, I would be better equipped for this eventuality than some, but that would be to underestimate the power of the life-long conversation that had been going on between us since the weekend we met in Vermont. Gil seemed to me so grown up in those days, though he was so much younger than I am now. Gil, tall and lanky and so graceful, mentally and physically, always. Gil, who seemed to remember every book he'd ever read; Gil, who could talk to anybody; Gil, so endearingly quick to find himself ridiculous; Gil, who thought the world delightful; Gil, who could always make me laugh, whose advice could always be trusted; Gil, who was always on my side.

Anyway. It's a lot to do without, when it's been the air you breathed for forty years. The silence that falls at the end of that conversation is deep and dark, and I'd been frightened for years that when it opened up before me I would fall in and never climb out.

Silence does affect people differently. Solitary confinement is a punishment for the most grievous kinds of transgressions. Yet for monks and hermits and others who choose it, it can bring tran-scendent joy, a sense of connection with all that is holy, an erasure of self that means erasure of personal disappointment and pain. It stands to reason that the emotional silence that comes at the end of a lifelong love must also be survived or not, a punishment or a prayer, depending on the character of the individual.

Are we ever done with tests of character in this life?

THE ONLY MARKER OTHERS NOTICED THAT GIL WAS SLOWING DOWN was that he'd switched from singles in tennis to doubles. He laughed just as much, finished double acrostics just as fast, and he could reliably clean my clock at backgammon. He was not planning on change or decay; he was halfway through *Remembrance of Things Past* in French. Then shortly before Christmas, he slipped on the ice, fell, and hit his head on a stone step. He was only briefly concussed and recovered consciousness quickly; the ER didn't even keep him overnight. But before he fell, he was a lively citizen of the world somewhere near the end of middle age. In one day he became an old man.

Althea came home from France. Gil and I had looked forward to celebrating Christmas at our house in Connecticut, but that hope was gone. He was sleeping a lot and taking things very slowly. Once Althea saw him, she canceled her other plans and stayed. We didn't meet for a month while he was convalescing; the best we could do was talk on the phone when Althea was out of the apartment. Althea was a better nurse than anyone would have expected, and he was grateful for the care she took of him. She wasn't young herself.

By February he claimed to be back in form, but his balance was uncertain, and he was understandably afraid of falling. He came to me two afternoons a week when he was supposed to be playing bridge at the Knick. Where once we would have headed into the park for a ramble or gone out to a film, we stayed in by the fire, sometimes reading or playing backgammon, sometimes just holding hands and watching the flames. I told myself that he still had years, but like a version of the pregnant woman's suitcase packed with everything she'll need at the hospital once she goes into labor, I also began taking care that I always had cash, a purse at the ready with reading glasses, my MetroCard, a list of his medications, and anything else one might need if something happened while he was with me. Or if I were suddenly summoned to a vigil in the middle of the night. But *would* anyone summon me? And if yes, who?

On the days when we couldn't see each other our habit was to "have tea" together. I would leave the shop and go up to my flat, brew a cup of decaf Earl Grey, and wait. Gil would call from his bedroom on a second telephone line he'd had installed for me. Was there ever a marital conversation about that line? I have no way of knowing. On a gray afternoon in early March I made my tea and sat down to wait, but no call came.

By five I was frantic. I called the line, a thing I'd done only once before, but this time it rang and rang.

I called downstairs and told Stephanie to close the shop when she was ready to go home, that I couldn't leave the apartment. Then I sat.

Do you know about the London *Times'* first Golden Globe sailing race? Of the two sailors competing to sail the fastest course single-handed around the earth, one fell so in love with silence that when he rounded Cape Horn, instead of shaping a course for England to finish the race and collect his prize, he kept sailing east, around the Cape of Good Hope and into the Indian Ocean again until he finally came to rest in Tahiti. The other, the only other candidate still in the running, same race, same silence, went mad and went overboard. His logbooks, found on his drifting boat, told the tale.

The phone rang at ten. I had it to my ear before the first ring had finished.

"Is this Loviah French?"

"Yes, speaking."

"This is Meredith Flood. We met—"

"You came to the shop."

"Yes."

Then our hearts failed us both, briefly.

"Something's happened," I said.

"Yes."

"Tell me."

"A stroke."

The thing he feared most, the thing I feared for him.

"A bad one?"

"Yes."

"May I come?"

"I think you'd better."

She told me where he was, and in minutes I was on the street, in a cab.

He was in the intensive care unit at a hospital where he'd served on the board for years. They'd given him a view of the East River, but it didn't make any difference and neither would anything else, as I understood when I stood at the gap in the curtains and saw him lying on his back, completely still. A nurse was unhooking the tubes that ran into his nose and the back of his hand.

I was still wearing the suit I'd dressed in for work that morning. I could have changed, but it hadn't occurred to me; I had been stuck in a state of waiting since I sat down with my tea so many hours ago.

Meredith stood with her back to the room, looking down at the river. She was crying. Althea was seated beside the bed, her hand holding Gil's cold one, her forehead leaning against white sheets. She appeared to be praying.

Meredith turned, and Althea looked up and found me standing there. Her face was lined and old. There were bags under her eyes, and her lipstick had bled into the tiny wrinkles around her mouth.

Our eyes met, and she held my gaze for a long moment. She didn't speak; she didn't have to. He had died in her arms.

The way the story ends tells you what the story means.

For a great while, I can't really say how long, I couldn't bear real conversation. Chat with strangers was fine, even desirable. Mrs. Oba knew without being told to keep silence with me, except on the simplest level: A tuck here? Let the cuffs down? Face the hem for another half-inch of length? I found conversations with customers—about the galas they were dressing for, the details of the stepdaughter's wedding—more than possible; necessary. A sort of soothing, dulling the consciousness, like knitting or strong drink.

My close friends grew anxious that I was spending too much time alone and tried with increasing pressure to get me to attend things they thought would divert me. A taping of Dinah's cooking show. A gathering for someone's tedious memoir. A house party in Millbrook, opening day at Belmont Park. In fact I went for the last one. A friend took us down to the paddock to see her horses saddled. There is something reassuring about being close to very large quadrupeds. It shakes your sense of scale. The horses were practically radiating life force, very beautiful and young. It was a nice day with the grass a bright strong color and the leaves all looking lime green. I won eighteen dollars on the fourth race. Gil would have loved it.

I wasn't in fact spending that much time alone. Instead, I was with new people, people who'd never met Gil. I went out to Southampton with a woman I swam laps with at the Colony Club. I went to films with single friends I'd known slightly for decades, and to the opera with one of Avis's young walkers. Little by little the days passed. Toward the end of the summer I paid some attention, not much, to talk of Fannie Mae and Freddie Mac and their problems. Richard Wainwright would call and say he thought I should sell this or move that. He sounded upset, but that barely registered. I told him to make any changes for me he thought right. Then Lehman Brothers crashed and burned, and even I woke up to the news that we were witnessing an end to prosperity as we had known it.

So I had something new to worry about.

I suppose I had better admit here that I was dealing with something almost more disorienting than Gil's death. Which, after all, we had both always known was coming. It was this: as you will have gathered, there was a place in Connecticut that had been ours, his and mine. It had come to him from his parents; Althea had never been interested. There was a small house of great charm, the place where we lived together as a couple. There were gardens, especially a rose garden planted and tended by me for many years. Huge deciduous trees like peaceful giants surrounded us with colors in the fall. He had always told me it would come to me, along with enough money to keep it up.

I can't explain it . . . it's not that I can't get along without a country house. It's the surprise. Well, the shock. My gardens. How many times had he seen me come in glowing after an afternoon of staking delphiniums, deadheading peonies, digging in the rose beds, knowing I thought they would always be mine?

I'll never know what changed. Or if this was always his plan. Nor will I ever be the same.

I found out at the funeral through an innocent conversation with the Floods' estate lawyer, whom I had met earlier that morning. The service was at the church of St. Vincent Ferrer, Althea's church, in the east sixties, right down Lexington Avenue from Hunter College. It's a neighborhood I know well, not far from my first flat where I lived when I worked for Philomena. The day was bright and dry, if still very raw, but I had dressed for a walk after the service. The reception was to be held at Gil and Althea's apartment, and of course I couldn't go there; instead I stood in the narthex waiting for Althea and the children to enter the small herd of limousines that idled outside and be whisked off, watching the friends and extended family pouring past me as if I were a rock in a streambed and they were the water. As they descended the church steps in the pale sunlight, they were already beginning to chatter to each other about the beauty of the service and whether to walk or look for a taxi, when the lawyer joined me.

He was just doing his version of mourning Gil, by musing

aloud about what a wise and thoughtful job Gil had done of planning for his loved ones, unlike some of his clients who seemed
truly to believe they were taking it with them. How carefully
Gil had weighed this against that so that all three children could
share equally in unequal things. He felt free to talk to me of such
matters, as he knew I'd been close enough to Gil to be a legatee.
He mentioned that Gil had left me a token sum of money and
his grandfather's gold pocket watch, which he'd been given on
his own twenty-first birthday. Gil carried it when he wore black
tie, which he rarely did with me. He had left my house to his
daughters.

The lawyer had no idea that he had just reached down my
throat and stopped my heart.

So. I HAD A LOT TO PROCESS.

But in the fall of 2008, so did everybody else. Richard had read
the tea leaves cleverly, and both Dinah and I were well insulated
from the rolling disaster going on down on Wall Street. And, as
we all learned to say eight times a day, on Main Street.

But my clients were not immune by any means. One of my
ladies had lived for decades in a palatial Park Avenue duplex. Her
husband had invested everything with the Ponzi schemer Bernie
Madoff. Overnight, they moved to a garage apartment in the suburbs, and at seventy-four she is selling cookware at a Bloomingdale's in a mall somewhere. Her husband has congestive heart
failure and sits all day in a wheelchair looking out the window.
Or so I'm told.

I sell a luxury product, and even those who could still afford to travel and dine out stopped spending conspicuously that winter. If you didn't actually need a new opera coat or fresh cruise wear, it seemed more appropriate to do without or to appear in "vintage." Plenty of my clients had pieces that had become vintage while hanging in their own closets; that's how it works if you buy good things that suit you and take proper care of them. They'd stop in wearing some suit I'd sold them in 1991 and thank me. By February 2009, I'd had to let Stephanie go and was running the shop myself. Mrs. Oba volunteered to take a pay cut and come in only three days a week. I was grateful, though I miss her on the days she's not there. Her daughter is now practicing medicine in Boston and her son lives near her in Brooklyn and has small children, so she has plenty to keep her busy.

I did not.

The hours were long in the shop, with virtually no custom. Life was gray. So I was particularly happy to see Avis outside pressing the bell for me to unlock the door on a blowy day in March. She came in, bringing the fresh smell of wind with her, her cheeks bright, her expensive loafers sodden.

"You look marvelous," I told her truthfully as she took off her wet things.

"I've been taking yoga with Grace. Bikram. I must say I feel sensational."

"That's the one in the hot room?"

"Yes, it's wonderful. I can stand on one leg for hours, and as Grace says, I am strong like ox."

"I'm quite jealous," I said, though I have never had trouble keeping my figure and I hate classes, as well as heat.

"I need a new evening skirt or two and maybe a jacket, if you have something with pockets."

"For here, or are you heading south?"

"Both. I'm taking Lindy and her parents to Sea Island for Easter."

"Lucky them," I said.

"You couldn't shake loose for lunch, could you?" Avis asked. "Could your girl cover for you for an hour or so?"

"I'll tell you what. Let me show you a couple of things and then I'll just close up. If customers show up without appointments, *tant pis.*"

"That's the spirit," said Avis.

AT THE BISTRO AROUND THE CORNER WE ORDERED CHEESE SOUFFLÉS and split a bottle of Sancerre. A little vacation in a glass, it seems, to have wine at lunch. I enjoyed myself, but I could see now that something was troubling Avis. She got around to it over coffee.

"Have you seen much of Nicky lately?"

I said not as much as I used to.

"How does he seem to you when you see him?"

I considered. To be truthful, he seemed drawn and touchy.

"I expect they're both exhausted. How's Grace?"

Avis paused, unhappy. Finally she said, "Could I tell you something in confidence? Really total confidence?"

I said of course.

THE LONG COURTSHIP. THE MONTHS NICKY SPENT ON THE WEST Coast. His seeming contentment there, so far from his wife, though the separations made Grace so unhappy. As soon as she started to talk I had the sense of suddenly hearing a disturbing noise that's been sounding in the distance for quite a while.

Avis had seated herself with her back to the room, and I was on the banquette across from her. She was wearing a black skirt and a gray Donna Karan jacket over a soft white open-collared shirt, and she had a long sheer linen scarf in charcoal that she wound around her throat, then removed again minutes later. Ladies of our age spend half their time reacting to their demented inner thermostats.

The restaurant had been crowded when we sat down, but by now the only occupied table near us was behind Avis, a foursome in the middle of the room who were absorbed in one another and having a jolly time. One of them was a lady known to us. I kept an eye on them as Avis leaned toward me, speaking softly.

" . . . says that . . . Well, that Nicky's *drive* isn't very strong. Even when they first fell in love, he was . . . tentative, I guess is the way she put it. Very happy to kiss and cuddle and leave it at that."

Oh. *That* kind of drive. This was really nothing I wanted to know about my beloved godson, and Avis was pretty rigid with discomfort as well.

I murmured something and kept a close watch on the table behind us. They were ordering dessert.

Someone came and poured us more coffee. Avis stopped talking. Like most people brought up with servants, she didn't interrupt conversation while being served except to say thank you, unless the topic was sex or money.

"So . . ." She took her scarf off again. "Since the baby, there's been . . . it's all stopped."

We looked at each other.

"Nothing? No . . . Nothing at all?"

"They haven't been . . . intimate"—Avis squirmed at the word, knowing she sounded like a down-market women's magazine—"since her fifth month."

Oh dear. I tried briefly to imagine having had this conversation with my own mother, or grandmother, or anybody, and failed. Poor Grace! But at the same time, I saw how truly close Grace and Avis must have grown, at last, that Grace had confided this. And how much it meant to Avis.

Dismayed and angry as I was about Gil, he had never been less than ardent as a lover and a gentleman in bed. I've led a sheltered life in that way, and I barely knew what to say.

"Have they talked about it?"

"She's tried. Nicky says . . ." I put my hand over hers, and she stopped speaking. Our acquaintance at the next table had risen, no doubt on her way to the ladies', and spotted us. As she penetrated our air space, we turned together and lit up our faces, all smiles.

"I thought that was the back of your head!" the woman trumpeted to Avis.

"Delia, what a treat! How are you?"

"Everything's fine. Actually that's a complete lie, but we won't go into it."

"You remember Lovie?"

Delia greeted me. Then said to Avis, "How is that precious grandbaby?"

"Perfect."

"Well, give her a hug for me," said Delia. "It is lovely to see you both." She blew us kisses and set off. At the table she had left, her three companions were leaning close together; then suddenly there was a loud burst of laughter.

"She's a beast," Avis said. "Tell me when it's safe to go on." When she could, she said, "Nicky says he doesn't see the problem. He said he had so much of that sort of thing when he was younger he just doesn't feel the need."

"But that's like saying you had so much food when you were young you've given up eating."

Avis nodded. I wondered how much of that there had been in her own marriage in the later years. Delia reappeared, and we fell silent again.

"What can Grace do?" I asked finally.

"There are really only two choices, aren't there? Give it time and hope it gets better, or leave him."

I was shocked. Avis, who had put up with so much with Harrison. And all our hopes for Nicky and Grace! All our shared pleasures in the match. The baby.

Custody fights. And my god, Dinah!

EASTER. GIL HAD BEEN A BELIEVER, BUT I HAVE ALWAYS BEEN MORE OF an atmospheric Christian. I love the flowers and the incense and the music, especially singing the hymns that seem conferred through DNA, but which I really acquired at boarding school. In those years we all went to church every Sunday morning and also sang hymns after supper while the math teacher hammered away at the upright piano in the Main Hall parlor. A clever piece of indoctrination, the hymns. Those melodies are emotional triggers that flood your system with the information that *This is part of you* and *You are part of all that it has been for centuries,* and *Whenever you return, you will be welcomed and taken in.* To find you know verse after verse, the alto lines, the descant, without having made any effort to learn or remember them, is a powerful experience.

Gil and I were normally in Connecticut for Easter; Althea preferred to observe Christian festival days in a Catholic country, specifically France. Easter is my least favorite part of Christianity—too triumphal for me—so Gil went by himself to the boxy stone Episcopal church in the next town over, and I worked in the garden for my Easter observance if the ground was soft enough, and if not, sat inside on the sun porch looking at garden catalogues, planning my annual beds.

This year, drawn by I'm not sure what, I went to the Palm Sunday service at the church that Gil attended in the city. It was odd to be greeting the season of resurrection with no crocus or snowbells or jonquils of my own to welcome back from the dark of the earth. I had filled my apartment windowsills with paperwhites in pots, and the violets twinkling amid dark green ground cover in Central Park and the daffodils and tulips along the median on Park Avenue would have to be my garden now. Walking north that Sunday morning with a weak spring sun warming my back, I remembered a beige linen spring coat I'd had in boarding school, with elbow-length bell sleeves, worn with a navy pillbox hat and long matching kid gloves. Very Jackie Kennedy. I could see myself walking with Meg to the Congregational church in the village, the feel of the garter belt tugging at my hips, the pinch of my stacked-heel pumps from Willy's Style Center in Ellsworth that never fit right. I could see the two of us, with all our lives stretching before us, and just about everything we then imagined those lives were going to be destined to be wrong.

Simultaneously I felt very much myself as I am now, a woman of a certain age who could barely resist stopping to pull the city's weeds out of the city's flower beds.

Could it be that I'd never been to Palm Sunday service in an Episcopal church? If I had as a child, I don't remember. I remember Sunday school dresses and Mary Janes with white socks, and being given two palm leaves to take home. You made a slit in one and pulled the second one through it to form a cross, and you tucked that into your mirror frame in your bedroom, where it stayed until it was time to burn it to make the ashes for the next year's Ash Wednesday.

This year, in this church, when it came time for the reading of the gospel, one of the deacons spoke the words of Pontius Pilate. The rest of us played the part of the crowd. "Meanwhile the chief priests and elders had persuaded the crowd to ask for the release of Barabbas and to have Jesus put to death," boomed Father Leonard in his purple Lenten robes with his rich baritone.

The deacon cried, "Which of the two would you like me to release to you?" and we all shouted "Barabbas!" *Shouted.* With what felt like enthusiasm.

"Then what am I to do with Jesus called Messiah?"

"Crucify him!" we shouted.

"Why, what harm has he done?" the deacon asked us.

But we all just shouted louder, "Crucify him!"

It was horrifying. I walked home in the sunshine feeling like a sac of poison. Feeling as if I didn't know who I was.

ONE AFTERNOON IN LATE APRIL I WAS WALKING ACROSS THE PARK after lunch on the West Side with an old classmate. It was a brilliant day, perfect weather for walking. The park smelled of warm earth and was full of foreign tourists carrying maps and guides to the city, a good effect, I suppose of a weak dollar, though I wasn't writing the Fed any thank-you notes; it was costing me more and more to buy from my European designers, let alone to go on scouting trips and pay for a decent hotel room with euros, and as I've mentioned, my clients were buying less and less. Eventually, I supposed I'd pass some tipping point, when the clients stopped coming to me at all because I had nothing in the shop to show them.

I could hear the babble and trill of small children playing as I neared the Fifth Avenue exit. For some reason I decided to look in at the playground, and as I approached, I caught sight of a very familiar profile. It was Nicky, still tanned from Easter in Georgia with Avis, sitting on a bench with the Irish and Haitian nannies. For the brief time I watched, when he believed himself unobserved, I thought he looked like the saddest man I'd ever seen.

His face lit up when he saw me. "Lindy-hop!" he called to his daughter. "Look who's here!" We embraced and Lindy looked up briefly from where she was busy filling her shoes with sand. She was wearing a pair of velvet corduroy overalls embroidered with bunnies that had the look of something Avis had chosen.

"What are you two doing way up here?" I asked, taking a seat.

"We have a playdate with Julian. Ginette's son." Ginette was a charming young woman with reddish quattrocento hair, a friend of Grace's from school, whom I'd met at Lindy's birthday party. She taught music. I could only suppose that a music teacher was able to leave school earlier than a homeroom teacher, and thus could take her own child to his afternoon playdate when Grace could not.

We watched Lindy hoist herself to her feet and careen toward us with a shapely pebble she'd discovered in the sand.

"What is that, Lindy?" Nick asked her.

"Gold!" she cried. Then she bombed off again to her excavation site.

"Did you enjoy Sea Island?"

"Lindy loved it, especially the beach. We have a world-class collection of sand dollars."

"And how is Grace?"

"Fine."

"I'm glad. And you? How's the screenplay?"

"All good. I'm shopping it to agents, and I'm working on a TV pilot."

My memory was that the screenplay was going to Alvin Grable's agent. So that hadn't worked out? Or had my memory failed me?

"Hello, sailor," said Ginette, who stood before us, extricating Julian from his stroller. She clearly had no memory of meeting me. As I left, they settled down together on the bench, and both children were leaning against Ginette's knees as she dispensed Baggies of goldfish crackers.

It was getting to feel like a pattern. When Casey Leisure stopped in at the shop one morning a week or so later, she had no memory of having met me either.

We were on the cusp of May, and the weather was warm, unseasonably. The flowering pear trees planted along the streets were dropping drifts of white petals at every breeze, and Casey had some in her sleek streaked hair, like freakish snow that never melts.

"Good afternoon," she said briskly, in a tone I recognized as reserved for servants and shopgirls. "Is Mrs. French in? I'm Casey Leisure, she sold my friend a pair of trousers I'd like to try, I'm very hard to fit. Long legs, you see, and a long rise as well, now *that's* a gorgeous piece," she said. She was pointing at a large polished ebony necklace in my accessories case.

"I'm Loviah French," I said.

"Oh!" She looked at me, surprised, then extended her hand.

I shook her hand and said, "I think we met at Marta Rowland's table at a benefit lunch; it's so nice to see you again." I wouldn't have mentioned it, but if she suddenly realized she had seen me before, it would seem as if *I* had forgotten *her,* which is not good for business.

"You're a friend of Marta's?"

"Tell me about the pants you're looking for."

"Literacy Partners?"

"Women Refugees."

"Oh yes," she said. "I remember."

She didn't. She had also managed to inform me of a different party at which I had not been included. "You're a size forty?" I asked.

"Oh, I never know European sizes. Eight above the waist, ten below."

Fortunately it was one of Mrs. Oba's days in the shop. She brought us trousers from two of my designers who do pants for well-toned ladies of a certain age, one German, one Danish. The cut of the German designer was perfect for Casey, and she took three pairs. This was easily the best sale I'd made all month. We settled down to adjusting the fit.

"How do you know Marta?" Casey asked, once the thrill of the hunt was over and her mind returned to more usual pursuits. She was standing on the fitting block, surrounded by mirrors. Mrs. Oba was on the floor, pinning up the cuffs of the pants; Casey's legs were not *that* long.

"We went to the same boarding school," I said. This was true, though we had not known each other there; Marta had graduated before I arrived. The very fact that I'd slapped down that credential told me Casey had irked me, and I should do a better job of hiding it.

"Ethel Walker," said Casey suddenly. She'd been trying to come up with which boarding school it was.

"Miss Pratt's."

"I meant Miss Pratt's. I never can keep them straight, those eastern schools, I'm from California."

"They're very close to one another."

"I know, my daughter dragged me to *all* of them when we were looking at high schools. And then in the end she stayed at Brearley all the way through! Do you have children?"

No. Score another for Casey.

Casey was now in her expensive underpants, standing on one foot to put on the next pair of trousers she'd chosen. These were a wool-linen mix in charcoal with a very faint lavender pinstripe, one of my favorite pieces. We only had a thirty-six and a forty-two left, but Mrs. Oba could take the forty-two in for her.

"Miss Pratt's," said Casey. "Then you know Avis Metcalf!"

She had just noticed the pear petals in her tawny blondish hair, and was now running her fingers through it to remove them. The hair fell perfectly back into place on its own, the sign of a very good cut. Casey raised and turned her chin slightly, admiring this effect in the mirror. I admired it too.

"I saw her two nights ago," she went on. "She seemed so cheerful, you could tell that no one has told her about Grace."

This landed hard. I was quiet for a moment, knowing she wanted me to ask her what she meant, knowing I'd be sorry if I did. I shouldn't have mentioned Miss Pratt's in the first place. Drop names in a certain company, expect to wind up with broken toes.

"Her daughter. Grace. You know her?"

"I do, yes."

"She's married to Nick Wainwright, the actor? You know, from that show?"

"I don't watch much television." I had watched every episode of that one, though, as long as Nicky was on it.

"Oh, I don't either, but sometimes when you've been out every night for weeks, don't you just love to crawl into bed with a baked potato for supper and watch a good sitcom?"

"How does that feel?" I asked, meaning the darts Mrs. Oba had pinned at the back and sides of the waist. Casey turned herself sideways, sucked in her tummy, and admired the view.

"Great."

Mrs. Oba set to work on the hems.

"Grace and my daughter knew each other from dancing school. Peter Varnum has been in love with Grace like *forever*. He followed her around Nantucket like a puppy. He was devastated when she married Nick. I always knew that was a mistake, that marriage. Isn't it ironic?"

I wasn't sure what she meant but suspected she was misusing the word.

Mrs. Oba had pinned one hem so there was a perfect little break at the ankle. She looked up at Casey in the mirror.

"Is that all right?" I asked her. "You're not going to wear a higher heel with these?"

"Not with pants," she said, as if I shouldn't have had to ask. "I walk *everywhere*. You can't wear heels in the daytime in New York."

News to me. But now I had Peter Varnum in focus. He was the tall one in white ducks who had come to dinner so often last summer when we were on Hulbert Avenue. A big bluff teddy bear of a man in a well-cut blazer.

"How do you mean? Ironic?"

She was pulling on the third pair of pants.

"Oh, you know. Sometimes you have to get married in order to end a relationship. To make it clear it won't work no matter what you do. And sometimes you have to break up to find out you can't live without each other."

It annoyed me that I thought this was actually a rather shrewd observation, although I was right, she was misusing *ironic*.

"Phyllis says Grace only broke up with Peter in the first place to annoy her mother. If I wanted a jacket to wear with these pants, what could you show me?"

I sold her a gray wool self-belted jacket with clever lapels that I happened to know would never lie quite right, and the big necklace of ebony beads she'd admired. When she had finally gone, I went upstairs and changed into loafers, now that I knew one could not wear heels in New York in the daytime, and went to the park for a long walk.

CONSIDER THE SOURCE. THAT WAS WHAT I KEPT SAYING TO MYSELF AS I quick-marched past the Temple of Dendur and up around the reservoir. I wanted to wear myself out. I didn't want to have heard this and was determined not to believe it. I was also furious with the messenger, and had half-resolved that if Casey Leisure came to the shop again I would simply say we couldn't serve her. But I wouldn't really do that; I couldn't afford it.

Nicky. Dinah! Poor trusting little Lindy. All the complicated pain to innocent bystanders that comes with divorce. Which Gil and I had been unwilling to cause. Didn't anybody else ever exercise any self-control?

I can't exactly explain what I did next.

I booked a rental car for Saturday morning. I had to get out of the city. To be alone, to be in motion, to be away from human voices, to see the spring in the countryside.

On the day, I dressed in slacks and walking shoes, took the subway to pick up the car, and drove to Connecticut.

I hadn't really meant to. I didn't have any particular plan. I'd thought I might drive up to Woodstock or maybe the Berkshires to visit The Mount and think about Edith Wharton, and a time when everyone in society understood the same manners. I could find a bed-and-breakfast and spend the night; there was nothing in New York I had to be home for. The dog was dead.

I was enjoying the classical music on the radio and the warm smell of turned earth through my open window when I realized what I'd done. As if on automatic pilot, I had chosen the route Gil and I had driven so often. I was practically in our village. Ten minutes more would bring me to our driveway. I drove into town, pulled into the library parking lot, and turned off the engine. What was I doing?

It was a heartbreaking spring day. Bright, with the light somehow golden. There was birdsong, there were children playing on the common, there was a soft-ice-cream truck doing good business down by the town playground. The question was, now that I was here, was I going to go through with it? Drive to the house, walk into the garden, or if someone was there, stand like a specter across the road watching who came and went?

If Meredith was there and she saw me, she might invite me in. In fact she would, I could picture it: she'd invite me in, and make me a cup of tea in my own beautiful blue-and-white Swedish teapot, put out a few cookies on my own blue-and-white porcelain plates. She might let me cut some of my own roses to take home.

If it was the other one, Clara, would she know me? If she knew me would she acknowledge me? Or leave me standing across the road, looking at the house like something inhuman from *The Turn of the Screw*?

I did not aspire to be a succubus. I had not lived my life, loved so much, come all this way, to become that. It was a gorgeous day. I had my health, I had my friends. One should never revisit a loved house once the life lived there was gone. I would drive to the next town, have a quiet lunch at a sidewalk table in the sun, perhaps a frisée salad with lardons and a poached egg on top with a glass of pinot grigio, drive home, go to the pound, and adopt a dog. I didn't think I could face training a puppy, but I could certainly rescue some sweet beast who had found itself bereft through no failing of its own.

Someone knocked on my window.

It was Mildred Connolly, the assistant librarian. She was bending down to smile in at me, her face inches from the window glass. They don't name girls Mildred anymore. What is it, old English? Like Alfred and Ethelred? I lowered the window; what choice did I have?

"I thought that was you, Loviah. It's so nice to see you back in town."

"Thank you, Mildred. How are you? How's Dennis?"

"Pretty good. We were sorry about Gil. I'd have written you but I didn't have your address in the city. I read the obituary in the *New York Times.*"

"He was quite a guy," I said, smiling as warmly as I could.

"We had no idea he'd done all those things. Come up to see the doings out at your house?"

"Really, I was just out for a drive. Such a pretty day."

"Oh, you should go see what they're up to. It's going to be something."

A pause.

I said, "What, exactly?"

"Two paddle tennis courts, and a spa beside it."

"Spa."

"A hot tub. Dennis did the bulldozing for it. Glad of the work."

"I see. I'm trying to think where it's flat enough to put paddle courts. Out past the garage?"

"No, right up next to the house, where you had your garden."

I suppose you saw that coming. I didn't.

THE NEW DOG IS ABOUT EIGHT, THEY THOUGHT AT THE SHELTER. SOME version of a cocker spaniel. She's cost me a fortune so far in treatments for worms, a rash, food allergies, teeth cleaning and shots, but she's a sweetheart. So grateful and eager to please. She doesn't bark much, and she wriggles with joy when she sees me. Tends to lose control of her bladder a little at the same time, but I've gotten very skillful at minimizing the damage. You could feel all her ribs when I first got her, and the pads on her paws were cut up; I think she must have been living rough quite a while before she was found. She's afraid of men. She growls and trembles if the super has to come into the apartment, but she's not all wrong about him. He doesn't like dogs. She is very cheerful and good on the leash, and she loves to ride in taxis. Her name is Edith.

ONE EVENING ABOUT A MONTH AFTER I GOT EDITH, MISLED BY some perversely glowing review I'd read somewhere, I bestirred myself to attend a performance of a Strindberg play at the Brooklyn Academy of Music. Why I thought I would like it, I cannot tell you; perhaps I thought that it would be like the lushly photographed Bergman of *Fanny and Alexander*. I left at intermission. That's one of the pleasures of a single life; if you want to leave, you don't have to negotiate with someone who wants to stay. You do, however, have to figure out the Brooklyn subways by yourself, and I made a hash of it and at first went the wrong way, deeper into Brooklyn instead of toward home. By the time I realized my mistake, I had to wait what felt like forever in a virtually empty station, all too aware of the simple but expensive watch I was wearing, and the other things about me that might encourage the wrong sort of person to see me as easy prey. The watch had been a long-ago present from Gil. It would be ironic, and I use the word advisedly, if it now got me killed. And if it did, who would take care of poor little Edith? How long would it be before someone thought of her?

Little as I relished feeling like a sitting duck, I had no idea what sort of world was overhead, whether there was a bustling brightly lit street full of taxis, or a neighborhood as dark and quiet above as the station below, so I felt I had no choice but to stay where I was and hope that a train arrived before something unpleasant did. At last a Q train arrived, not a line I understand at all, but it was brightly lit and going toward Manhattan, neither of which you could say about the bench where I'd been sitting, so I got on.

We went one stop, then halted. The subway is like that after-hours. What had possessed me to go to an outer borough at night by myself? There was an announcement, very loud, of which I understood no word. A middle-aged Muslim couple sat quietly at the other end of the car, and I decided that if anyone alarming got on, I would move down to sit near them. I wished I had something to read, but I didn't, so I sat gazing through the window, across dark and filthy tracks to the opposite platform.

The frame of the subway car window made the scene beyond it a little like something in a film. Which is why it seemed hardly real when a couple came down the stairs and onto the lighted platform. They looked anxious and unhappy. The young woman, who was Grace, and who had no good reason for being in Brooklyn at this time of night that I could think of, looked at her watch. Then the man, who was Peter Varnum, bent to kiss her on the mouth, a kiss she returned as a train drew toward them from the opposite direction from mine. Through the windows of two train cars I saw the doors open and Peter boarding the outbound train. The doors closed behind him, and the train began to move. By the time the last car had left the station, Grace was gone, and my own train jerked into motion again.

I DIDN'T INTEND TO TELL DINAH. I STAYED AS FAR AWAY AS I COULD from them all that summer, though Avis had taken the house in Nantucket again and invited me to join the family there.

By fall, I found I was missing Dinah. I wanted to snarl about the paddle tennis courts with someone who would make me laugh. I wanted a little fun in my life. We had a Girls' Night Out, down in Tribeca at a jolly dive with delicious food where we wouldn't meet anyone we knew. We had a happy time planning revenges on Gil's daughters that we'd never carry out. It felt wonderful to join in Dinah's great rattling warm colorful belly laugh. It was like being young again. We ordered another bottle of wine, why not? Of course, part of our being young together had always been that I found myself telling Dinah things I never meant to. Dinah felt so helpless in the face of Nicky's sadness, his feeling that his life, so full of promise, had been derailed, and neither of them could understand how or why it had happened. And after all, Nicky was my godson, and I loved him.

For a day or two Dinah was obsessively angry at Grace. She called me multiple times and railed about how she had practically adopted her back in the day when Grace had no use for Mrs. Gotrocks. She said things about Grace, and Avis too, that were not kind or fair. Or very ladylike. She wanted to shield Nicky; she wanted to force Grace to think of her husband and her child and the vows she had made. She wanted to protect Nicky from experiencing the bad thing that had happened in *her* marriage. She thought of how to confront Grace. But then, as I understand it now, she moved on to another stage.

Why would it be so bad if Nicky and Grace divorced? If Nicky sued for custody, he'd win. Nicky was a blameless full-time parent. Grace was the unfaithful wife and absent working mother. True, in court, in a battle of who could hire the best lawyer, Nicky might lose, but what about the court of public opinion? Grace and Avis had far more to lose there than Nicky and would certainly cave in and settle long before it came to the glare of the spotlight. Shared custody and spousal support for Nick must not have sounded so bad to Dinah. Nick could get his career back on track, she and Nick could have Lindy for the summers on the Vineyard, and Dinah wouldn't have to pretend to enjoy her losing competition with Avis for Grandmother of the Year anymore. There was a lot for Dinah to like in this new vision of the future.

BLIND ITEMS BEGAN APPEARING ON THE SOCIETY BLOGS AND WEB SITES:

What well-heeled celebutante has been seen getting cozy with an old beau while hubby is home minding the baby?

Or:

What handsome TV actor doesn't know what they're saying about his schoolteacher wife and her extracurricular activities?

The Web sites would make sure to run photographs of Grace and Nicky together, smiling for a camera, at a book party for some hot new novelist, or a fund-raiser for the ballet or for the Robin Hood Foundation. Did these items have Dinah's fingerprints on them somewhere? It certainly seemed to me that they did. And I was shocked.

On nights when Grace was going to be late getting home, Nicky often brought Lindy uptown to have supper at Dinah's. One such evening sticks in my mind. We'd finished our meal, and Dinah was playing Ride a Cockhorse with Lindy as I cleared the table. Nicky sat staring at the candles, in another world. Each time Dinah got to the line "she shall have music wherever she goes," she let Lindy tip all the way backward, gurgling with laughter.

"Oh, you are my little pigeon pie," said Dinah when Lindy was right side up again. "You would make a delicious lunch." And she'd plant her lips on Lindy's neck and blow, making a sound that makes all small children laugh as if something naughty has happened. "And didn't you like your mac and cheese? Wasn't it good?" (Another rude noise vibrated against Lindy's skin as she shouted with glee.) "Isn't it sad poor Mommy didn't get any? Where is Mommy? Do you want to take her a cookie? Whoopsie Daisy!" and she turned Lindy upside down to more shrieks of excitement.

Suddenly Nicky pushed away from the table and took Lindy from her. "Mom, stop it. You've got her all hopped up." Lindy started to cry and wriggle angrily, and held her arms out to Dinah. Nicky carried her out of the room and we could hear a battle begin as he wrestled her into her parka and shoes. We looked at each other, both a bit unnerved, I think, by the sudden end of our little party. Dinah got up and went to them out in the hall, and I followed her. Nick barely spoke to us as he planted the now-screaming child in her stroller, put one arm into a sleeve of his own jacket, and went out the door.

AVIS SAW THE ITEMS IN THE PAPER AND ON THE WEB; "FRIENDS" MADE sure of it. I believe she talked with Grace about them, because Peter Varnum developed a deal he had to attend to in London and left the country, but it didn't help.

HUMILIATION IS A SCALDING EMOTION. MANY OF US LEARN TO CONCEAL that we feel it, as it is not a condition that inspires sympathy, but

264 / BETH GUTCHEON

we all know the terrible heat of it, flooding the system like a vicious shade of red.

Late one Tuesday afternoon in the dead gray weeks of midwinter, Nick brought Lindy to his mother's apartment to spend
the night. It was shortish notice, and Dinah had to cancel a theater
date with me in consequence, but she sounded not displeased. "I
have a date with my grandchild" trumps most things for women
our age. Dinah kept a couple of plastic crates full of toys under
the bed in Nicky's old room, where Lindy stayed when she came
to visit. Special rails were attached to the sides of the bed so she
couldn't roll out. It had been her first "big girl" bed. She was rumored to greatly prefer it to the hand-painted "youth bed" that
Avis had provided at her apartment.

Lindy arrived dressed entirely in pink, except for her shoes.

"What can I tell you, we're in a pink mood," Nicky said. "I got
her pink tights last week and it sort of grew."

"Come here, my pink girl," said Dinah. Lindy ran to Dinah.

"I'll be back in the morning. What time do you need me?"

"I have a class tomorrow night, so I have some prep work to do."

"I'll be here by ten."

"Don't rush. Lindy and I are working on our waffle recipe,
aren't we, pink girl?"

"Waffles!" said Lindy, and wriggled out of Dinah's arms so
she could rush into the kitchen.

"I'm off, Lindy-hop," Nicky called after her. "Do I get a kiss?"
But Lindy was busy in the cupboard Dinah had designated as
hers, from which she was allowed to pull all the pots and arrange
them upside down on the floor and beat them with spoons if she
wanted, and she usually did want.

Nicky followed her into the kitchen to give her a hug. He kissed his mother and thanked her. He wasn't exactly ebullient, but he was calm. Well within normal range, in the opinion of the person who knew him best in the world, which as we all know now was not well enough.

For some time, Grace had been unusually careful about keeping her laptop with her. She needed it to run presentations on the Smart Board in her classroom. She needed it at night, for entering grades and comments, and for keeping in touch with the parents of her students. But the last time her mother talked to her, which was right before lunch on that Tuesday, Grace had called to see if she had left her cell phone at Avis's. She hadn't.

That evening when she walked through the door, at the time of day when the living room was usually flooded with western light and Lindy should have been having her supper, the apartment was quiet.

"Hi, pup, I'm home," she called to Nick. And then, "Lindy? I'm home, little widget . . ." Then she saw her cell phone lying in the middle of the otherwise empty dining table.

Nick came out of their bedroom. "Hi, pup," he said. They looked at each other for a long minute.

"Where's Lindy?"

"At Mom's."

"Ah."

So it had come. She probably didn't know if she felt dread or relief. Probably both.

"I'm sorry I didn't call as I was leaving. I left my phone," said Grace, looking at it, pulsing on the table.

"No, you didn't. I took it out of your bag this morning."

So. There was no chance that it had been a simple mistake on her part, a helpful act of retrieval and return on his. We can only guess at the list it contained of numbers called. How many were to and from London? The text messages—hundreds? More? Even pictures?

And then what happened? I can imagine—so can you. She may have cried. She may have been cool. She may have told him she loved him, she may have told him she didn't. She may have said she wanted to try again with him. She may have said his lawyer should talk to her lawyer. Whatever she said and did, it was clearly and absolutely the wrong response for that situation, with that man, because instead of accusing her or blaming her or threatening her, he killed her.

SHE WAS IN THE BEDROOM WHEN THE POLICE ARRIVED. NICKY WAS IN the living room, quietly waiting, comforting the dog. The cell phone was gone and has never been found.

She fought hard. Nicky had rake marks down his cheeks where she had scratched him, but he was simply bigger, heavier, and much, much angrier. The matter under her fingernails was packed with his DNA, though why they bothered to test it I don't know. He never denied he had done it. He strangled her until she was dead, then put a pillow over her face so he didn't have to see the protruding tongue, the terrible eyes, and then put out the

light, as if she were sleeping. He went out to the kitchen to telephone. Grace lay there on their king-size bed in her slim tweed
skirt and lambswool cardigan, heart stopped, lungs collapsed, re-
leasing the contents of her bladder onto the expensive linens.

I'VE HEARD THE TAPE OF THE 911 CALL ON THE NEWS. YOU PROBABLY
have too. He gives his name and address and calmly explains that
he's just killed his wife. That tape isn't going to help him at all, if
it comes to trial.

THE POLICE CALLED ME FIRST, BECAUSE NICKY ASKED THEM TO. HE
needed me to get the dog.

The dog and I were with Dinah when Avis's lawyer arrived
at ten o'clock that night to take Lindy. Dinah didn't fight it. How
could she? I wanted to go to Avis as well, but I couldn't leave
Dinah. You wouldn't have either. I was up most of the night with
her. She kept waiting for Nicky to call her, but he didn't. Her suf-
fering was indescribable. So is Avis's, but at least she has Lindy.

The next afternoon Ursula was on Avis's doorstep, having
read the papers and rushed to help. She has been in charge of
Lindy since then, except when Avis sent her downtown to collect
Lindy's things. I went with her. Avis couldn't bear to go into the
place herself.

While I was there I packed up Grace's jewelry to keep for
Lindy. I could barely touch the clothes. They are too alive for me,

too much a museum of moments with Grace laughing, talking, teasing her mother, gossiping with me as she stood before the mirror in my dressing room. I did have to bring back clothes for her to be buried in. I chose a green wool sheath that had brought out the beauty of her eyes. An Hermès scarf she had loved, to hide any bruises on her neck; very few would know it was a scarf Nicky had given her. Jimmy Choo shoes. Underwear. Fresh panty hose. I took them all to the funeral home and handed them over.

I went through her desk to be sure there were no letters, no diary, no keepsakes that would hurt or embarrass Avis if the press got hold of them. I found only a few things and destroyed them. I'd have taken her computer if it had been there, but it wasn't. The police must have it.

The next day I had to go down again with Dinah. She wanted to pack up some of Nicky's things to take to him at Riker's. She wasn't thinking very clearly; she'd been crying for several days. I can't imagine they'll let him have his own things at Riker's. We had to get the super to let us in. Avis had a key to the apartment but Dinah didn't. Interesting.

The yellow crime scene tape was already down. I guess since Nicky has confessed, and his account matches the evidence, there wasn't much point in treating it like a mystery. Dinah didn't know I'd already been here since the murder. The apartment seemed as dead as Grace, the air stale, the blinds drawn. Reflexively Dinah opened the refrigerator. She looked at Lindy's juice boxes and yogurts, at the open containers of milk in the shelf of the door, strawberries in a green plastic basket shriveling in the dehydrating air, and a package of chicken legs in the meat bin that smelled of rot. She closed the door again.

I followed her as she went into the master bedroom. She spent a little time opening drawers in Grace's desk while I watched and hoped she wouldn't find anything I'd missed. She packed up Nicky's wash kit and a small suitcase of socks and underwear, shirts and jeans, a sweater, and a pair of sneakers. Then Dinah went to the baby's room. She saw at once that the toys and clothes were gone. There was a stuffed yellow chicken with a squeaker in it lying on the floor. We hadn't done a very tidy job of closing drawers or the closet door after we'd cleaned them out; the place looked as if it had been ransacked.

A framed picture of Dinah with Lindy at the beach had been left on the painted dresser. Dinah took that.

AVIS'S APARTMENT IS FULL OF FLOWERS AND VISITORS, AS YOU WOULD expect after the death of a young person. Avis wanted to bring Grace home to lie in the living room, but she was persuaded that it would be very much the wrong thing for Lindy. The corpse that had been Grace stayed at Frank Campbell's. Her room there too was packed with flowers, and there was one long ghastly afternoon when Avis stood receiving Grace's friends, saying the same things over and over. *Yes. Thank you. She does, doesn't she? Thank you for coming. You were one of her favorite people.*

I stood by the door and reminded people to sign the guest book. Avis had no idea whom she was talking to; her eyes were blank. Someday she'll want to know who came. The funeral home did a remarkable job of restoring Grace's face to a normal expression. I don't know what violence they may have done to her down in their horrible workroom to achieve their effects. She was coated in makeup, which made her look like a familiar but slightly wrong representation of herself. Her face seemed too big, and her hair was weirdly wiglike. I was no longer sure that the scarf had been a good idea, but it was too late to fix it. As with so many things.

On the sidewalk outside Campbell's the press was thronged six deep. They snapped and shouted when they recognized people going in or out; I can only suppose they had studied the photo vaults in their morgues for hours so they would recognize the people in Grace's life. They even called to *me* by name, trying to ask me questions, and outside a very small circle, I am nobody. You can imagine the hoopla when they caught sight of the famous actress from Grace's class at Nightingale, or the boldfaced names among Avis's social friends. Between that day and the funeral itself we went through two guest books and started on a third. You'd be amazed at the list.

The press gauntlet was the same outside Dinah's apartment. They harassed anyone coming out about Nicky and Dinah. At one point they caught the woman whose daughter Nicky had bitten when he was three. I saw this on the evening news; thank God all she said was that everyone in the building was terribly sorry for the family. A reporter then asked her if Alvin Grable was coming to the funeral.

They liked asking everyone if they were surprised. What the hell did they expect people to say?

Inside Dinah's apartment, the atmosphere was far stranger than at Avis's. A young life had ended there too, but neither Miss Manners nor Emily Post had covered the situation. Richard and Charlotte came in from Ardsley to sit with Dinah the first day.

Richard is devastated. If he blames Dinah at all, he didn't show it. People telephoned but didn't know what to say. Charlotte and I took turns answering. Nicky's friends arrived wanting to help, wanting to offer condolences, but then didn't know how. Two of them fell to reminiscing about funny moments they had shared with Nick in happier times, but instead of eliciting smiles from the mourners, they found the family staring at them in confusion. Dinah moved through minutes that took forever to build into hours, as if she were underwater. More than anything, she seemed bewildered.

Her sisters from Canaan Hamlet went to Avis's first, to pay their respects, and then came to sit with Dinah. Treena seemed aphasic, she was so distraught. She said that Avis had been very gracious to them and seemed to be holding up. Dinah just stared at her. I could see her framing the question in her head: *You went to Avis's? You went to Avis's first?* But in the end she said nothing. They had loved Grace. Avis had been nothing but kind to them. What were they to do?

In the evening, when most people had left, Dinah asked me if I thought *she* should go to see Avis. She was completely unmoored. I said no, the funeral would be circus enough for both of them to get through. I led her sideways into a talk about what she would wear.

YOU'VE SEEN THE TAPE OF NICKY WALKING INTO THE COURTHOUSE FOR his arraignment. The perp walk. Everyone's seen it, the local news shows ran it over and over that day and evening while repeating what they considered his vital statistics. Out-of-work actor, former

star of *The Marriage Bureau,* fired for punching Alvin Grable at a
bar in a quarrel over a girl. Now being arraigned for the murder
of his socialite wife, Grace Metcalf. On the screen you see Nicky
walking quickly but with none of the ducking and squirming of
the typical accused. He holds his handsome head up and looks
calmly ahead of him into his ruined life as the cameras flash. His
hands are cuffed behind him, and police hold both his elbows. On
sound, you hear the 911 call. He says, "I need to report a murder."
The operator asks for his name and address. He gives them. The
operator asks, "Do you need an ambulance?"

He says, "No, she's dead."

"Who is dead, sir?"

"My wife. I killed her."

You can hear the operator talking excitedly to a dispatcher;
then: "Can you stay on the line, sir? Can you tell me what happened?"

He says, "I killed my wife."

"Yes, sir. Can you stay right there, sir? Help is on the way."

"Yes, I'll stay with her."

Help wasn't what was on the way. But whatever he had called
for, he sat quietly until it came for him.

INSOMNIA. DO YOU HAVE THAT? IT'S LIKE A NASTY LIGHT YOU CAN'T
put out no matter what you pour on it.

Is this a very American story? Boy meets girl, boy loses girl,
boy kills girl? If yes, I don't see why. People who go unhinged belong to some separate country with no history or culture. Though

your country and mine is already getting its hands all over it. Indictments will be brought. For manslaughter or first degree? Does taking the child to his mother's house prove Nick had decided in advance to kill? Does keeping the dog at home prove he had not?

Will they understand it any better when it's over? I doubt it. Murder is always bound to be more than the sum of its parts.

The funeral. It was at St. Thomas, where they had been married. Officially married. Two hundred or so of us had cards of invitation, which in theory entitled us to seating in the reserved pews in front, but the place was packed to the rafters, and even with cards you were out of luck if you hadn't arrived at least three-quarters of an hour before time. The church staff as well as some private security—I assume that's who those men in black suits with the earpieces were—did their best to keep out the press, but plenty of them found their way in, and with little digital cameras they got enough pictures to feed the gossip sites and tabloid columns for days. Avis had hired an event planner to handle the details; she was in no shape to do it herself. But it was still she who had to decide about sending reserved seating cards to Dinah and the rest of Nick's family.

Of course she sent them.

AT DINAH'S HOUSE, ONCE THE FIRST GRUESOME SHOCK HAD BEEN SURvived, the axis began to move off center, first a degree or two, then more and more until Dinah's universe was at right angles to Avis's. Grief for Grace faded back a little as feelings, complex though they were, for Nicky, who was still alive, moved to the fore. He had snapped; he had fallen very far and hard. But did he jump or was he pushed?

There is even a soundtrack for this question. There was a long conversation in the family about choosing a defense lawyer and how to pay him. About an insanity defense. The case for manslaughter. The fact that Nicky has so far showed no wish to do anything except plead guilty. Which is not exactly the same thing as showing remorse. He seems to think it's as if he'd fought a duel, done something illegal but quixotically manly.

Dinah assumed I would sit with her at the funeral. Nicky's godmother, after all. Dinah, who had positioned herself as an outsider all her life, now found herself with the Establishment ranks arrayed against her, with their silken tents and banners flying, armor in place and parade weapons at the ready. She sees, at last, what a formidable force it is.

Avis invited me to join her in the rector's study and walk into the sanctuary with them after the mourners and others were seated. Dinah and her family would have to fight their way down the aisles, clutching their tickets like everyone else. Instead I managed to arrive late and alone and slip up a side aisle. Casey Leisure saw me and signaled to me; she made room for me in her pew by squeezing her daughters aside and putting all their coats on the floor, which was kind of her.

Avis walked down the center aisle, supported by her stepdaughters and their families. Her head was high, and she looked like a carved ivory icon, dignified and drained of blood. She must have taken something. In the center of the aisle she bowed to the cross, then turned directly to enter her pew, completely avoiding looking to the right, where Dinah and her family were sitting.

Then the casket was carried down the aisle on the shoulders of
eight pallbearers, four weeping friends of Grace's and four stout
men from the funeral home. We all stood as it passed, and I
caught sight of Mike Allison and his new wife on the other side of
the aisle. She was not the one from the doctor's office, not a trophy
wife at all, but a friendly-looking Town Club dowager with gray
hair and a pleasant face.

The music and flowers were magnificent. The rector, who had
barely known her, gave a rote eulogy, referring to Grace as Gracie.
A long—too long—parade of Grace's friends came forward and
spoke; it was touching, moving, a cause for laughter and for tears,
as well as of frustration at the sloppy diction of the young, which
caused many of us to miss the point of the stories. Finally, a piano
played the adagio from Beethoven's *Pathétique* sonata as the pallbearers carried Grace back out into the winter sun, followed by
Avis, head down, face raddled with weeping and looking twenty
years older than when she had come in, and the stepsisters and
their families, all also in tears. I'd be pleased if I never had to hear
that piece of music again. When I finally saw myself in a mirror
an hour later, there were black smears of eye makeup down my
cheeks. I should have known better than to wear mascara.

Dinah stayed in her pew for a long while. I got up with the
bulk of the crowd and made my way slowly along with the current, surrounded by people greeting friends, putting away their
hankies, beginning to make their plans for the afternoon.

Across the church, in a similar sea of people, I saw Peter Varnum. He was alone. He was freshly barbered and wearing a clean
shirt but looked as if he'd been crying for a week. When he finally got up he put on mirrored sunglasses that hid his eyes before

he left his pew. He stood up straight and tapped the side of the funeral program against his wrist in a vacant tattoo as he slowly moved toward the sunlight along with the distant acquaintances and the sightseers. What will his life be like now? What will he tell his children about this day?

Outside, I waited to see Dinah make her exit. I could have ridden to the reception in one of the family limousines, but the weather was mild for winter, and one could easily walk from the church to the Colony Club.

Dinah finally appeared under the Gothic arch of the door. The dress we had chosen draped well, and she too was wearing large dark glasses. The press surged toward her, cameras clicking and flashing, and began shouting questions. Richard and Richard Jr. with their children formed a flying wedge in front of Dinah. With Charlotte and Laura at her sides, they muscled her through the crush and into a car that quickly left the scene.

I saw a tall woman with auburn hair moving toward me as we descended the dark stone steps in the sunlight. She reached me and said, "Loviah, it's Meredith Flood," at the same time as I said, "Meredith. Hello." I didn't offer my hand.

"I'm so sorry," she said, touching my arm.

You should be, I did not say out loud, wishing she meant sorry about my garden.

"I know how close you are to Avis and Grace. It's so, so sad."

"Thank you."

A pause. I didn't help her. "Well. I just wanted to say that, to say how sorry I am. We all are." She moved on past me.

It had been graceful of her. I just wasn't in the mood for it.

⤫

I DON'T NEED TO DESCRIBE THE RECEPTION TO YOU, YOU WERE THERE. Balloon glasses of chardonnay in every hand, and platters of funeral food. Clumps of young women leaned together in their too-short dresses, weeping. The young men looked restless and miserable and tried to check their watches without being seen. It *was* a workday. No one from Dinah's side came, unless you count me.

Sherry Riggs came up to me. I think I mentioned her, Sherry Wanamaker, my new-girl roommate at Miss Pratt's. She had been crying. She said to me, "Lovie, was I a bitch to you at boarding school?"

I just looked at her. She said, "Never mind. Don't answer. But I'm sorry." She wandered off, following a tray of hot canapés.

DINAH IS GIVING UP THAT APARTMENT AT LAST. SHE MAY MOVE UP TO the Vineyard full-time. Avis has settled into a routine of work and Lindy. Lindy will go to nursery school in the fall, which is good. A child shouldn't be alone in a silent apartment with two old ladies so much of the time. *Grave* is not the word you want to think of when you think of a child-centered home.

I don't sleep well anymore. As I've mentioned. Sometimes in the very dark hours of some morning, I think about my garden. There was a Cécile Brunner climbing rose on the back wall that I had taken out because there was too much pink in that section of the perennial beds, and it was common. I regret it now. The Lady Banks I put in instead would have been lovely, but it never did well. I have no idea why not.

I've been seeing a lot of Casey Leisure. She was widowed suddenly and doesn't seem to know what to do with herself, and she talks too much for most people. She has her good points. She likes to go on cruises now and play bridge with people she meets on the ships. My bridge game has gotten fairly good; if I have to close the shop, I may try one with her. There's a tour of the Baltic I like the look of; we'd see the cities of the Hanseatic League and end in St. Petersburg. The white nights of summer are so lovely there.

At least that's what people tell me.

ACKNOWLEDGMENTS

SO MANY PEOPLE HELP A BOOK ALONG ITS PATH. SANNA BORGE FEIR-stein has been deeply generous, *again,* this time providing guidance on the course of Loviah's young professional life. Jennifer Mitchell Nevin was similarly invaluable on the subject of Avis's career, and I thank them both. Thomas Mifflin Richardson, Anthony Fingleton, Phil Norris, Katherine McCallum, Gail Monaghan, Ramon Rodriguez, Don Barney, and Richard Osterweil all enriched these invented lives, and I'm grateful to have them in my actual life. Lauren Belfer and Elizabeth Oberbeck kindly read the manuscript for me at different stages and provided essential advice and support. I thank Wendy Weil, who has been my friend and my agent for over half my life, for her wisdom, her loyalty, and the pure fun of being a member of her tribe. I am grateful to my editor, Jennifer Brehl, for her skill and her lovely spirit, and to all those at William Morrow who do what they do so well. And first, last, and always, I am grateful to Robin Clements.